EYEOPENERS II

Beverly Kobrin earned an undergraduate degree in Music Education from the New England Conservatory of Music in 1957, a master's degree with a major in Education from Stanford University in 1972, and a doctorate in Elementary Curriculum and Instruction from Brigham Young University in 1978. She has supervised music in the elementary grades in Mount Lebanon, Pennsylvania, and taught general music in junior high school in Quincy, Massachusetts. Dr. Kobrin has taught the fourth, fifth, and sixth grades as well as gifted children from first through eighth grades in Mountain View, California. Since 1980 she has published *The Kobrin Letter*, the only periodical to review and recommend children's nonfiction literature exclusively.

Dr. Kobrin also conducts workshops on the use of children's nonfiction books at home and in the classroom. By November of 1994, she had addressed 32,187 parents, teachers, librarians, and others at 396 sessions in 208 cities in the United States and Canada. (She keeps a computerized list.)

Beverly Kobrin lives in Palo Alto, California, with two cats and her very, very patient husband. Her son David connects kids and good books as the tap-dancing, origami-folding Tapigami Man.

EYEOPENERS II

CHILDREN'S BOOKS TO ANSWER CHILDREN'S QUESTIONS ABOUT THE WORLD AROUND THEM

Beverly Kobrin

SCHOLASTIC INC.

NEW YORK   TORONTO   LONDON   AUCKLAND   SYDNEY

Photo credits: Cover: Top left: © David Young-Wolff/PhotoEdit; top right: Wide World. Middle left: Fred Mang, Jr./National Park Service; middle right: Stock Editions, Inc. Center and spine: © Richard Hutchings/PhotoEdit. Bottom left: Stock Editions; bottom right: © Myrleen Ferguson/PhotoEdit.

ISBN 0-590-48402-8

Library of Congress Cataloging -in-Publication Data
  Kobrin, Beverly.
  Eyeopeners II / by Beverly Kobrin.
  p.   cm.
  Includes bibliographical references and index.
  ISBN 0-590-48402-8
  1. Children's literature—History and criticism. I. Title.
PN1009.A1K598 1995 809'.89282—dc20 95-36183 CIP

12 11 10 9 8 7 6 5 4 3 2 1   5 6 7 8 9 0/0 9
                    Printed in the U.S.A.
              First Scholastic Printing, September 1995

To my sister Binese Goldberg,

my son David,

and my husband and coauthor, Don,
who lets me take all the credit—
and, of course, the responsibility for
any eye-opening errors and omissions.

Contents

Acknowledgments

With an undergraduate degree in music and a doctoral dissertation on the use of the hand-held calculator, it may seem strange that I am now the author of a book on how to choose and use children's nonfiction literature. My circuitous route has been shaped and my life enriched by many talented people whose paths I've crossed.

While my gratitude extends to scores of people, I'd like to acknowledge these individuals for their help and their inspiration: my mother, Pearl Mason, who read to me and taught me how to read; my father, Morris Mason, who taught me how to work; Dorothy Grenbeaux, my now-retired principal, under whose wise guidance students and teachers learned and grew as individuals; Barbara Armstrong and Beth McLean, teaching colleagues whose creativity fired mine; Jim Jacobs, whose class in children's literature changed my life; Andrea Stryer, with whom I co-taught my first children's nonfiction literature course; Jan Lieberman, whose friendship, creativity, and boundless enthusiasm for the best in children's literature buoys me; Elaine Griffin and the other gifted teachers and librarians who patiently tolerated my repeated requests for details about their books-to-kids connections; the authors and illustrators of the children's books that enthrall me as an adult as much as they did when I was a child.

And to Deborah Brodie, who gave me the welcome opportunity, at age fifty-three, to become an author; and Kate Waters, who made it possible once again, at age sixty-one.

What's in
This Handbook?

A re you a teacher, a librarian, a parent, parent proxy, a friend
of one, about to become one, or any combination thereof? If
so, this book is a bundle of ideas just for you—a passel of per-
suasive prose about the pros of children's nonfiction books.

The more than 800 books I've reviewed will interest just about
everybody. These eyeopeners are a delight to look at, a pleasure
to read, and a source of fascinating information on subjects that
hold children, and adults, spellbound. Get some and see for yourself.

Nonfiction books published for the general public are called
trade books. A trade book is "not a textbook, not a technical trea-
tise, but the sort of thing that could [and the publisher hopes will]
interest everybody," as *Webster's Third International Dictionary*
explains. If you thought that "nonfiction books" meant textbooks
or turgid, data-filled tomes, you are in for a wonderful surprise.

AMONG THE VERY BEST

The attractive, nonfiction books I recommend present factual material in imaginative, enriching, exciting ways. I've culled them from the best of those published in the United States, Canada, and Great Britain. All were in print and available in the U.S. in the winter of 1994-1995.

I believe nonfiction trade books are essential in the education of all children. I explain why in Chapter 2 and describe how I came to integrate them into my classroom teaching in Chapter 3.

PERUSE, CHOOSE, USE

In Chapter 4, you'll read how teachers and librarians can use nonfiction to encourage reading, enhance a child's innate need to know, and complement any curriculum. I've included many immediately useful tips to help you incorporate books into day-by-day teaching. See also Chapter 6 about Non-Book Reports for a way to use my titles and tips as stepping stones to more reading or other activities.

If you are a parent or parent proxy, Chapter 5 will suggest ways to ensure that books will become an integral part of your child's life, from infancy on.

YOUR CHILDREN'S LINK TO LITERATURE

Although I espouse nonfiction, I do not believe it better or more valuable than fiction. They are literary coequals. In the Guide you'll find nonfiction titles linked to complementary works of fiction.

I've recommended more than 800 books in the Guide which begins on page 51. You are entitled to know how I selected them from the cornucopia of choices the publishers send me each year. (I received and scanned more than 2,800 books in 1994.) In Chapter 7 I've summarized my criteria to provide you a quick checklist you may wish to use when evaluating nonfiction for your children.

Please remember that my recommendations are a guide—not gospel. Ultimately, it is *your* attitude and the enthusiasm of *your* recommendations that most influence your youngsters' willingness to read.

I've arranged my choices in the Guide by topics—50 of them. This is browsing territory—for good books and good ideas. Look up a topic that fascinates your youngsters and you'll find a group of books on the subject. (These are by no means the only worthwhile books available; they're the ones I could fit into the pages my publisher has allowed me.)

Those of you familiar with the first edition of *Eyeopeners* will notice that there are fewer categories and more titles in this edition. In *Eyeopeners II*, I've opted for depth over breadth.

FIND IT FAST!

If you, or a student hunting information for a research project, need books on a particular topic, turn at once to the Quick-Link Index starting on page 271. You'll be led to appropriate books regardless of their titles: *Giants in the Land* for example, when you search for books on trees and *To the Top of the World* for books on wolves. I've explained how to use the Quick-Link Index on page 53.

A conventional, alphabetical listing of the titles, authors, and illustrators of the books I've mentioned follows the Quick-Link Index.

Now, reach into the book bundle and pull out some ideas!

Good reading,

2.

Why Nonfiction?

Why a book devoted to children's nonfiction books?

Good question! Let me count the whys:

1. CHILDREN ARE FASCINATED BY THE REAL WORLD

As infants, they reach out and touch—everyone and everything. They explore, taking things out of whatever they're in and putting them into whatever they're out of. As soon as children speak, they're a fountain of questions. I often thought my son David was born with a silver question mark in his mouth. He was a steady stream of whos, whats, wheres, whens, and whys. As author Anne Weiss has said, "Kids are born hungry to learn. That's why the word *why* was invented."

Eye-opening nonfiction books, books about real people, places and things, begin to satisfy that curiosity. The best nonfiction answers questions and inspires even more.

2. NONFICTION RAISES SELF-ESTEEM

Slow Reader

I-am-in-the-slow
read-ders-group-my-broth
er-is-in-the-foot
ball-team-my-sis-ter
is-a-ser-ver-my
lit-tle-broth-er-was
a-wise-man-in-the
in-fants-christ-mas-play
I-am-in-the-slow
read-ers-group-that-is
all-I-am-in-I
hate-it.

—Allan Ahlberg
from *Please Mrs. Butler*
(Kestrol, 1983)

Would you feel comfortable if every book you used let your colleagues know how your reading ability ranked against theirs?

Neither do children.

You don't read only those books on your "reading level." Why should children? Yet that's what we force them to do when we rely upon graded texts.

Children don't feel stigmatized when we give them books for readers of all ages, books that are attractive, engrossing, and challenging: adult photo-essays or artfully illustrated information books, picture books with few or no words, and "first" books.

They may not be able to read all the text in the adult books, but children will certainly learn from the pictures. The photos and art in books of few words may inform as eloquently as any prose. And if a good book for older children has no pictures, you can read an excerpt aloud or share something fascinating that you learned when reading it. Pique their curiosity, and they'll want more.

Children ordinarily in the bottom reading group will discover that they can learn from "hard" books: Motivated by the illustrations and the subject itself, they'll work to make sense of the text. (I've yet to find a middle-grade reader too "low" to read the *Guinness Book of World Records!*) Children in the top reading groups will discover that they can learn from simple books. Carefully distilled texts and illustrations provide effective, confidence-building introductions to any subject for readers of all ages.

3. KIDS NEVER SAY NO TO NONFICTION

Will you read an enticingly written book with first-rate illustrations about a subject you find fascinating? So will children.

You can create more effective assignments for introducing, reinforcing, and reviewing skills with books students want to read. If one child likes dinosaurs, another basketball, and yet another space exploration, gather together books about dinosaurs, basketball, and space exploration.

This strategy works, even for "difficult" children. When I discovered that one of my students, a belligerent eighth-grader, had pet rats, I rounded up a few good rat books. The day I took them to school I became ill, so I stopped by his homeroom to explain that I'd had to cancel class but couldn't wait until the next day to deliver the books I'd brought in especially for him. This usually antagonistic young man looked at the books, paused a moment, and bent over (he was a head taller than I) to put his arm around me. He hugged me gently, and said he was sorry I was sick and hoped I'd feel better soon. He straightened up, reentered the room, and quietly slid himself into his seat and the books into his desk.

The next time we met, he told me that he and his mom had read and reread the books and could he *please* keep them for a few more days. He caused no more disturbances in my class. Don't underestimate the power of books!

4. NONFICTION BOOKS HELP KIDS LEARN HOW TO LEARN

Do you believe everything you read?

Neither should children.

You don't base your decisions upon an isolated bit of information, why should they? Yet that's what we teach them when we hand them one text and one workbook for each subject. A single source of reference conditions children to assume all the answers can be found in one book or one computer file. If we want them to become critical thinkers, we must teach children how to learn. That means checking and cross-checking what they read.

Set aside the textbook/workbook routine with its right-or-wrong answer activities. Surround your children with many books on the same subject. My rule is "At Least Three," whenever possible, on whatever subject, when my students gather books for reports. I want them to read critically, and chances are three books will present different views of the same subject.

When studying astronomy, for example, children must understand that the books they read are out of date as they come off press. That what we "know" about our solar system changes almost daily, in part because of data sent back from satellites such as Viking, Explorer, Voyager, and the Hubbell telescope.

As they do their research, my students and I talk about what one book reports that the other doesn't. We compare photographs and illustrations. Occasionally, we find typographical errors or authors who don't agree. We play the "Who's Older?" game: Who's older, the reader or the books? (That's a sneaky way to teach kids to look for a book's copyright date and the age of its information.)

Dates of copyright, authors' qualifications, acknowledgments, photo credits, and accompanying bibliographies take on added importance when children refer to many books on a single subject. They begin to appreciate that information's value depends upon its source and age.

5. CHILDREN AREN'T GETTING ENOUGH NONFICTION BOOKS TO READ

The adults in kids' lives simply aren't as familiar with nonfiction as they are with fiction. Many hear the negative-sounding term *nonfiction*, think *ugly*, and lose interest. (Imagine naming a daughter "nonSally"!) Author Jane Yolen says the word *nonfiction* sounds as if it had been in a contest with fiction—and lost!

Some people equate nonfiction with the dull, boring textbooks they had to read in school. Truth is, good nonfiction is everything most textbooks are not; it is well-written, well-illustrated, and well-designed by first-rate authors, illustrators, editors, and art directors. You'll find more than 800 in this Guide—just to get you started!

6. NONFICTION BOOKS ARE GOOD FOR TEACHERS, TOO

Nonfiction books keep us as enthusiastic, excited, and involved in learning as they do our students. We learn little and are challenged less when we use texts and workbooks that are, no matter how their titles or publishers change, virtually the same each year—someone else's plans for Everychild. In all my years of teaching, I have yet to meet Everychild.

With carefully selected nonfiction, you needn't struggle to make students interested in what you teach; they already are. Relevant books keep kids and, just as importantly, *you* learning. Instead of burdening children with texts that bore you year after year (how many times can you teach a subject with the same texts and workbooks and avoid burnout?), you'll read new books—the ones your kids read. You will be constantly challenged to find those books, devise new lessons, and teach whatever skills are necessary.

You will learn and grow along with your students. As did an Idaho teacher, whose elementary students "...stood on a model of a Tenochtitlan causeway and fended off the enemy...touched three-million-year-old stromatolites and mammoth-tooth fossils...visited the ancient Anasazi ruins in Chaco Canyon...and were mesmerized by Gary Paulsen's passionate writing about the Alaskan Iditarod. We fell through our day like Alice in Wonderland," she wrote, "soaking up ideas, experimenting with and stretching our talents. We were civil engineers, archeologists, art critics, computer nerds, teachers, and community planners. We used technology, bright construction paper, dog-eared books, parents. We used our imaginations, our background knowledge, and our intuition. We went home exhausted and satisfied."

Nothing is as versatile as nonfiction to match a child's interest and needs. Whether you are teaching math, science, or history, whether children are gifted, average, or struggling! Whether they are young children or young adults, you can find books they will want to read.

By providing the right books at the right time, you can direct your youngsters toward a self-motivated, lifelong interest in reading and learning. For pleasure and information.

Starting on page 57 you'll find more than 800 books to consider. So consider!

3.

How I Began...

"**M**rs. Kobrin! Mrs. Kobrin! You know that book I read? My dad and I went out after dark to look for the North Star like it said...."

"Mrs. Kobrin! Mrs. Kobrin! They ate the whole thing! I picked one of the recipes from that cookbook and made it for my family last night. Mom says...."

"Mrs. Kobrin! Mrs. Kobrin!..."

I didn't always have kids bursting into my classroom, erupting with excitement about books, homework, or what we'd read in class. I used to be greeted by rather stoical children prepared for another day (yawn!) with paper, pencil, and texts.

On a warm fall day in 1969, I walked into Whisman Elementary School in Mountain View, California, enthusiastic about inspiring kids to read and learn. I began teaching the fourth grade the way I had been taught to teach: Use textbooks and workbooks. For everything. Ad infinitum.

After a few weeks on the job, I found that textbook-per-topic teaching unrealistically separated each area of the curriculum into periods regulated by the clock: Reading Time, Math Time, Social Studies Time, Science Time. Related workbook assignments conditioned my children to strive for "right" answers, rather than to think creatively. And the whole process meant hour after hour of Correcting Time for me! What had seemed practical in college theory proved impractical in classroom practice.

My students were learning that each subject began with a capital letter, came at a certain time of day, and always had questions that were marked *right* or *wrong.* They were not learning about how closely subjects were related, or that what we did in the classroom had relevance to their lives away from school. *I* was instructing and correcting. *We* were not exploring and challenging. I was bored and so were my kids.

So I abandoned the routine. Little by little, I replaced textbooks with trade books. I surrounded my students with an ever-changing assortment I perused and picked especially for them. My classroom bulged with books borrowed from nearby public libraries. Books about motorcycles, mummies, dinosaurs, Disneyland, and Bigfoot. Baseball, popcorn, pirates, space ships, and whatever else they expressed interest in.

The effect was electric.

TRADE BOOKS DID THE TRICK

Enthusiasm replaced ennui. My children demanded more reading time. They simply couldn't wait to open the books I'd brought. And once opened, they were read—by those who requested them and others who caught their excitement. Nothing is as effective as kids' personal endorsements in a classroom. Every time one child said "Wow! Mrs. Kobrin, look at this!" or "That was baaaad!" (read: "Not to be missed"), everyone else wanted the book. The room buzzed with energy and book talk.

I did away with workbooks. Each week my youngsters reported on at least one of the books they read. I read every one, then created Non-Book Reports, assignments designed to use each book as a stepping stone to other books and subject areas. Assignments that involved the youngsters' families, whenever possible. (You'll find my ideas on Non-Book Reports in Chapter 6.)

By 1977, I had been teaching by the book—library book, that is—for almost a decade. During the summer, while at Brigham Young University completing requirements for my doctorate, I registered for Children's Literature #628.

The first morning of class, Dr. James Jacobs, Associate Professor of Elementary Education, asked us to sign up for a small group project. We were to select one category from his list (fantasy, folk tales, historical fiction, and the like) and, at the end of the term, "sell" our choice to the class as a whole.

I was fourth from last when the sign-up sheet reached me. Every topic was spoken for but one. Surprised, I raised my hand. "Dr. Jacobs, no one has chosen nonfiction...."

Before I could finish the sentence, my classmates, experienced teachers all, reacted as though I'd nicked a nerve. "Nonfiction? It's so BORING!"

I was amazed. Nonfiction was the backbone of my teaching. We couldn't have been thinking about the same thing. When I asked why they'd reacted so strongly, I learned, sadly, that they equated nonfiction with textbooks.

Even then, there were few activities I enjoyed more than talking about teaching with good books—particularly nonfiction. I signed my name under nonfiction and persuaded the three still-undeclared teachers to join me. Seven weeks later, our eye-opening presentation received a standing ovation from our classmates. They were sold on nonfiction. That presentation is where this book began.

BIRTH OF A NONFICTION ZEALOT

I returned to California after my summer at BYU. In 1979, in addition to teaching in elementary school, I began teaching university extension classes; speaking at reading and library association conferences; and conducting workshops for teachers, librarians, and parents. Each presentation had a single focus: How to use children's nonfiction literature in school and at home.

In September of 1980, I began publishing *The Kobrin Letter*, still the only periodical devoted exclusively to the review and recommendation of worthwhile children's nonfiction.

Since then I've been selling the virtues of nonfiction to every teacher, librarian, and parent I can reach. And the books continue to receive standing ovations.

When I review the anonymous evaluations after each workshop, I read... "I see nonfiction now as a way to stretch the imagination, not just for information. It's a whole new world."

"I've always been a fiction pusher, but I'm thinking of changing my stripes."

"I feel that I won't be able to sleep tonight. I don't know of any bookstore open this late. I know what I'm going to be doing this weekend."

"I will use nonfiction more often than just to teach facts. There are many ideas that grow from one book—the book is just the beginning."

Readers, I hope this book of eyeopeners will be *your* beginning.

4.

For Teachers
and Librarians

Education is what remains after we've forgotten what we've learned.

Prof. James Freeman
San Jose State University, CA

LIBRARIANS = TEACHERS

Though this chapter is headed "For Teachers and Librarians," it might well have been merely "For Teachers," because librarians *are* teachers—among the most effective teachers in children's lives. The opening ideas are for classroom teachers working closely with school and public librarians; the chapter concludes with summer project concepts and resource-stretching hints for librarians which can be adapted easily for the classroom.

CHILDREN ARE LITTLE ENGINES THAT CAN

Think of your students as locomotives. They have the power to go anywhere, but they'll go only where you lay the track. And that small fraction of the day when you're in charge—about 20 percent of their waking hours—is track-laying time. That's when you must forge an attitude toward reading and learning that will set their course for the rest of the time—actually for the rest of their lives.

How can you "lay track"? First of all, remember that what you do is what you teach. Your actions deliver the message, not your words. If you integrate books—nonfiction and fiction— throughout your curriculum, odds are your students will learn that reading is a natural, necessary, and neat part of everyday life. Not just for Reading Time in school.

LIBRARIES AREN'T ONLY FOR LIBRARIANS

Put books within easy reach: Keep your classroom library well stocked. When I taught full time, I surrounded my students with book bargains I'd acquired at Friends of the Library sales, thrift shops, second-hand bookstores, and garage sales, as well as publishers' promotional bonuses and giveaways and books borrowed from the public library. I kept them on the windowsills, floor-to-ceiling bookshelves my husband built, and every horizontal surface not otherwise covered. My kids couldn't say, "I don't have anything to read."

Transform every available surface into billboards that publicize books and reading. Set aside at least one bulletin board for books-read pinups. In the fall, for example, have youngsters write the title and author of every book they've finished on a two-inch paper-pumpkin pinup they've designed and cut out. By the end of October, you'll have a bulletin board filled with paper pumpkins. Clear the board so your youngsters can take the pumpkins home to show parents what they've accomplished and start a new collection, of book-marked snowflakes and sleds, or raindrops and umbrellas, if you live in a part of the country where winter brings rain instead of snow.

Have your children make advertisements for the books they've read and put them in your windows. Ask your librarian, or local children's bookseller, if you can borrow any extra posters acquired at reading/library association conferences. Put them on the ceiling when you run out of wall space. Send a stamped (two ounces worth of postage), self-addressed, 6" x 9" envelope to the Children's Book Council, 568 Broadway, Suite 404, New York, NY 10012, to learn about the beautiful posters, bookmarks, and book-related materials it sells, as well as the free and inexpensive materials available from publishers. Make bookmarks during art periods with variegated selvage garnered from local printers.

Call attention to those drab but worthwhile books. Take a tip from Helene Treat, co-owner of the Red Balloon Bookstore in San Antonio, Texas, and prominently mark a section "Bad Cover, Good Book."

Set aside special areas that invite readers. Stitch or tape together colorful rug remnants for a reading rug that kids can spread out on during silent reading periods. Pile it high with old pillowcase covers children have brought in, stuffed, and decorated with blurbs for a favorite book. Visit a large appliance store and ask for empty dishwasher or refrigerator boxes your kids can turn into miniature reading-room retreats to be enjoyed during earned free time.

LET CHILDREN CHOOSE

When children start to choose their own books, never admonish them with "That book's too easy (or hard) for you. Put it back and take one that's harder (or easier)." Books that are "right" for children are the ones they want to read—or look at—now!

No one chastises us for flirting with books that are too easy or too hard. As adults we can take pleasure in beautifully illustrated books designed for toddlers and read nonfiction children's books as an introduction to unfamiliar subjects. We browse through weighty tomes, taste the language, look at the photographs and illustrations, and perhaps read the captions in books far too technical for us to understand. And we relax on occasion with an indulgence of romances, mysteries, fantasies, mass-market blockbusters, and other fast-read publications that provide a breezy change of pace.

Allow children the same freedom. A book is its own reward. That reward is unique to each reader. Kids cannot learn which books are "right" for them until they—on their own—have discovered which ones aren't.

CREDIT BOOKS, NOT PAGES

When you ask youngsters to select books, please don't make them count the pages. Wherever I speak, librarians tell me that teachers frequently impose minimum page counts. That is, a child cannot receive "credit" for reading a book unless it is at least 100 pages long. As if the length of a book were a measure of its quality!

Take biographies, for instance. With a 100-page minimum for credit, children would be discouraged from reading Karen E. Hudson's 64-page *The Will and the Way: Paul R. Williams, Architect* (Rizzoli, 1994); Diane Stanley's and Peter Vennema's colorful 48-page collaborations, e.g., *Cleopatra* (Morrow, 1994); or any of Wendy Thompson's 48-page series on composers, among them *Wolfgang Amadeus Mozart* and *Ludwig van Beethoven* (Viking, 1991).

Help students understand that good things can come in small packages. Teach them how to recognize quality without imposing false standards. Use analogies: tell them Leonardo da Vinci's Mona Lisa is only 21" by 30"; tell them *I* am 4 feet, 9 1/2 inches tall!

READING IS MORE IMPORTANT THAN CLASSIFYING

To young children, everything is real: mud and the Muppets, manatees and monsters, magic and magnets. With maturity comes an understanding of the difference between real and make-believe. And that's fine. The terms are unimportant. What is critical is that you open children's eyes to good literature. Popular, contemporary, classic. Prose, poetry, plays. Fact and fiction.

Unfortunately, Melvil Dewey used a fact/fiction dichotomy as the basis for his decimal system, and this orderly method of shelving books split literature down the middle. The division into fiction and nonfiction, however, is often clearer to adults than to children. Youngsters who have experienced emotions described in a story "know" the story is true. After all, the same thing happened to them! And kids who hear about the vu quang ox, a recently discovered species of wild cattle with goat-like antlers, might consider it pure fiction. After all, they've never "seen" it.

Often it's difficult to draw a sharp line between fiction and nonfiction. In this nonfiction guide, you'll find reviews of Kate Waters's *Samuel Eaton's Day* (Scholastic, 1993); Ted Dewan's *Tiger Trek* (Macmillan, 1990); and Abderrahman Ayoub's *Umm El Madayan, An Islamic City Through The Ages* (Houghton, 1994). The "Samuel Eaton" photographed at Plimoth Plantation was seven-year-old Roger Burns; the trekking tiger is not "a" tiger, it's a "typical" female; Umm El Madayan never evolved from a North-African Phoenician colony. Each person, place, or thing is the author's creation, the fruit of skillful research.

Whether you label them fiction or nonfiction is unimportant. Don't let the terms close your eyes to the power and worth of both. Supply your youngsters with good literature. There are more than 800 volumes of it right here. Though I've devoted 90+ percent of this book to nonfiction, it does not mean I believe nonfiction to be more important than fiction. On the contrary, children need both.

TAKE A BREAK

Have you read any children's books lately? That may seem like a silly question, yet I often find myself addressing teachers, intent upon encouraging their students to read, who tell me "I know I should be more familiar with the books my kids read, but I just don't have the time."

Keeping current with the best children's books, especially nonfiction, is an essential part of being an effective teacher. Here's a quick and easy way you can add to your repertoire. I call it "Beverly's Brief Book Break."

Once a month, ask your librarian—school or public—to select

books (one per teacher, including the principal) for your faculty meeting: New books or older ones that she knows may be unfamiliar to you. Set aside two minutes for Sustained Silent Reading (SSR) during which everyone (1) scans a book and (2) thinks of one idea for using it creatively in the classroom. Just two minutes, no more. Use a stopwatch.

When the time's up, form groups of three. Allow each person two minutes (use the stopwatch again) to share with the others in the trio the teaching idea and its inspiration.

Is it possible to "see" enough in two minutes to learn about a book and think of a way to use it in the classroom? Absolutely! It's fun and the whole routine takes less than 10 minutes per week.

If you do this once a month for the nine months of a school year, in three books per session, you will have discovered 27 new eye-opening books, exchanged as many teaching hints with your colleagues, and (perhaps best of all) enlivened your faculty meetings.

I use this strategy in my workshops to introduce the people in my audience to half-a-dozen new books in about 10 minutes. Those of you who also teach children's literature courses can adapt it to your classes. After your prospective teachers or librarians have shared something they noticed about the book and a way they might use it with a child, have them also link at least two nonfiction books to each book of fiction and vice versa. This practice will help them appreciate how easy it is to connect fiction and nonfiction. It is essential that they provide their youngsters with both.

READING REINFORCES ROUTINES

No matter how frequently you say that books and reading are important, you must *act* as though they are, or your children will not believe you. Remember that kids are impressionable; they take home gut feelings about books and learning. You determine that feeling. Make reading a noticeable part of your agenda. Be sure your children see you read. One of the most appropriate times would be during Sustained Silent Reading (SSR) periods. When I taught in the classroom full time, I renamed our SSR...

SQUIRT

SQUIRT stands for **S**ustained **Q**uiet **U**n**I**nterrupted **R**eading **T**ime. If SSR isn't yet in your lesson plans, jot it down. SSR helps children acquire the habit and discover the pleasure of being alone with something good to read. It also gives you a daily opportunity to catch up on children's books, in addition to the Brief Break (see above) during periodic faculty meetings.

I always began the school year with a daily 10-minute SQUIRT and gradually increased it until, by June, my youngsters were wrapped up in reading silently every day for 25 minutes. Me too. It's tempting to want to use that time to correct papers or finish other chores, but if you don't read during SSR time, a children's book or one of your own, children will assume that SQUIRT (or whatever you name it) is just another keep-the-kids-quiet-and-in-their-seats-while-I-get-more-important-work-done technique.

After you've tried SSR in your own classroom, spread the word. Perhaps you can influence your whole school or district to drop everything for a book. Since 1990, the teachers and students at San Diego, California's, Crawford High School have done just that during a daily Read to Succeed (RTS) period. Every teacher gets together with about twenty-five youngsters from all grade levels for the 35-minute silent-reading sessions. Special funds are allocated for the nonfiction and fiction RTS books, which remain in the room so that they're always available. Not surprisingly, reading scores have improved.

THE READ-ALOUD RITUAL

Make reading aloud another daily activity. I read aloud to my students each day, immediately after lunch. Fiction and nonfiction. Picture books and photoessays. Poetry, joke, and riddle books. Children's books and adult books. I read aloud from magazines and newspaper articles and shared noteworthy art, photographs, or prose from adult books I've enjoyed. It doesn't matter whether or not youngsters understand all the words you speak; what matters is that they hear fluent, literate language. The more language children hear, the more they will use; the more fluently they speak, the easier reading becomes.

When you read aloud, try to read expressively, because when it's their turn, children will pattern their style after yours. On occasion, let children volunteer to practice an upcoming section. The self-esteem of poor readers in my room rose a noticeable notch or two after they'd practiced and read a portion fluently. Ask youngsters to read excerpts that might be difficult for you. I need assistance during particularly sad parts: David Kherdian's Boston Globe-Horn Book Award acceptance speech for *The Road from Home* (*The Horn Book*, vol.LVI, no.1 [February, 1980] pages 97-99), for example. I start to read it aloud whenever I recommend the book to middle-school students. No matter how often I try, however, I cannot finish the description of Mr. Kherdian's mother reacting to his book. I must ask a student to finish for me.

READ NONFICTION ALOUD, TOO

The Read-Aloud Handbook (Penguin, 1982) has probably done more to encourage parents to read aloud to children than any other book. It is making an important contribution to the raising of children. After reading Jim Trelease's book, however, you might infer that only fiction is suitable for reading aloud. Nothing could be further from the truth. You *can* read nonfiction aloud to children. I know!

Nonfiction books make me and my students laugh over jokes and riddles, cry over Anne Frank's diaries, become angry over hunger in America, be more resourceful over recycling, feel powerless in the face of the panda's impending extinction, and be awed at the insides of a whale. You do not have to read makebelieve to entrance children. By their very nature, they are information sponges. They want to know about the real world.

By the way, you don't have to read aloud whole books. Much nonfiction is particularly suited to reading in bits and pieces. Feel free to pick and choose from many books and to mix and match excerpts from nonfiction with fiction. And if your children want to draw or color while listening, let them.

PUBLICIZE PROCEDURES TO PARENTS

Take every opportunity to keep parents informed about what you do! Provide recommended reading lists for gift suggestions and vacation reading so that parents can link children and books at home. Share ideas from Chapter 5, "For Parents and Their Proxies."

Before your students leave school, review the day's activities with them: Remind them that they've vicariously experienced the flight of a bat, for example, or have finished another chapter or two in a good book. Encourage them to share what they've done with their families.

If "What did you do in school today, dear?" elicits "Nothing, the teacher just read to us," it's easy to understand why 20 minutes of reading aloud can seem like a waste of time. But if the answer is "Wow! The teacher read to us and I began to feel like a bat...my fingers seemed to grow...did you know the bat's wings are his hands?...and...," then the 20 minutes becomes time well spent.

As a teacher, you are aware that reading aloud to children is not just a time filler—that it stimulates visualization and exercises imagination, that sustained silent reading gives children practice in concentration and in reading for the sheer pleasure it brings. But it's not enough that you know. You must also make sure parents—and their children—understand as well. To the folks at home, youngsters are both your medium and your message. Make it loud and clear.

BOOKTALK THE BEST OF BOTH WORLDS

As you select tales that you hope will entice listeners to become readers, remember that the truth can be as spellbinding as fiction. And that the beauty of storytelling nonfiction lies in its ability to sell itself—it can be so visual.

Take *Steven Caney's Invention Book* (Workman, 1985). Imagine how youngsters will clamor for it after you roller-skate to the front of the room, earmuffs on head, Band-Aid™ on hand, to tell the stories behind the three inventions. You could even sip soda through a straw as you paraphrase its creation! Or, having wheeled out the volumes you are about to booktalk in a shopping cart borrowed (with permission) from a nearby supermarket, you describe its origin. Until the inventor tricked them, shoppers wouldn't touch Mr. Goldman's contraption, as you will discover in Don Wulffson's *Invention of Ordinary Things* (Lothrop, 1981; Avon, 1991).

Barb Dean, Manager of Children's Services at the Prince George (British Columbia) Public Library successfully grabs fifth to tenth graders when she reads "Portrait of Death" from Don Wulffson's *Amazing True Stories* (Cobblehill, 1991) and connects it to Caroline Cooney's *Flight #116 Is Down* (Scholastic, 1992); Elizabeth Lutzeier's *The Wall* (Holiday, 1992); and Carol Matas's *Daniel's Story* (Scholastic, 1993). She gives kids the ghost IQ test from James M. Deem's *How to Find a Ghost* (Houghton, 1988; Avon 1990), then connects them to Daniel Cohen's *Phone Call from a Ghost* (Putnam, 1989) and Betty Wright's *The Ghost of Mercy Manor* (Scholastic, 1993).

Coauthors, Betty Carter and Richard F. Abrahamson, write that "all literature... represents the appropriate raw materials for booktalking," in *Nonfiction for Young Adults: From Delight to Wisdom* (Oryx, 1990). They've connected science fiction to Brian Aldiss's *Trillion Year Spree: The History of Science Fiction* (Atheneum, 1986); recommended mysteries be expanded to include books on finding solutions, such as David Macauley's *The Way Things Work* (Houghton, 1988); and suggested Jane Louise Curry's *Me, Myself, and I* (McElderry, 1987) and similar fictional titles be shared along with collections of experiments when science fair time arrives.

MAGNIFICENT MUNIFICENCE

Every month, Kim Pepper of Somesvile, Maine, buys a children's book at Oz Bookstore in nearby Southwest Harbor and gives it to her public library. She also buys "tons" of books for her own children.

Such remarkable year-round gift giving is rare, but teachers can probably stimulate an addition or two to a child's classroom, or school's collection, with a judicious hint to parents. Include them on a list of recommended titles you send home when parents ask for gift-giving ideas.

Suggest that they make wonderful presents for parents to give to their children, children to give to each other, or as a group gift in lieu of the expendable miscellany kids generally select for teachers. With their signatures on a specially prepared bookplate, the class can leave behind a present that teachers and children will enjoy together for years to come. Choose from any of the books in this guide: They are cornucopias of facts that can launch research for either classroom or homework assignments.

START A BACK-TO-BOOKS CLUB
OR COLLEAGUES' READING CLUB

Have you read any books *not* written for children lately? That, too, may seem like a silly question, yet I frequently find myself in the presence of teachers who have not perused a nonprofessional, nonchildren's, nonmagazine in years. They tell me, "I just don't have the time."

Keeping in touch with reading's pleasures is as essential to the effective teacher as any other endeavor. When connecting kids to books, the memory of great-books-once-read palls against the mention of great-books-one's-reading. Start reading again—with a district book group for you and your colleagues.

In the September 1989 issue of *The Kobrin Letter*, I asked my subscribers if they read enough. I told them I thought I did until the previous June when my husband took me (and an armful of books) to a "secret" vacation spot with no TV, radio, or other diversions. Just a bucolic view, a large porch, and comfortable chairs. We read, each of us, four of the sort of books we'd always meant to read, but never seemed to have the time for. It was an eye-opening experience!

Upon our return, I joined the Peruse and Schmooze (P.S.) Society, a book club my husband had started; watched TV less; and read more. I recommended my readers start a book group, too. A teacher at one of my workshops later that year told me she had started one and that the opportunity to discuss literature is a distinct contrast to the usual faculty room chatter.

BRINGING BOOKS TO BROOKLINE

Naomi Gordon, Elementary Language Arts Coordinator for the Brookline (MA) Public Schools, told me that Brookline's Literature Study Group has met since 1989. Anyone in the district can attend the eight monthly meetings during the school year and typically fifty to sixty people show up.

Before each meeting, while everyone else has refreshments and schmoozes, volunteer facilitators get together for 15 minutes to share insights and outline conversational approaches to that month's book. The facilitators then lead individual groups of ten to twelve people in a 90-minute discussion.

The groups, which are made up of participants from a range of grade levels and specialities, stay the same from session to session, so members can get to know each other. Whole-group sharing takes place after the small-group discussions on a voluntary basis. Once or twice a year, a guest speaker enlivens the get togethers. A storyteller and jazz combo helped celebrate the study group's fifth anniversary.

Ms. Gordon said that among the book group's many benefits participants have particularly noted the pleasure they get when they (1) read books they would not have chosen otherwise and (2) have the opportunity to discuss them with other teachers. Knowing in advance they will be talking with colleagues about the book in hand allows them to read with friends' "voices in their heads" and wonder about their reactions.

Two activities have spun out of their book group: One is Brookline Read, where students' parents and faculty members are linked with the help of the public librarians. Participants meet in the fall to discuss two books, one fiction and one nonfiction. First they discuss the books in small groups, then assemble to hear authors and other guest speakers. Additionally, at all Brookline schools, the librarians and teachers have begun to meet each month to read and discuss children's books: a single book, books by one author, books on one topic, or whatever. Brookline's teachers are readers!

There are infinite ways to organize book discussions. Most groups I know about meet monthly and rotate the choice of book from member to member. Some limit choices to a particular type of book, such as nonfiction or contemporary novels. Our group has no such limitations and we've bounced from nonfiction best-sellers to classic novels.

Whatever your process, the important thing is to read. And when you share the joy of reading with peers, the students can't help but get the message. So, to be the example you'd like children to emulate, find the time to read for pleasure, too. It's there.

FOMENT REVOLUTION—
A TEACHER/LIBRARIAN CONSPIRACY (TLC)

Have you done your homework lately? The homework you assign to students, that is. From examples librarians cite during workshops, it would seem that too many assignments are merely time wasters.

Some children arrive at the library for information on a subject about which little is written, or that exists only for older readers in a form too complex to decipher. Other children appear with a ban against encyclopedia use and a list of questions unanswerable with the trade books at hand. Yet others appear with a questionable book-report mandate: "...a nonfiction book...100 pages long" or "a fiction book about prejudice...100 pages long."

With homework like that, a trip to the library becomes a source of anxiety rather than the start of an adventure. If you spot a colleague making such assignments, suggest s/he make certain that assignments can be done and that the library contains, in a readily readable form, what students are looking for. Sometimes that does require the use of an encyclopedia. And remember: A book chosen merely for its length is better left unread—it will be, anyway!

TLC advocates that teachers consult with librarians in advance of lesson plans (remember "reserve" books in college?). Librarians can then share their knowledge of the collection and help teachers capitalize on what's available or what can reasonably be ordered. They can estimate the time necessary to pull books together and to request, receive, and catalogue new ones. Forewarned, they work more effectively with young researchers.

TLC recognizes that all students need not have identical assignments. Teachers and librarians collaborate on a menu of homework options, employing a wide variety of resources that might otherwise sit unused on the shelf.

Since collections always change, assignments change, too. TLC keeps homework fresh and interesting, both to students and teachers. Librarians gain more satisfaction as they plan how their collections are shaped and used. To make homework stimulate, not inhibit, a taste for the written word and the search for knowledge, try a little TLC.

KEEP COLLECTIONS CURRENT

There are classics in fiction that will live forever, but the nonfiction you set out for children must reflect today's world. Texts that depict a snub-nosed Brontosaurus, two-mooned Neptune, undiscovered Titanic at unreachable depths, and a United Soviet Socialist Republic serve only to confuse and mislead. Pull them out.

Occasionally I hear, "I won't have anything left on the subject, if I throw out the old books!" Better fewer books than bad books! Particularly when librarians enter collection titles into a central data base for interlibrary loan. Mary D. Lankford, Director of Library and Media Services for the Irving Independent School District in Texas, and children's book author, urges librarians to form teams when it's time to weed. Fewer dated books are retained when the resident librarian must overrule the team to justify their shelf—and computer—space, for colleagues can quickly suggest alternatives.

Once library collections are keyed into an automated system, she notes, it will be easier to search for dates of publication to keep nonfiction titles current. Ms. Lankford recommends that librarians who must hand weed without benefit of computers "divide and conquer." Taken a shelf at a time, over an extended period, the task becomes more manageable.

ALL FOR ONE AND ONE FOR ALL

It's axiomatic that your library budget isn't large enough to do everything you'd like to stimulate kids' reading. In the community at large, though, there are most likely many untapped sources of help—fiscal and otherwise. You're not alone out there, though it sometimes must seem you are.

The Indianapolis-Marion, Indiana County Library has a cornucopia of creative co-sponsorships for its reading programs. In one three-month period, Chris Cairo and her colleagues conspired with a local pizza parlor in a dinosaur book read-aloud program for families, using coupons for free pizzas as incentives; initiated a library treasure hunt with a Native American theme co-sponsored by The Indiana Association for the Gifted; and launched a "Read the Zoo" incentive program funded by *The Indianapolis Star and News.* With the help of its co-sponsor, each program was well-larded with appropriate flyers, posters, pins, and stickers. These activities were all aimed at elementary school-aged children and their families, with other programs for preschool and day care.

MAKE FAIRS FAIR TO BOOKS

If you are asked to help organize a book fair, please be sure that the purpose is to raise literary consciousness and not merely to raise funds. There's no doubt that book fairs raise money. I've seen it done many times. Local book dealers and distributors cooperate because they profit, too. They fall into two classes, however: Those who are in it primarily for profit and those who really care about the quality of the books they offer children. Both will help your short-term cash needs, only the latter can aid the long-term mental growth of your children.

The excitement of a book fair and the involvement of parents or other volunteers provide you a rare opportunity to "sell" the very best books available, so please keep the quality standard high. It goes without saying (she says) that nonfiction books should be prominently displayed.

What does one *do* with the money raised at a book fair? One invests it in the library, of course. If the playground needs a new swing, let someone organize a swing fair. But to use book fair profits for anything but books, why, it's simply not fair.

CALL IN NEIGHBORS

Children's librarian Jan Lieberman of Santa Clara, California, told me about on-going happenings where professionals outside the library world made in-kind contributions to the City Library's reading programs: a dinosaur authority from a nearby college visits with slides and artifacts; a model plane enthusiast lends planes to the library for display, conducts workshops on their construction, and—of great interest to children—shows videos of spectacular crashes of model planes; scuba divers bring equipment for the kids to try on; a Gilbert and Sullivan group casts children into a two-minute sample of *The Mikado's* chorus and processional; The Bee Man visits with a swarm; a string quartet plays and the members explain their instruments using hoses and straws to demonstrate; my son, The Tapigami Man, teaches simple dance routines and origami; there are toy shows, other music groups.... And everyone connects kids to books.

PROMOTE YOUNG AUTHORS

When you help children celebrate the books *they* write, illustrate, and publish, you demonstrate in a most impressive way that books are worth celebrating. You also enlarge youngsters' knowledge of literature's scope and provide insight into the literary process. And you give them an outlet for creativity and a meaningful way to use the language arts.

Pickerington, Ohio, Elementary second graders discovered this when, with the help of art teacher Mary Sheridan, they wrote and illustrated *Who Lives at Pickerington Pond* as part of a "Good Earth = Good Education" theme. Ms. Sheridan told me that the volume provided the youngsters both "a sensitive and sensational record of observation" and unexpected funding for more school-made books. It documents the youngsters' visit to a nearby wetlands under the guidance of naturalist/children's book author Ron Hirschi. Each color-photocopied page is a composite of an annotated photo of pond flora or fauna, set against a background of original art. When Ms. Sheridan sent a copy to the photocopier's manufacturer, the school was granted $3300 worth of equipment to help students continue publishing.

Since 1977, the Reading Council, School Librarians Association, and Office of Education in my county, Santa Clara, California, have promoted and sponsored a Young Authors' Fair. In April, authors, illustrators, and publishers in kindergarten through ninth grade display, at a central location, the books they began in the fall. There, their families, teachers, librarians, and the general public admire them; and each child receives a certificate: a certificate of recognition—fairs are not competitions.

TRUST THE KIDS

Children will read if you surround them with books about subjects that capture their fancies. You'll attract them with books that take them to the scene, behind the scene, or to any other place they cannot ordinarily go. You'll enthrall them with books that reveal what lies beneath their skin, nestles in the niches of the planet, or soars through other solar systems. You'll captivate children with what is, what was, and what might be—in fact and fiction.

Whether you're a school or public librarian, a teacher or a parent, youngsters' enthusiasm and excitement about good literature—fiction and nonfiction—depends upon your ability to promote it to them and to those who reach them.

Jo Carr prefaced her insightful book *Beyond Fact* (American Library Association, 1982) with "A child is not a vase to be filled but a fire to be lit."

Fire 'em up!

5•

For Parents
and Their Proxies

Knowledge cuts up the world; wisdom makes it whole.
> David Maybury-Lewis
> Host of *Millennium,*
> PBS special, 1992

It's up to you, you know. You're in charge. Teachers and librarians can do only so much in the limited time available. Most of the job of linking kids and books must be done before and after school, on weekends and vacations—during the approximately 80 percent of a child's waking hours spent outside of the classroom.

How can you connect kids to books?

Remember that kids are copycats. If *you* set aside time for books and reading, odds are the children you care for will. If you don't, chances are they won't.

TAKE A TIP FROM TEACHERS

Teachers set aside time for sustained, silent reading every day, to help children acquire the habit and discover the pleasure of being alone with something good to read. I call it SQUIRT for **S**ustained **Q**uiet **U**n**I**nterrupted **R**eading **T**ime. SQUIRT isn't reserved for schoolrooms alone, though.

As my son was growing up, I set aside a short reading-to-myself time each day while he was up and about. I was out of bounds, but David could set his reading chair or spread out on the rug next to me to look through his own books. As long as there was "No Talking." Pretty soon, *my* reading-to-myself time became *our* reading-to-myself time. At first, we were alone together for a very short time, so that David could become accustomed to the rules. As his attention span increased, so did our reading time. But I kept it just beneath his limit. We never went beyond 15 minutes. The duration was unimportant; it was the repetition—and ease— that was essential.

READ WITH YOUR CHILDREN

I wanted to establish a custom. We read to ourselves every day and, as I had hoped, it became a habit—as much a habit as my reading aloud, another daily event. Our days were never complete unless we shared both times. He doesn't remember that he pulled his chair up to mine with "Reading time, Mom," but I do. He doesn't remember—but he still reads.

Plan alone-together sessions with your youngsters. Make certain that they have many books to peruse and that they understand that no talking is the rule. Keep the first experience short to guarantee success. Stop before their span of attention ends, so that they look forward to tomorrow's session when they can be "grown up" and "read" quietly. Remember you want to establish a habit of enjoying a private time with a book.

Read as a family. Set aside 20 minutes every night for a family alone-together reading time. Read the newspaper, magazines, comics, *TV Guide*. Scan packets of money-saving coupons, cookbooks, small appliance manuals. We are surrounded by practical nonfiction that is both fascinating and enlightening. Even phone books. In many areas they are a handy, quick reference for community and emergency services, lifesaving techniques, and time zones.

The phone book brought my son countless hours of pleasure as soon as he was able to identify his name. He loved to see it in print and no matter how often we went to the library, he'd head for the phone book collection to see where in the world he could find a Kobrin. These days he'd be scouring microfiche and other databases as well. If you have computer-based information available in your home, share that with children too. (Though they may be way ahead of you there!)

Whatever you read, do it together. I've been told that any activity done twenty-one consecutive days becomes a habit. If you and your children start today and read together every day for a month, you will begin a habit that's likely to endure. You will establish the positive attitude toward books and reading that will help your youngsters become better readers and thinkers.

Reserve a day a month to demonstrate the fine art of browsing by visiting a bookstore as a family. Make part of your vacation budget a new book the whole family will enjoy. Pick it out together. Buy books as birthday presents for your children's playmates, cousins, and classmates. Giving a book as a gift helps a child understand that it is something of value.

MAKE READING THE RAGE

As they get older, let your children join the ranks of read-alouders. While my husband was recovering from recurring bouts of illness, David read aloud to him from the *Guinness Book of World Records*. Together, they pursued trivia (long before the game was invented) from the assorted books and almanacs in his collection—nonfiction was and still is his favorite reading. Long automobile rides were dramatically shortened as all of us (except the driver) took turns reading aloud.

David read aloud recipes to make certain we didn't forget any thing as meals went together. At the end of the day, he became the "real, live TV newsman" with newspaper cartoons, squibs, or other interesting articles as his script. He'd read to us from the mound of junk mail to see if it contained anything we needed.

Use every opportunity: Before a trip have children read about the destination. As you travel, let them read maps and estimate times and distances. Read movie reviews together. Have your child keep a weather log, getting information daily from the newspaper. Slip notes to your youngsters in their lunch boxes—jokes, riddles, or mini-puzzles they and their classmates can enjoy.

As for books, don't limit yourself to children's literature. Read adult nonfiction aloud. It doesn't matter if youngsters don't understand all your words, what matters is that you speak new ones. They'll pick up the meaning of an unfamiliar word from the familiar words that surround it. That's how their vocabulary increases. When children are young, you buy clothes that are a little too big so that they can grow into them; the same should be true for books. The more language children hear, the more they will use; the more fluently they speak, the easier reading becomes.

NO BOOK IS TOO OLD OR TOO YOUNG

You'll find this advice elsewhere addressed to teachers and librarians, but it bears repeating:

When children start to choose their own books, *never* admonish them with "That book's too easy (or hard) for you. Put it back and take one that's harder (or easier)." Books that are "right" for children are the ones they want to read—or look at—now!

No one chastises us for flirting with books that are too easy or too hard. As adults we can take pleasure in beautifully illustrated books designed for toddlers and read nonfiction children's books as an introduction to unfamiliar subjects. We browse through weighty tomes, taste the language, look at the photographs and illustrations, and perhaps read the captions in books far too technical for us to understand. And we relax on occasion with an indulgence of romances, mysteries, fantasies, mass-market blockbusters, and other fast-read publications that provide a breezy change of pace.

Allow children the same freedom. A book is its own reward. That reward is unique to each reader. Kids cannot learn which books are "right" for them until they—on their own—have discovered which ones aren't.

BEDTIME IS ONE OF THE BEST TIMES

And, of course, remember books at bedtime. Few moments with children are as warm, loving, and long-remembered as those between tucking in and the last sweet-dreams kiss. Many adults say their strongest childhood memories are of a bedtime reading ritual. I remember my mother reading to me as vividly as if I'd fallen asleep to the sound of her voice just last night. Share counting books, alphabet books, books about trains and dinosaurs, sharks and space flights, knights and motorcycles. Use wordless picture books, newspapers, magazines, comic books, and books of lists and world records. In whole or in part. One book or many. Once or over and over and over again. Fact or fiction. Both.

PARENTS AREN'T THE ONLY ONES

Odds are that both parents of small children work today. Though they may reserve time to read with their young ones—or spontaneously read when the opportunity arises—there is seldom enough time. Grandparents and other proxies who care for small children represent a reservoir of time unpressured by normal parental pressures. That's an easy assignment, because nothing is more satisfying than reading to or with a child, especially one on your lap.

You who are grandparents are most likely the best audience kids have. If a book they share triggers a thought or a question, you have the time to listen and take the question seriously. Children are information sponges; they'll absorb what you impart. Talk is important to children; the more they talk, the easier reading becomes. You can introduce children to books you remember from your children's youth. The memories they evoke are even richer when shared with grandchildren.

As you plan vacations, read travel books with your grandchildren or other children you help care for, so they will know where you will be going and what you expect to see. When you return, don't forget to include among your gifts at least one children's book from the place(s) you visit. Books can help you "be there" whether you are in the same room, thousands of miles away, or gone forever.

Dream with grandchildren, or other young charges, about your past and their future. They're linked. You can bring *your* generation alive. On joint visits to the library, ask the reference librarian for newspapers and magazines published during your youth. Look through them together. Talk about the cars you rode, the movies you saw, the TV programs you watched, the world events that affected you. See if any of the books you read as a child are still in print. If they are, read them together.

Grandparents, ask your grandchildren to write down or record your memories; and together work on a book that will become a treasured family keepsake. "We must share our stories with one another," writes grandmother Roslyn Bresnick-Perry in *Leaving for America*, for they create a "connection, an empathy, a reaching out.... They cross generations, dissolve time and space, overcome differences and barriers."

When older, your grandchildren will harvest recollections of your talks and read with interest what you wrote together. Your book about real people, places, and things in their heritage will nourish the memories you shared. Those are the recollections they will pass on to their children. In *their* own special nonfiction books.

KEEP KIDS THINKING CRITICALLY

If children are to be critical readers and thinkers, it's essential that they learn to check and double-check what they've read in one place with what's written in another. Teach your children not to believe everything that's said. If they read something or hear something on TV that they distrust, encourage them to react. Show them how to look up facts, how to check several sources, how to challenge a position with one of their own.

Encourage children to write letters to editors, authors, publishers, TV and radio stations to thank them for good work, agree or disagree with what they say, or ask for more information. (Klutz Press specifically asks children to write for the background story of any photograph published in *Earthsearch* [1994].) If your local newspaper does not review books for your children, have them write and suggest one.

IT'S OK TO NOT KNOW

"I don't know, let's look it up," should come readily to your lips. It's never wrong to admit you don't know the answer to a child's question; it's better, though, to initiate a search for the answer. When children are very young, you'll have to do most of the research; as they get older, they will. If the answer can't be found at home, aim them at a reference librarian, or have them find the answer at school and bring it home. Finding answers is an important source of pride for children.

PROVIDE A READY-READING PLACE

Reading rooms and reference desks aren't only for libraries. In your own home, or wherever your children gather, set aside a comfortable place to read. It doesn't have to be a whole room. Any nook or cranny with a comfortable chair—even pillows on the floor—will do. Make sure there's good lighting. Make sure there are special places to keep books neatly—on bookshelves or tabletops reserved for books-being-read. Children treasure such special book places at grandparents' homes, too, whether it be a shelf, a drawer, or a secret storage box.

Provide your youngsters with special places for their personal collections as soon as you begin collecting books for them. Books do NOT belong in a toy box any more than your favorite CDs belong in a tool box. Make or purchase decorative bookmarks and bookplates. Treat books as honored guests.

Build a home reference center. Start with the reference works you may already have—dictionary, atlas, almanac, phone book. Add books on subjects of interest to your children—sports, camping, space travel, dinosaurs, presidents, whatever.

SUPPORT YOUR LOCAL LIBRARIAN AND BOOKSTORE

Make going to the public library a weekly event, at the very least. This is a wonderful opportunity for kids and parents or proxies to explore together. Introduce your child(ren) to the librarian. A dedicated children's librarian can have a profound influence on an inquisitive young mind. By guiding book selection from a child's early years through the time that a child makes his or her own choices, the librarian can raise and sustain interest in good books. A quick check of your municipal records will confirm that librarians' rewards are not received in the form of high salaries. Their satisfaction is derived from the pleasure of their patrons—your children and you.

Support your school librarians, too. School is the best place for children to learn what librarians offer, what their specialized training and knowledge of the literature can add to learning. If the fabric of knowledge is woven of books, skilled librarians are among the master weavers. Employ them.

By the way, what is the relative ratio of books to sports gear at your child's school? Is the school library as up to date as the athletic equipment? Nonfiction especially requires constant updating to keep information relevant. Lobby for adequate library funds with school administrators.

And if your neighborhood is blessed with a shop that deals exclusively with books for youngsters, you'll find that the proprietor and staff will know about or will have read most of the stock. They know the literature and can suggest books that are "right" for your child, from fanciful fables to books about bugs. As with the librarians, it helps if the booksellers know your child. Introduce them.

YOU ARE THE MOST IMPORTANT RESOURCE

Your youngsters' principal route to reading is—you. Children learn by observation. If you respect good books, have them around, frequent their habitats, demand their use in school, and, most importantly, read them yourself, then you are well on your way to developing children who'll read. And when those books are nonfiction, your readers will become critical thinkers as well.

With nonfiction titles from this guide, suggestions from your youngsters' teachers, and ideas from librarians and your local bookshop proprietors, you can give the gifts that use no batteries and require no assembly. Eye-opening gifts that can be shared, savored, and cherished by generations of children.

The Non-Book Report

WHY DO I CALL THIS A NON-BOOK REPORT?

Because just plain "book report" brings to mind those every-
one-does-the-same-thing, no-nonfiction-allowed-unless-it's-a-
biography, describe-the-setting, who-are-the main-characters,
what-is-the-plot, paper-pencil assignments that children anticipate
with as much pleasure as adults contemplate root canal work.

Non-Book Reports are assignments children thoroughly enjoy.
Everyone does something different, all books are allowed, and the
reports are not necessarily written.

Rather than be constrained by one format, why not make the
assignment a creative experience—for both teacher and student?
Teachers who have adopted creative book report strategies to
involve kids with books (I didn't originate the idea, I just named
it) find that they greatly improve attitudes toward reading and
learning. Children don't want to stop.

You'll notice that the Non-Book Report form is almost a blank
page. I developed this open-ended form after a few years in the

classroom. It has proven to be the simplest, most effective tool to keep my kids and me interested in books, reading, and learning.

THE NON-BOOK REPORT

```
                              Name_____
                              Date_____
   Title _____
   Author _____
   Illustrator_____
   Publisher _____
   Date of Copyright _____
   Project _____

   _____
   _____
   _____
   _____
```

HOW NON-BOOK REPORTS WORK

1. Upon the completion of any book they chose, my students picked up one of these forms and filled in the blank spaces after name, date, title, author, illustrator, publisher, and date of copyright.
2. They slipped the form into the book and put both on top of the piano in my classroom. (The only horizontal surface not otherwise occupied!)
3. I took book and form home, read the book, and made suggestions for a "project". I linked what I'd read with what I knew about the child's interests and academic strengths and weaknesses.
4. Back in the classroom, I returned the book to the child who worked on the project, slipped it or a note that it was finished into the book, and returned both to the piano top.
5. We conferred and checked out the project together.

Occasionally I assigned different children similar projects, but usually each child had a different one. The last few years I taught full-time, my youngsters were responsible for one book and one project a week. By June, almost every student had fulfilled that requirement and most of my youngsters had far exceeded it— some reading between 75 and more than 100 books during the nine months. And many of them had created their own projects, more challenging than any I might have suggested.

THE SUCCESS SECRET

Step 3 above holds the secret to the success of this strategy: I read every book my students read. If we don't read the books we promote, our students will look upon our words as just another version of "Take this, kid, it's good for you (but I wouldn't touch it with a 10-foot pole)"!

I read every book. And yes, that meant reading or refreshing my memory on 30 to 35 books a week. Wait! Before you slam shut this book and exclaim that you don't by any stretch of the imagination have time to read 35 books a week, please understand that I didn't start that way.

When I began this system, my students were responsible for one book a month. Any teacher can read 30 or so elementary-grade-level books a month. The next year, I raised the requirement to one book every three weeks, and it wasn't until two years later, when I was familiar enough with the literature, and comfortable enough with the system, that I set the one-book-a-week rule. By then, I had to read only a few new books a month.

My youngsters thrived on the challenges I set them. I might ask a youngster with reading difficulties, for example, to pick a few paragraphs or pages (depending on the size of the book) and practice until she or he can read them aloud to me—fluently. I've asked children to read aloud to me or to the class, memorize poetry, build dioramas, locate on a map the places mentioned in the book, prepare a recipe for their family (cookbooks are popular), write to an author, or make up their own assignments.

They've interviewed parents or other relatives on book-related topics, polled the school for opinions, made a life-size image of an animal or person, conducted experiments, made a five-minute audio-cassette about the book (my school didn't have a video camera), visited another classroom and "sold" them on a book, or demonstrated or taught them something they had learned from it. As often as not I have used each book as a stepping stone to another one.

ELAINE GRIFFIN'S BOOK PROJECTS

After she attended my workshop in 1987, teacher Elaine Griffin, in Chiniak, Alaska, adopted and adapted Beverly's Brief Book Break (see page 18) and the Non-Book Report. Two months later Elaine told me that she, her students, and their parents couldn't be more enthusiastic about the results. She permits her fifth through eighth-graders to read *any* book in the school library, regardless of the reading level. They select a book (most often nonfiction, she said), design a related project, and present their finished work to the class. They have no other homework.

Her students have become so excited about their self-motivated assignments, that many spend the whole weekend immersed in projects—often with as-interested parents.

In 1994, I asked Elaine if she and her husband/coteacher, Ned, remained enthusiastic about their reading program. She said that it is so effective, parents change residence to be close enough to enroll their children in the school with "book projects." One of the many pluses of these projects is their value in a multi-cultural setting, she said, because the required parent involvement calls for no reading or writing.

To illustrate, Elaine told me about an especially moving book project that came about when a new student, native to Palau in the Caroline Islands, took home an article on mapmaking. His dad knew exactly how to construct the navigational tool used by early Polynesians and, under his guidance, the boy made the device and presented it to the class. "I can't tell you the magic we all felt," Elaine exclaimed. "Actually holding this artifact from another time period and culture in our hands...we imagined what it was like to look through it, to match wave patterns...it was wonderful!"

When the boy's mother, who neither reads nor writes English, came into the school and saw the tool on display, she was proud of her son and appreciated his being "in a school that values our culture."

The youngster's next self-motivated project on Leonardo da Vinci progressed from a pop-up book through children's and adult books on the artist to a presentation that included a mirror-writing display and videotape. Having come from a school where everything had been "lock-step and dittos," his father noted, the child's new-found freedom to choose what he read and how he would "report" created a marked change in attitude.

Elaine reiterated that the strategy is successful because it combines freedom and structure. The children select the topic and the project, and the Griffins help them find and implement a structure for its presentation. With their compliments, here are the forms they've devised for their projects.

STOP PRESS!

At the urging of one very pleased parent, Elaine completed and submitted the necessary forms to a teacher-of-the-year selection committee. In October, 1994, she became the Kodiak Teacher of the Year; in November, 1994, she was named Alaska Teacher of the Year; and in April, 1995, President Clinton presented her on television as the National Teacher of the Year!

THE PROJECT PLANNING SHEET
Elaine and Ned Griffin

NAME _____ BOOK TITLE _____ DATE _____

DAY	PLAN	ACTUAL WORK DONE	TIME SPENT ON PROJECT	PAGES READ IN: __(title)__	TIME SPENT READING	PARENT INITIALS
FRIDAY & WEEKEND						
MONDAY						
TUESDAY						
WEDNESDAY						
THURSDAY						
			TOTAL		TOTAL	

PARENT COMMENTS:

Was the work done and shown to you on a daily basis? _____

How was the difficulty level? (challenging, just right, too easy…) _____

Comment on time management and organization: _____

What sort of learning took place? _____

Effort? _____

Other: _____

1. On Friday, each student chooses a book, makes a plan, and writes down what s/he'll do at home that weekend in the PLAN column.
2. Students indicate what was done in the ACTUAL WORK DONE column. The planning sheet is brought to school on a daily basis for the Griffins to learn what was accomplished the night before.
3. Every day during lunch, the Griffins and their students talk as a group about the projects.
4. Before students go home each day, they fill out the next block in the PLAN column.
5. In the TIME SPENT ON PROJECT column, students indicate how much time they devoted to working, not reading.
6. In the PAGES READ IN: (title) column, students note how many pages were read—in books related to this project and/or any other book.
7. The TIME SPENT READING column is for noting time not used for constructing, writing, etc.
8. The PARENT INITIALS column keeps parents involved on a daily basis.
9. PARENT COMMENTS are filled out by parents on Thursday nights and handed in by the students on Fridays with the completed project. All projects are presented and shared on Fridays and put in the display case for the next week. Displays change weekly.

INITIATE YOUR OWN READING RENAISSANCE

Adopt the Non-Book Report habit. It develops the enjoyment of reading. Now that you've finished this chapter, turn to the Guide (page 51) and scan the tips for using a book. They are marked with an eyeglasses icon. You'll find that they're frequently adaptable to books other than the one they accompany. Try them or their variations with your children. Before you realize it, you'll find yourself delighted by a room filled with Non-Book Reporters.

7.

One Critic's Criteria

There is nothing proprietary about evaluating books. You can do it as easily as I. Whether you are selecting a single nonfiction title or a library full, however, it's useful to have a checklist as you skim and scan. Here's mine.

Take it along the next time you sift through books and make it yours by adapting it as you deem necessary.

1. Attractiveness
    - Does the cover beckon, the design encourage perusal, and do the photographs and illustrations engage and enlighten?
    - Unless the writing mesmerizes, say NO to ugly books, period!
2. Tone
    - Does the writing "grab" and hold the reader? Any subject can be made interesting. Insist on it.
3. Rhetoric
    - Does the author carefully distinguish between fact, theory, and opinion?

4. Appropriateness
   - Is the style and language appropriate?
   - Does the information match the child?
   - Did the author start at the beginning and proceed in a logical manner?

5. Format
   - Do headings and subheads break up long blocks of type?
   - Is the scope and sequence logical and easy to grasp?
   - Are text and pictures complementary?
   - Are there a table of contents, an index, and other appropriate appendices?
   - Are pages numbered?

6. Reliability
   - Can you take the author's word? Is there evidence—on the flyleaf, copyright page, acknowledgments, photo credits, or bibliography—that the author's resources are up to date and credible? If not, check with a librarian, the review media, or a local authority—perhaps a friend or relative.

7. Accuracy
   - There's no practical way to judge the accuracy of everything you read. So make certain your children have at least three books on a topic in order to compare and contrast for as close to an accurate answer as is reasonably possible.

8. Illustrations
   - Are relative sizes obvious, or is there a recognizable scale of reference?
   - Are enlargement or micrograph magnifications noted?
   - Are photographs and illustrations crisp, clear, and uncluttered?
   - Remember: Black and white can be as effective as color—except when used to illustrate something colorful. Scientifically accurate renderings can often provide more information than photographs, and vice versa.

9. Stereotypes
   - Avoid them: Not all scientists wear glasses, nor are all pilots men, nurses female, senior citizens stooped, sharks dangerous, nor inhabitants of third world countries starving.

10. Cautions
- Are dangers noted and precautions advised?
- Does the author dissuade readers from emulating professionals and provide warnings about potentially injurious activities?

Don't expect every good book to excel in all respects, but
defects should be heavily outweighed by overall excellence.

The ultimate test a book must pass is this: Does reading the
book become as much an aesthetic as an intellectual experience?
If so, you are holding an eyeopener.

THE GUIDE

More Than 800
Books for Inquisitive Kids

How to Use this Guide
and the Quick-Link Index

I've coded the entries in my Guide for easy reference. Here's an example:

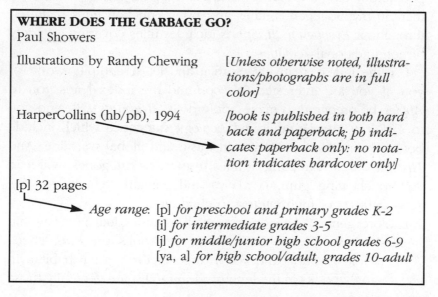

WHERE DOES THE GARBAGE GO?
Paul Showers

Illustrations by Randy Chewing   *[Unless otherwise noted, illustra-
tions/photographs are in full
color]*

HarperCollins (hb/pb), 1994   *[book is published in both hard
back and paperback; pb indi-
cates paperback only: no nota-
tion indicates hardcover only]*

[p] 32 pages

Age range: *[p] for preschool and primary grades K-2*
[i] for intermediate grades 3-5
[j] for middle/junior high school grades 6-9
[ya, a] for high school/adult, grades 10-adult

To make entries in the guide easier to scan, I've shortened publisher's names. You'll find the complete name listed in the Key to Publishers on page 267.

The age range is only to help, not limit, the linking of books to children. Junior high photo-essays can be as enriching to primary graders just looking, as their "first" books can be to junior-highers just beginning new subjects.

Reviews prefaced by include teaching tips and/or additional related titles.

THE QUICK-LINK INDEX

The Quick-Link Index will make it easy for you to find books linked by subject matter—even when the subject is not obvious from the title. Take *Giants in the Land*, for example. Would you know that it was about trees? Probably not. Yet if you were interested in the subject, the Quick-Link index would bring you right to this book when you looked under *Trees*.

Biography and its cross-references lead to more than 70 books about real people; the books under *Careers* point out titles about people pursuing their life's work; *Fiction* pulls together the more than 30 myths, legends, tales and non-nonfiction titles scattered throughout *Eyeopeners II*. *Sports* includes titles covering a variety of non-traditional activities.

Use the index creatively. Scan it and let serendipity work for you. If you are interested in *Food* and the index leads you to *Apples*, be prepared to make apple dolls; *Habitats* will send you to *Children and Families* and *Ecology*, categories which include books about life in the Amazon Basin and global warming. And *History*, with its sampling of titles from many categories, will lead you to chewing gum, cowboys and cowgirls, chocolate, and cats—subjects of high interest to children.

Explore general categories as well as individual items within them. For example, when looking for books on *Bats*, check *Animals* and *Habitats* and you'll discover *Cave*, a bat habitat. In fact, the only books in the lengthy *Animals* list are generally those without specific animal names in their titles. *Bats, Cats, Dogs, Dinosaurs, Whales*, and other species have listings of their own.

SIMPLY FOR STUDENTS

There are few listings under *Anatomy, Archeology, Biology, Geology*, or other "ology" terms. Look instead under *Bodies, Mummies, Plants*, or *Rocks*—the terms children are more likely to use. And, for easy spotting—particularly when confronted by restless children on a rainy day—I've asterisked (**) the books not listed under Experiments that contain investigative, experimental, or arts/crafts activities. This is not a scholar's index. It has been developed to suit my teacher's instincts and to satisfy the needs of parents and other educators working with children. You'll find it guides you into strange areas where you'll be presented with unexpected learning opportunities. It is meant to be practical—to make fast connections.

CATEGORICALLY SPEAKING

Would that there were more room in the Guide for more categories. I've had to leave out groups of books that I know kids love. If a subject you seek is not included, perhaps it will appear in a **EYEOPENERS III**. In the meantime, you can keep abreast of the best children's nonfiction by subscribing to *The Kobrin Letter*, 732 Greer Road, Palo Alto CA 94303. You'll find a coupon you can photocopy on page 307.

AIDS

DOES AIDS HURT?
Marcia Quackenbush and Dr. Sylvia Villarreal
Network (pb), 1988/1992
[a] 149 pages

A clearly written, cogent explanation of why young children must learn about AIDS and how to talk and teach about the disease. The authors suggest ways to answer youngsters' questions and the values to stress while so doing. In addition to specific age-appropriate information and discussion/teaching strategies for boys and girls up to age ten, the coauthors also discuss what adults should know about AIDS. They write about the relationship between school and home—for example, how to interact with HIV-infected students or staff in school—and provide background and additional information sources on AIDS.

Jeanne Moutoussamy-Ashe wrote and photographed *Daddy and Me: A Photo Story of Arthur Ashe and His Daughter Camera* (Knopf, 1993), from her five-year-old daughter's perspective. To Camera, having AIDS meant not feeling well and just needing someone to love and take care of you. The Ashes hope to give other parents a way to discuss AIDS with their young children. This book will.

CHILDREN WITH THE AIDS VIRUS
Rosmarie Hausherr
B/w photographs by the author
Clarion (hb/pb), 1989
[p, i] 48 pages

Share this as soon as little ones start asking questions about AIDS. The author discusses the body's immune system in simple terms, allays youngsters' fears of catching the AIDS virus from everyday items, and explains how the disease spreads. She focuses on one youngster who was transfused with AIDS-contaminated blood and another who was born with AIDS. There are two texts: One to read aloud and the other, in smaller type, to supplement the first with more detail, if needed.

BE A FRIEND: CHILDREN WHO LIVE WITH HIV SPEAK
Lori S. Wiener, Aprille Best, and Philip A. Pizzo, Ed.
Illustrations
Whitman, 1994
[i, j] 40 pages

Dr. Wiener asked HIV afflicted children to complete such sentences as "If only..." and "I often wonder...." Their poignant answers and drawings give testimony to AIDS's devastation and the yearning they have to be accepted by their healthy peers. The publisher's profits and Dr. Wiener's royalties are being donated to the Pediatric AIDS Foundation.

EVERYTHING YOU NEED TO KNOW ABOUT AIDS
Barbara Taylor
Illustrations and b/w photographs
Rosen, 1988/1992
[j] 64 pages

Aptly designed for reluctant or less-capable junior high and high school readers, the well-organized, sharply focused, simply written chapters are set in large, but not too large, type. Ms. Taylor begins with a description of the AIDS virus and its lethal effect. She discusses how the disease spreads and its prevention. She concludes with a Q & A section, a glossary, and a list of sources for AIDS information and help.

LYNDA MADARAS TALKS TO TEENS ABOUT AIDS: AN ESSENTIAL GUIDE FOR PARENTS, TEACHERS, AND YOUNG PEOPLE
Lynda Madaras

B/w illustrations
Newmarket (hb/pb), 1988/1995
[j] 110 pages

Ms. Madaras covers topics most people are not comfortable with in a nonjudgmental, honest, straightforward, explicit, and thorough manner. Though she promotes and stresses abstinence, she realistically provides alternatives for the sexually active. She writes about "outercourse" and provides detailed instructions—with illustrations for correct condom use—on safe sex. She presents the facts and destroys the myths associated with AIDS and its transmission. She suggests ways teenagers can join the fight against the disease. The preface should be read by all concerned adults.

For a quick reference with answers to pertinent questions frequently asked by youngsters and adults, turn to *100 Questions and Answers About AIDS* (Beech Tree, 1993) by Michael Thomas Ford.

FIGHTING BACK: WHAT SOME PEOPLE ARE DOING ABOUT AIDS
Susan Kuklın
B/w photographs by author
Putnam, 1989
[j, ya] 144 pages

The literature on AIDS is not all about statistics, prohibitions, and techniques. There are also emotion-laden narratives of the ill and their allies. Photoessayist Kuklin was warmly welcomed into a team of volunteers who help AIDS sufferers and their loved ones so that she could document details of the lives and deaths of PWAs—Persons With AIDS. You and your high school students will surely be moved by the loving care which volunteers of all lifestyles bestow, and by the variety of ways that PWAs handle their illness.

KIDS MAKING QUILTS FOR KIDS: A YOUNG PERSON'S GUIDE FOR HAVING FUN WHILE HELPING OTHERS AND LEARNING ABOUT AIDS AND SUBSTANCE ABUSE
ABC Quilts
Photographs and b/w illustrations
Quilt Digest (pb), 1992
[i, j] 44 pages

As of late 1994, some 155,000 children-made quilts have been donated to hospitals for babies with HIV/AIDS, alcohol, or drug-related problems, thanks to Ellen Ahlgren. This retired teacher/counselor who began the now worldwide ABC Quilts project was motivated by the knowledge that most children have great anxiety about these problems, that quilting bees provide an ideal environment for discussion, and that afflicted babies would be comforted with a quilt of their own. In addition to clear directions for making quilts, the editors have included suggestions and facts and discussion starters for parents, teachers, youth leaders, and others interested in starting a quilt project with youngsters.

When I spoke to Ms. Ahlgren, she told me about the Noble Jr. High eighth graders in Berwick, Maine, who won first prize for a state-sponsored creative writing contest. They'd written about their quilt projects as seventh graders and used their prize money to help other seventh graders on their quilt project. You'll find directions for *Incredible Quilts for Kids of All Ages* (Quilt Digest, 1993) in Jean Ray Laury's colorful paperback.

AIRPLANES

When youngsters fancy flight, it need not be a flight of fancy: They can pilot across the country and back, accompanied by an adult pilot, as nine-year-old Rachel Carter did in March 1994, solo in a sailplane at 14, pilot a powered plane at 16, and earn a private pilot's license at 17. Tie the excitement of flying to history, science, math, biography, adventure, and just about any other area of the curriculum and you may expand horizons—literally.

BEFORE THE WRIGHT BROTHERS
Don Berliner
B/w photographs
Lerner, 1990
[i, j] 72 pages

Don Berliner vivifies the attempts of aviation pioneers and their peers, among them George Cayley, the airplane's originator; Otto Lillienthal, the first aviator; and Gustave Whitehead, who may have flown a controlled, powered, fixed-wing aircraft four years before Orville and Wilbur.

AIRBORNE
Richard Maurer
Photographs and illustrations
Simon (hb/pb), 1990
[i, j] 48 pages

The author conveys the exhilaration of challenge, discovery and accomplishment in the search for the secret of flight. He explains flight theory and its application with easy-to-follow instructions for making a hot air balloon and other working models. By the time they finish this first-rate book, readers will have a working knowledge of the principles of flight.

FLYING MACHINES
Norman Barrett
Photographs and illustrations
Watts, 1994
[i, j] 48 pages

Past, present, and future airliners, helicopters, and airships appear on every page. One of the "Visual Guides" series, this is sure to appeal to browsers and perusers (particularly reluctant ones) as a starting place for reports as well as an ideal read during sustained silent reading periods. Annotations and commentary recount aviation history as well as record-breaking achievements.

👓 Add a poetic dimension to plane talk with Diane Siebert's evocative *Plane Song* (HarperCollins, 1993), illustrated by Vincent Nasta. It tells of "planes of every shape and size/that taxi out/takeoff/and /rise/ above a world of/ tundras/ trees/ fields and farmlands; cities/ seas. . . . "

THE VISUAL DICTIONARY OF FLIGHT
Photographs and illustrations
Dorling, 1992
[i, j, adult] 64 pages

Dramatically displayed across the 10" x 12" pages are the individually itemized parts and cross-section diagrams of flying machines, from balloons, airships, and "pioneer" airplanes to helicopters, ultralights, VTOL, and modern military aircraft. As they pore over its pages, readers will be able to identify by name what they'd only known by sight; scouring its index, they'll locate and then see what they'd known only by name. An introductory paragraph with historical and pertinent technical detail accompanies each breathtaking spread.

PLANES
Michael Johnstone
Illustrations by Hans Jenssen
Dorling, 1994
[p, i, j] 32 pages

These views beneath the surface of flying machines are from a somewhat different perspective than the book above. Here, in addition to revealing what lies beneath the surface, the cross-sections show pilots, crews, and passengers in situ. A glossary and illustrated aircraft timeline of thirty planes from the 1903 Wright Flyer to the 1980s Stealth Fighter wrap up this eyeopener.

EUREKA! IT'S AN AIRPLANE!
Jeanne Bendick
Illustrations by Sal Murdocca
Millbrook, 1992
[i] 48 pages

This introduction to flight, from an inventor's point of view, is a first-rate blend of lucid writing and humor. Ms. Bendick begins with Newton's Laws of Motion and goes on to explain how an understanding of aerodynamics shaped the airplane's evolution and how its engines and controls work.

THE AIRPLANE BOOK
Cheryl Walsh Bellville
Lerner (hb/pb), 1991
[i] 48 pages

Author/photographer/pilot Bellville's historical overview of flying includes shots of classic and modern planes, from the Sopwith Camel to the F-16 Flying Falcon. The photos and illustrations will attract readers, especially reluctant ones.

Contact and invite a local flight instructor or private pilot to share first-hand experiences. Suggest s/he bring along navigation maps so children can learn how pilots make their way on the "highways" in the sky.

LINDBERGH
Chris L. Demarest
Illustrations by the author

Crown, 1993
[p, i] 36 pages

FLIGHT
Robert Burleigh
Illustrations by Mike Wimmer
Philomel, 1991
[i, j] 32 pages

Mr. Demarest recounts how Charles Lindbergh's mechanical ability, evident from childhood on, and his love of flying led to his historic flight. Segue from his biography into Mr. Burleigh's account of that flight, which comes alive with Mike Wimmer's powerful paintings.

RUTH LAW THRILLS A NATION
Don Brown
Illustrations by the author
Ticknor, 1993
[p, i] 32 pages

Eleven years before Lindbergh's trans-Atlantic flight, Ruth Law set an American nonstop cross-country flying record of 590 miles. Though aimed at primary graders, Mr. Brown's words and pictures are not childish. Share it with older students to familiarize them with the accomplishments of a woman whose name they'll not have heard elsewhere.

FLYING FREE: AMERICA'S FIRST BLACK AVIATORS
Philip S. Hart
B/w photographs
Lerner, 1992
[i, j] 64 pages

AT THE CONTROLS: WOMEN IN AVIATION
Carole S. Briggs
B/w photographs
Lerner, 1991
[i, j] 72 pages

Few aviation histories mention the names of the intrepid men and women featured in these two volumes. They were adventurers who became pilots in the face of seemingly insurmountable opposition and are worth meeting, whether or not flight is the topic. Their determination, resourcefulness, and refusal to give up will inspire youngsters to persevere.

HOW AN AIRPORT REALLY WORKS
George Sullivan
B/w illustrations
Lodestar, 1993
[j] 128 pages

Mr. Sullivan not only provides facts about airport sizes (the largest, in Saudi Arabia, is one-tenth the size of the entire state of Rhode Island) and operations (the first piece of luggage should leave planes within 45 seconds of landing), but he also spices his narrative with details about scaring off birds from runways, caring for pets in transit, and pickpocketing.

A natural progression from planes in books is planes in the air—paper planes, that is. So you must have handy Seymour Simon's *Paper Airplane Book* (Puffin, 1976); Neil Francis's *Super Flyers* (Addison, 1988); or E. Richard Churchill's *Instant Paper Airplanes* (Sterling, 1990) for youngsters ages 7 up.

VOYAGER
John Kauffman
B/w photographs
Enslow, 1989
[j] 64 pages

After an introduction to its designer and copilots, Mr. Kauffman takes readers on the compelling journey of the first plane to circumnavigate the world. From sketch to success, he explains the problems involved in designing, funding, and piloting what was essentially a flying gas tank.

 **ALPHABETS**

All too frequently, teachers tell me that colleagues strike alphabet books from their upper-grade library's book order list. That's sad, for the best alphabet books are for everyone. Lois Ehlert's *Eating the Alphabet* (Harcourt, 1989), for example.

You can share it as (1) a simply beautiful alphabet book; (2) a sampling of edible plants that youngsters can categorize (i.e., leaf or root, crunchy or slurpy, yellow or green), whose origins can be pinpointed on a map, or whose preparations reflect cultural similarities or differences; (3) a collection of fine watercolor collages that anyone can try; (4) an information book with glossary entries that are models of tightly constructed, information-laden, two-to-four sentence paragraphs.

ALPHABET ANIMALS
Charles Sullivan
Color and b/w illustrations
Rizzoli, 1991
[p, i, j] 48 pages

Prints, paintings, photographs, and sculpture from artists as diverse as Rembrandt and Warhol open youngsters' eyes to an impeccable and exhilarating selection of fine art.

NATURAL HISTORY FROM A TO Z:
A TERRESTRIAL SAMPLER
Tim Arnold
Full-color and duotone illustrations by the author
McElderry, 1991
[i, j] 58 pages

A refreshingly designed and stimulating introduction to familiar and not-so-common plants and animals and the basic principles of biology.

ALISON'S ZINNIA
Anita Lobel
Illustrations by the author
Lothrop, 1990
[all ages] 32 pages

Every blooming page of this alliterative bouquet of blossoms is a delight, from the amaryllis Alison acquired for Beryl to the zinnia Zena zeroed in on for Alison.

Between Adam's arrival in Amsterdam and Zachary's zigzagging in Zaandam, a band of beaming boys bounce into 22 other towns *Away From Home* (Greenwillow, 1994) in Ms. Lobel's traveling companion to the book above.

AARDVARKS DISEMBARK!
Ann Jonas
Illustrations by the author
Greenwillow, 1990
[all ages] 40 pages

Having emptied his ark of its creature cargo (alphabetically, of course!), Noah descended Mt. Ararat, passing paired zebus, you yous, xerus, and scores of other creatures that have or are about to become extinct. Ms. Jonas's unique slant (both figurative and literal, as you will discover at first glance) dramatizes the precarious state of the earth's animals.

AFRO-BETS BOOK OF BLACK HEROES
Wade Hudson and Valerie Wilson Wesley
B/w photographs and illustrations
Just Us (pb), 1988
[i, j] 54 pages

Among the noteworthy men and women highlighted are Chicago founder Jean Baptiste DeSable, dancer Katherine Dunham, and Supreme Court Justice Thurgood Marshall.

ILLUMINATIONS
Jonathon Hunt
Illustrations by the author
Bradbury, 1989; Aladdin (pb), 1993
[i] 44 pages

Mr. Hunt culled representative people, terms, and things from medieval myths, legends, and life; and illustrated them on pages designed to reflect the era's beautifully embellished or illuminated manuscripts.

THE DESERT ALPHABET BOOK
Jerry Palotta
Illustrations by Mark Astrella
Charlesbridge (hb/pb), 1994
[p, i] 32pages

Whatever his focus—the desert, or *Icky Bugs, Yucky Reptiles, Frogs, Flowers* or Furry creatures, to name but five other subjects he's addressed alphabetically (all Charlesbridge, 1986-1991)—Mr. Palotta's witty prose creates a feeling of warmth and undisguised delight at the marvels of nature. A teacher-par-excellence, he understands that the best lessons are those taught with laughter.

In her 32-page *Agave Blooms Just Once* (Harbinger House, 1989), Gisela Jernigan focuses, in rhyme, upon flora and fauna indigenous to the Sonoran Desert. With her text-in-verse as a model, suggest youngsters select any subject under study and create a list of related people, places, and things. Have them then add appropriate descriptors, build phrases and sentences, and replace and rearrange initial words until they have a "report" written as a similar alphabetical progression of rhyming couplets.

GEOGRAPHY FROM A TO Z
Jack Knowlton
Illustrations by Harriet Barton
HarperCollins, 1988

[p, i] 48 pages

Sixty-three well-chosen words contain simple, clear definitions of some of the terms with which we identify Earth's physical characteristics. From archipelago to zone, this is an excellent glossary.

LETTRES ACADIENNES: A CAJUN ABC
Don Goodrum
Illustrations by the author
Pelican, 1992
[i] 30 pages

You can almost hear the zydeco band as you peruse these 26 audacious paintings plus boldly hand-lettered alliterative descriptions in Cajun patois. The joyous Acadian ambiance is unavoidable.

CARIBBEAN ALPHABET
Frané Lessac
Illustrations by the author
Tambourine, 1994
[p] 32 pages

Evocative paintings, one per letter, capture the Caribbean life and experiences that make up everyday island life.

Suggest youngsters (alone or with a younger primary grader) paint alphabetical arrays of scenes for their state, city, home, school, or room alphabets similar to Ms. Lessac's.

EIGHT HANDS ROUND: A PATCHWORK ALPHABET
Ann Whitford Paul
Illustrations by Jeanette Winter
HarperCollins, 1991
[i, j] 32 pages

I still have the patchwork baby-blanket Mrs. Somers made for me in 1934. Its pattern's name was the first thing I looked for when this delightful alphabet arrived. Suggest youngsters discover what designs they have on quilts at home, use the 26 patterns as models for paper patchwork projects, or just enjoy this simple, engaging history of one colorful aspect of women's creativity.

In 1988, a retired school teacher and counselor initiated a project that included *Kids Making Quilts for Kids* (Quilt Digest, 1992). See page 60.

THE HANDMADE ALPHABET
Laura Rankin
Illustrations by the author
Dial, 1991
[p, i, j] 32 pages

Keep this around toddlers to introduce or review letters or as an alphabetical guessing game. (What is each hand holding?") Hand it to elementary graders as a guide to signing letters; a multicultural adjunct (the colored-pencil-on-charcoal-paper hands are of varied size, age, and shade); or rich stimulus for creative writing (Whose hands are they...what are they going to do with the object they hold...etc). Share it with everyone for the pleasure of its exquisite beauty.

Connect the book above to Camilla Gryski's HANDS ON, THUMBS UP (Addison, 1991) for an assortment of handy practicalities, pleasures, and pastimes, including silly hand shakes, "hand" idioms, hand signs, hand tricks, right-and left-hand facts, and enough other hand-related miscellany to entertain, inform, and stimulate projects throughout the year.

A SWIM THROUGH THE SEA
Kristin Joy Pratt
Illustrations by the author
Dawn (hb/pb), 1994
[pre, p, i] 44 pages

From angel to zebrafish by way of xiphosuran (no X marks the spot here!), this stunning menagerie of marine life is beautiful to look at and full of facts. Point out to aspiring author/artists that the hard-working Ms. Pratt wrote this, her second book (first was her alphabetical *Walk in the Rainforest* [Dawn, 1992]), while in high school.

 Have youngsters use the books above to create their own alphabet on a family member, subject of a biography they've just read, someone in the news, a classmate, neighbor, pet, or any other person, place, or thing of special interest.

ANCIENT EGYPT

INTO THE MUMMY'S TOMB
Nicholas Reeves
Photographs and illustrations
Scholastic (hb/pb), 1992
[i] 64 pages

Egyptogolist Reeves's account of the discovery of King Tutankhamen's burial site is simply the best on the subject that I've found for children. Archival photographs of discoverer Howard Carter's work-in-progress, contemporary shots of artifacts, and detailed drawings of the tomb are artfully arranged so that readers see what Dr. Reeves describes.

Artist/author Robert Sabuda's exquisitely illustrated *Tutankhamen's Gift* (Atheneum, 1994) depicts the young king as a shy, unassuming child who restored his people's freedom to worship their old gods when he became pharaoh.

THE GIANT BOOK OF THE MUMMY
Rosalie David
Illustrations

Lodestar, 1993
[p, i] 12 pages

Chances are this 16" x 24" board book will be grabbed immediately when youngsters catch sight of King Tutankhamen's
magnificent coffin on the cover. And once they've peeked
behind it, they'll be intrigued by a simply written, cleverly
designed introduction to the young pharaoh, his life, his tomb,
and its treasures.

Suggest youngsters reading about ancient Egypt compare
similarities and differences between the pharaohs and
China's first emperor. They will meet the military genius
in Caroline Lazo's *Terra Cotta Army of Emperor Qin* (New
Discovery, 1993), where they'll learn that he united
China, built the Great Wall, and made an approximately
8,000-piece, life-size, model army to accompany him in
his tomb—more than 1,000 years before the pharaohs
built their pyramids.

GROWING UP IN ANCIENT EGYPT
Rosalie David
Illustrations
Troll (hb/pb), 1993
[i] 32 pages

ON THE BANKS OF THE PHARAOHS' NILE
Corinne Courtalon
Illustrations
Young Discovery, 1988
[i] 36 pages

In complementary books, the authors describe farming in the Nile
Valley; the food, clothing, homes, gods, and everyday activities of
average and wealthy Egyptians; pyramids and hieroglyphs.
Though addressed to younger readers, older readers beginning
research projects will find both to be excellent first references.

ANCIENT EGYPT
Geraldine Harris
Illustrations, photographs, maps
Facts, 1990
[i, j] 96 pages

This lavishly illustrated "Cultural Atlas" begins with a history of the pharaohs and spans the almost 3,000 years from Egypt's unification to the arrival of the Romans. It concludes with an archaeological journey down the Nile, from Lower Nubia, south of Egypt, to the Mediterranean coast.

Read aloud Ms. Harris's (see above) versions of ancient Egyptian children's familiar stories from the 132-page *Gods and Pharohs from Egyptian Mythology* (Bedrick, 1982). She reconstructed them from remnants found in hymns, prayers, temple inscriptions, and the like.

ANCIENT EGYPT
Judith Crosher
Illustrations
Viking, 1992
[i, j] 48 pages

This detail-laden volume includes overlays that readers lift to discover what's behind the walls of a palace, tomb, temple, and town house. Chapters on childhood, women, arts and crafts, education, and writing will allow today's youngsters to compare many facets of their lives to those of ancient Egyptians.

THE ANCIENT EGYPTIANS
Vivian Koenig
Illustrations by Veronique Ageorges
Millbrook, 1992
[i, j] 64 pages

Ms. Koenig's exposition is enhanced by splendid illustrations and a conversational narrative which includes details not generally covered elsewhere: The English word "pyramid" derives from the

Greek "pyramis," or "little cake," for example; and (always of interest to children) the Egyptians did have toilets, though they were rare.

THE RIDDLE OF THE ROSETTA STONE
James Giblin
B/w photographs
HarperCollins (hb/pb), 1990
[i, j] 84 pages

An engrossing account of the unsuccessful attempts to translate hieroglyphs prior to the Rosetta stone's unearthing, and Jean-Francois Champollion's brilliant discovery that hieroglyphs represented both things and sounds.

HIEROGLYPHS FROM A TO Z
Peter Der Manuelian
Illustrations by the author
Rizzoli, 1993
[p, i] 48 pages

Mr. Der Manuelian's illustrations are based on carvings or paintings found on the walls of Egyptian tombs and temples. On each page, the author/artist accompanies the English letter and its hieroglyphic counterpart with an image identified in both languages. In conclusion, he explains the script, how its written, and the story of its decoding.

 Suggest youngsters correspond with a friend or classmate using either the stencil included in Der Manuelian's book or Styrofoam stamps of their own making.

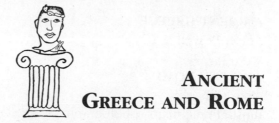

ANCIENT GREECE AND ROME

Most trade books for children about Ancient Greece and Rome are found in series. In the paired series titles that follow, you'll find a refreshing absence of distracting bold type to indicate a word's presence in the glossary.

OVER 2,000 YEARS AGO: IN ANCIENT GREECE

OVER 1,600 YEARS AGO: IN THE ROMAN EMPIRE
Philip Sauvain
Photographs and illustrations by Graham Humphreys; Harry Clow
New Discovery, 1992
[i] 32 pages each

Sidebars that highlight how we learned about these cultures enrich the six 4-page overviews of the two civilizations, from general lifestyle to such specifics as the Roman Army and Olympic Games.

THE ANCIENT GREEKS: IN THE LAND OF THE GODS
Sophie Descamps-Lequime and Denise Vernerey

THE ROMANS: LIFE IN THE EMPIRE
Charles Guittard and Annie-Claude Martin
Illustrations by Annie-Claude Martin
Millbrook, 1992
[i, j] 64 pages each

Straightforward, flowing narratives are enhanced by the continuity of a single artist's illustrations and by sidebars that highlight details of particular interest to children, lifting this series above the ordinary.

ANCIENT GREECE
Anton Powell

ANCIENT ROME
Mike Corbishly
Illustrations, maps, photographs
Facts, 1989
[j] 96 pages each

These 9 1/2" x 12", lavishly illustrated atlases are first-rate introductions to their respective cultures. You can use the well-organized presentations as lesson plans guides. Your students will find the two-page subtopics ideal introductions to subjects they'll want to research further.

THE GREEKS

THE ROMANS
Pamela Odijk
Illustrations and photographs
Silver, 1989
[i, j] 48 pages each

Ms. Odijk's instructive books are specifically designed for report writing: A timeline and map precede chapters which detail topics youngsters are likely to list when webbing, clustering, or otherwise setting down appropriate areas of interest prior to investigation.

THE GREEKS

THE ROMANS
Susan Peach and Anne Millard
Illustrations
Usborne, 1990
[i, j] 96 pages each

Here is a rich lode of data accessible to beginning as well as accomplished researchers because of the illustration-integrated text that is the hallmark of Usborne books. Key-date charts, maps, cross-sections of constructions, reproductions of art, and the details of clothing, jewelry, and hair styles are among the specifics dotting the narrative.

THE GREEKS

THE ROMANS
Roy Burrell
Illustrations by Peter Connolly and photographs
Oxford, 1990
[j] 112 pages each

Mr. Burrell's imaginative presentations are written in a relaxed conversational tone. He creates verisimilitude with occasional you-are-there dialogue: a "conversation" with a worker on the reconstruction of the palace at Knossos, for example, and a young Roman en route to the public baths.

GREEK CITIES
Barry Steel
Illustrations
Watts, 1990
[i] 24 pages

Mr. Steel's simple, straightforward descriptions of home, school, religious, and recreational life provide easily grasped basic facts for a discussion of the similarities and differences between today's children and their ancient Greece counterparts. His fully illustrated book is particularly appropriate for older, reluctant students.

ANCIENT ROME
Simon James

ANCIENT GREECE
Rowena Loverance
Illustrations, photographs
Viking, 1992

[j] 48 pages each

Among the features in these fact-laden volumes are overlays read-ers lift to discover what's behind the walls of homes and other gathering places. Chapters on children, the family, and everyday life will allow today's youngsters to compare many facets of their lives to those of their Ancient Greek or Roman peers.

GREEK MYTHS
Marcia Williams
Illustrations by the author
Candlewick (pb), 1995
[p, i, j] 40 pages

Readers, from reluctant to eager, will be attracted by the colorful illustrations, the artistry, and the wit with which Ms. Williams depicts the tales of Theseus and the Minotaur, Daedalus and Icarus, and six other classics from Ancient Greece. Her comic-book style presentation both entertains and enlightens.

THE LEGEND OF ODYSSEUS

THE ROMAN FORT

POMPEII
Peter Connolly
Photographs; illustrations by the author
Oxford (hb/pb), 1988
[j] 10 up 80 pages each

Mr. Connolly's expertise, enthusiasm, and excitement for the era is a pleasure to experience. His comments and annotations on the maps and photographs interspersed among chapters reflect a familiarity with and considerable knowledge of relevant artifacts, reconstructions, and excavations.

THE LOST WRECK OF THE ISIS
Robert D. Ballard with Rick Archbold
Photographs and illustrations

Scholastic, 1990
[i, j] 64 pages

Dr. Ballard recounts the exciting adventure in which he and his crew recovered artifacts from a Roman cargo ship that sunk in the Mediterranean during the second half of the fourth century A.D. In alternate chapters, he conjectures about the ship, its crew, and its passengers.

COLORING BOOK OF ANCIENT GREECE
Line drawings
Bellerophon, 1990
[i, j] 56 pages

The drawings are copies of gods, goddesses, and a few mortals as they are depicted on vases, cups, and other artifacts found in museums around the world. Just for the fun of it—and the learning that accompanies the attendant attention to detail—youngsters can fill in the blank spaces with crayon or felt-tip pen or trace them to emboss clay or Styrofoam trays for subsequent printing.

ANIMAL POTPOURRI

CRINKLEROOT'S 25 BIRDS EVERY CHILD SHOULD KNOW
Jim Arnosky
Illustrations by the author
Bradbury, 1994
[pre, p] 28 pages each

Warm watercolors provide a friendly look at common wildlife: birds here, and *...Fish*, *...Mammals*, and *...More Animals* in Mr. Arnosky's other *Crinkleroot's 25...* books (all Bradbury). In each, a few words about general attributes precede one or two individual portraits per page. Couldn't be simpler—or nicer.

A TIME FOR PLAYING

A TIME FOR SINGING
Ron Hirschi
Photographs by Thomas D. Mangelson
Cobblehill, 1994
[p] 32 pages each

Poetic prose and photographs here and in *A Time For Sleeping* and *A Time For Babies* (both Cobblehill, 1993) will delight little ones as they learn how animals live in the wild.

SOMEWHERE TODAY

AND SO THEY BUILD

WHEN HUNGER CALLS
Bert Kitchen
Illustrations by the author
Candlewick, 1992, 1993, 1994
[p, i] 28 pages each

The impeccable paintings in these volumes, which respectively depict 12 animals in unique postures, constructing habitats, and attacking prey, add an aesthetic to youngsters' views of wildlife rarely equalled.

EGG!
A. J. Wood
Illustrated by Stella Stilwell
Little, 1993
[p, i] 26 pages

EGG: A PHOTOGRAPHIC STORY OF HATCHING
Robert Burton
Photographs by Jane Burton and Kim Taylor
Dorling, 1994
[pre, p, i] 48 pages

Chickens Aren't The Only Ones (Putnam; Sandcastle, 1981), as Ruth Heller deftly puts it–the only egg layers, that is. And these titles nicely supplement her classic on the subject. Ms. Wood's "what-will-they-be" question/answer format uses clever folds to first hide then reveal the hatching ovipara. Mr. Burton's annotations introduce and describe the closeup sequences of 27 animals, from ostrich to slug, as they wriggle out of their shells or sacs.

TERRIFIC TAILS
Hana Machotka
Photographs by the author
Morrow, 1994
[pre, p] 32 pages

Here and in her earlier titles, *Breathtaking Noses, What Neat Feet!* and *Outstanding Outsides* (all William Morrow, 1991-1993), Ms. Machotka's engaging photos and simple text focus upon the single body part of different animals. When comparing them, youngsters can see how each part suits its owner's specific needs.

For more on the ways in which animals have adapted to their habitats, supplement Ms. Machotka's books (above) with Mark J. Rauzon's photoillustrated *Skin, Scales, Feathers, and Fur* and *Horns, Antlers, Fangs, and Tusks* (both Lothrop, 1993), and *Feet, Flippers, Hooves, And Hands* and *Eyes And Ears* (both Lothrop, 1994).

SKELETONS: AN INSIDE LOOK AT ANIMALS
Jimmy Johnson
Illustrations by Elizabeth Gray
Reader's Digest, 1994
[p, i, j] 46 pages

The images of eighteen skeletons, strikingly set on black pages, are enhanced by detailed annotations and insets that show how each animal moves and its relative size to a human adult. This oversize volume will grab readers of all ages.

DO THEY SCARE YOU? CREEPY CREATURES
Sneed B. Collard III
Charlesbridge (hb/pb), 1992
Illustrations by Karen Kest
[p] 32 pages

SCARY ANIMALS
Jean de Sart
Illustrations by Jean-Marie Winants
Charlesbridge (hb/pb), 1994
[i] 43 pages

By providing facts and challenging myths, both authors reassure children that, under ordinary circumstances, they need not fear most animals with bad reputations.

When animals are on the agenda, aim for kids' funny bones with Teri and Robert Sloat's *Rib-Ticklers* (Lothrop, 1995). It's a joyously illustrated, delightful jumble of jokes, limericks and riddles about fauna—from Tyrannosaurus to tuna.

TOAD OR FROG, SWAMP OR BOG?
A BIG BOOK OF NATURE'S CONFUSABLES
Lynda Graham-Barber
Illustrations by Alec Gillman
Four Winds, 1994
[i] 48 pages

WHAT'S THE DIFFERENCE? A GUIDE TO
SOME FAMILIAR ANIMAL LOOK-ALIKES
Elizabeth A. Lacey
B/w illustrations by Robert Shetterly
Clarion, 1993
[i] 70 pages

Ms. Graham-Barber pinpoints the telltale differences between 22 pairs of often misidentified animals (frogs and toads, for example), plants, and natural phenomena. Ms. Lacey elaborates on the general as well as distinguishing characteristics of seven pairs of animal look-alikes.

THE SERENGETI MIGRATION;
AFRICA'S ANIMALS ON THE MOVE
Lisa Lindblad
Photographs by Sven-Olof Lindblad and illustrations
Hyperion, 1994
[i] 40 pages

The excitement is palpable in this chronicle of a half-million wildebeests and 750,000 zebras on their annual north-south migrations across Africa's great plain. They're stalked every step of the way by lions, leopards, cheetahs, wild dogs, and hyenas, while crocodiles await them at river crossings.

MAKING SENSE
Bruce Brooks
Photographs
Farrar, 1993
[i, j] 74 pages

In effortless, amusing, down-to-earth prose precisely tuned to intrigue intelligent young readers, Mr. Brooks proves that nonfiction can be as gripping and insightful as the finest fiction. This third volume in his "Knowing Nature" series addresses animal perception and communication; the previous two, *Nature By Design* and *Predator,* (both Farrar, 1991), are on, respectively, animal architecture and the quest for food.

I've mesmerized audiences by reading aloud excerpts of Mr. Brooks's books. Try it! You'll like it—and so will your students.

ANIMALS OBSERVED: A LOOK AT ANIMALS IN ART
Dorcas MacClintock
Photographs and illustrations

Scribner's, 1993
[i, j] 56 pages

Ms. MacClintock comments on both artist and subject in this sampling of drawings, paintings, and sculptures of mammals, which include Inuit stone carvings, a Rosa Bonheur oil, and a Ugo Mochi cutout. All breathtaking.

WILDLIFE RESCUE: THE WORK OF DR. KATHLEEN RAMSAY
Jennifer Owings Dewey
Photographs by Don MacCarter
Boyds, 1994
[i, j] 64 pages

Begin, and you won't be able to stop reading this—alone or aloud. It sizzles with the energy and intensity Dr. Ramsey and her nurturing staff devote to sick and injured birds and other animals at the Wildlife Center she established in 1985. And when you finish, your eyes, like mine and the good doctor's, will become teary when she releases a bobcat, hawks, and a bald eagle she's healed.

SAFE IN THE SPOTLIGHT
Elaine Scott
B/w photos by the author
Morrow, 1991
[i, j] 80 pages

Many animals seen in movies, advertisements, and on magazine covers—from mice to elephants—are employees of Len and Bunny Brooks's Dawn Animal Agency and Sanctuary for Animals. Ms. Scott's photoessay describes the couple and their able-bodied animal actor/models whose fees support all of the 100-acre sanctuary's residents, many of whom are too old or sick to work.

GUINEA PIGS
Mark Evans
Photographs
Dorling, 1992

[i, i] 40 pages

This is one of the outstanding "ASPCA Pet Care Guides for Kids" that helps them become caring and responsible pet owners. Youngsters learn about their pet's physical characteristics and how to select one as a pet. They're told what equipment they'll need and how to house, feed, clean, and keep their pet healthy. And they're provided a checklist of weekly and yearly responsibilities. Among the other titles in the series are *Puppy, Kitten, Rabbit, Hamster, Fish*, and *Birds* (all Dorling, 1992-1994).

ART

TAKE A LOOK:
AN INTRODUCTION TO THE EXPERIENCE OF ART
Rosemary Davidson
Photographs
Viking, 1994
[j] 128 pages

Ms. Davidson discusses the difference between looking and seeing and demonstrates how a viewer's background influences what is seen. She explains why people create art, answers questions about how it is made and what makes it work, and poses some questions she leaves unanswered. A time line, glossary, suggestions for further reading, and comprehensive index conclude her work.

ENJOYING ART WITH CHILDREN
WORLD OF PLAY
Gladys S. Blizzard
Photographic reproductions
Thomasson, 1990/1993

[p,i] 32 pages each

Each of 12 paintings in these oversize (10" x 10") volumes is paired with a facing-page of text devoted to information about the artist and questions that encourage perusal, reflection, and dialogue. These, and other titles in the four-volume "Come Look with Me" series, are as easy to share with a small group as with a single youngster snuggled close. *Exploring Landscape Art With Children* and *Animals In Art* complete the series.

Preschoolers can discover how *A Painter* (Greenwillow, 1993) creates art and some tools of the trade in one of Douglas Florian's "How We Work" titles.

MARY CASSATT
Susan E. Meyer

ANDREW WYETH
Richard Merryman
Color illustrations by the subject artists
Abrams, 1990/1991
[i, j] 32 pages each

Richly illustrated, artfully designed (including a four-page gate-fold), and intelligently written, these biographies are enclosed within an irresistible, full-color, full-cover reproduction of the featured artist's work. These and others of the exemplary "First Impressions" series are consistent in approach, yet each author's voice and style is distinct. All are unusually respectful of the intended young adult audience. Biographies of Monet, Frank Lloyd Wright, Audubon, da Vinci, Picasso, and Rembrandt are among the others currently available.

If your public library, like mine, circulates large, framed reproductions, make art a natural part of your youngsters' environment. Borrow and hang them in your room throughout the year.

INSPIRATIONS

VISIONS
Leslie Sills
Whitman, 1989, 1993
[j] 64 pages each

FRIDA KAHLO

FAITH RINGGOLD
Robyn Montana Turner
Little, 1993
[i] 32 pages each

These titles from exceptionally well-produced and complementary series on women artists contain first-rate reproductions. Each author's simple, conversational style reveals insights that vivify the artists and their works. Ms. Sill's two volumes focus on a quartet of artists: Georgia O'Keeffe, Frida Kahlo, Faith Ringgold, and Alice Neel in the first title; Mary Cassatt, Betye Saar, Leonora Carrington, and Mary Frank, in the second. Other subjects in Ms. Turner's "Portraits of Women Artists for Children" are Rosa Bonheur, Mary Cassatt, Georgia O'Keeffe, and Dorothea Lange.

Photography as fine art is the subject of Sylvia Wolf's fine *Focus: Five Women Photographers* (Whitman, 1994). Ms. Wolf follows brief biographies of the artists with interpretations of representative photographs. The artists range from pioneer portraitist Julia Margaret Cameron (1815-1879) to Lorna Simpson, (1960—).

WHAT MAKES A DEGAS A DEGAS?

WHAT MAKES A VAN GOGH A VAN GOGH?
Richard Mühlberger
Reproductions
Metropolitan Museum of Art/Viking (pb), 1993
[j] 48 pages each

Two of the compelling "What Makes A...A..." series in which Mr. Mühlberger's insightful explanations of why and how the artists painted as they did will hold readers spellbound. Before highlighting details of twelve paintings, the author introduces the featured artist with a brief biography. On the final page, he enumerates signature stylistic devices. Bruegel, Monet, Raphael, and Rembrandt are the other subjects.

Suggest youngsters look at their own creative expressions and isolate a few characteristics that make their art uniquely theirs, as Mr. Mühlberger does with his subjects.

CHILDREN OF PROMISE: AFRICAN-AMERICAN LITERATURE AND ART FOR YOUNG PEOPLE

HERE IS MY KINGDOM: HISPANIC-AMERICAN LITERATURE AND ART FOR YOUNG PEOPLE
Charles Sullivan, Ed.
Color and b/w reproductions
Abrams, 1991/1994
[i, j] 128, 120 pages

An impressive and select assemblage of culturally representative photographs, paintings, sculpture, poetry, lyrics, excerpts from speeches and other artful expressions comprise these engrossing anthologies. Biographical notes on the artists precede the lists of illustrations and acknowledgments conclude this compilation by the seemingly inexhaustible Mr. Sullivan.

Horace Pippin, one of the African-American artists featured in *Children Of Promise* (see above) didn't begin painting until he was 43 years old. Intermediate-grade youngsters and older can learn more about him in Mary E. Lyons's biography, *Starting Home* (Scribner's, 1993), which is illustrated with photos and reproductions of his "primitive" works.

ROY LICHTENSTEIN
Lou Ann Walker
Photographs by Michael Abramson
Lodestar, 1994
[i, j] 48 pages

Full-page-and-more photos capture the mood of the pop artist's studio which is draped with massive paintings drenched by light from skylights in its 20-foot-high ceilings. Readers will learn exactly how Lichtenstein plans and executes his paintings. More importantly, though, s/he'll learn the importance of perseverance and the virtue of pursuing artistic impulses, wherever they lead.

Segue from the closeup of Mr. Lichtenstein and his work to the work of other contemporary American artists via Jan Greenberg's and Sandra Jordan's *The Painter's Eye* (Delacorte, 1991)—or vice versa. Whichever way you go, the coauthors' biographies of and knowing introduction to the works of such artists as Helen Frankenthaler, Andy Warhol, and Sam Gilliam will help readers appreciate what 20th-century artists mean to say.

SELF-PORTRAITS

DOGS
Peggy Roalf
Color and b/w reproductions
Hyperion (hb/pb), 1993
[i, j] 48 pages

In these and others of her "Looking at Paintings" series, Ms. Roalf shows young readers how artists—men and women from many cultures and eras—see the same subject. Her simple design of full-page reproduction and facing-page of lucid descriptive prose succeeds admirably. Other subjects currently include families, seascapes, horses, children, dancers, cats, landscapes, the circus, flowers, and musicians.

A WEEKEND WITH DIEGO RIVERA
Barbara Braun

A WEEKEND WITH MATISSE
Florian Rodari
Color and b/w illustrations
Rizzoli, 1994
[i, j] 64 pages each

In the guise of their respective artists, the authors of these and others in the "A Weekend with..." series tell young readers about themselves and their work. The first-person enthusiasm and air of congeniality and the plentiful illustrations makes these volumes as captivating as they are enlightening. Youngsters can also spend weekends with Van Gogh, Degas, da Vinci, Picasso, Renoir, Rembrandt, Rousseau, Velazquez, and Winslow Homer.

DIEGO
Jonah Winter
Illustrations by Jeanette Winter
Knopf (hb/pb), 1991
[p] 40 pages

A charming, simply told account, in Spanish and English, of the life of Diego Rivera, the Mexican muralist whose art is said to cover more than two and a half miles of walls throughout Mexico and North America.

A YOUNG PAINTER
Zheng Zhensun and Alice Low
Color illustrations and photos by Wang Yani
Scholastic, 1991
[i] 80 pages

Fascinate children with this photo-biography's revelations about the awesomely talented teenager Wang Yani and her father's understanding and nurturing of that talent.

In addition to keeping them readily available on your

shelves, suggest parents keep Kim Solga's "Art and Activities for Kids" books on hand for vacation, weekend, or not-well-enough-to-go-to-school-but-not-sick-enough-to-rest-quietly- at-home days. Ms. Solga's easy-to-follow directions, illustrated with life-size photographs of materials and insets of youngsters at work with the various media, is an appealing incentive for children to *Make Prints* (1991), *Draw* (1991), partake in *Paint Adventures* (1993), *Make Clothes Fun!* (1992), or engage in endeavors suggested by the other titles in the artfully designed series (all North).

COLOR
Ruth Heller
Illustrations by the author
Putnam, 1995
[p, i] 36 pages plus overlays

With jaunty poetry, vibrant paintings, and clever use of overlays, Ms. Heller demonstrates how printers use black ink and three primary colors to produce the rich, full-color illustrations.

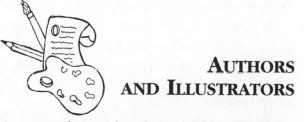

AUTHORS AND ILLUSTRATORS

Authors' biographies or autobiographies help children realize that some of their favorite books' creators are real people whose experiences often become characters, incidents, and scenes in their stories.

BIGMAMA'S

SHORTCUT
Donald Crews
Illustrations by the author
Greenwillow, 1991; 1992

[pre, p] 32 pages each

Artist/author Donald Crews lovingly portrays the halcyon summers of his youth, when his mom, brother, and sisters visit his grandmother's home in Florida. *Bigmama's* recaptures the wonderful sense of freedom that came with the shedding of shoes, and the subsequent rush to renew acquaintance with every nook, cranny, and creature around the farm. In *Shortcut* he tells how he and his siblings once took an unexpectedly scary shortcut to Bigmama's via the railroad tracks.

DON'T YOU KNOW THERE'S A WAR ON?
James Stevenson
Illustrations by the author
Greenwillow, 1992
[p, i] 32 pages

In the fourth of his autobiographical gems, Mr. Stevenson recalls the 1940s and the wonderful innocence of the elementary grader he then was. His watercolors, appropriately detail-less, are as fuzzy as most memories of times past.

Children will discover that some things never change, when you have them create their own *Fun, No Fun* (Greenwillow, 1994) lists to compare with Mr. Stevenson's, in his fifth recollection of times past.

BEST WISHES
Cynthia Rylant
Photographs by Carlo Ontal
Owen, 1992
[i] 32 pages

SURPRISING MYSELF
Jean Fritz
Photographs by Andrea Fritz Pfleger
Owen, 1992
[i] 32 pages each

These titles, along with others of the exemplary "Meet the Author" series, belong in every school library. Readers will feel they've had a few private moments with each of the authors, learned how and where they wrote, met family and pets, and enjoyed each others' company.

 Older readers can learn more about the two authors above in Ms. Rylant's *But I'll Be Back Again* (Orchard Books, 1989; Beech Tree Books, 1993), and Ms. Fritz's *Homesick: My Own Story* (Putnam, 1982), and *China Homecoming* (Putnam, 1985).

THE PIGMAN AND ME
Paul Zindel
B/w photographs
HarperCollins (hb/pb), 1991
[j] 168 pages

Fan's of the fictional *Pigman* (HarperCollins, 1968) will enjoy meeting Frankie Vivona, the real one. When Mr. Zindel was a teenager, he, his mom, and his sister shared a house with Nonno (grandpa), Frankie's daughter, and her children. In the breezy, irreverent vernacular of his audience, the author writes about those teen years and Nonno Frankie's profound effect on his life.

ANONYMOUSLY YOURS
Richard Peck
B/w photographs
Messner (hb/pb), 1991
[j] 122 pages

"Anonymously" because he feels he's "never written a conscious line of autobiography in my novels...." Yet, his autobiography is filled with people and events that appear in his novels in one guise or another. Among the insights embedded throughout Mr. Peck's recollections is "A Teenager's Prayer" which ends "And give me nothing I haven't earned so that this adolescence doesn't last forever."

THE MOON AND I
Betsy Byars
B/w photographs
Messner (hb/pb), 1991
[i] 96 pages

Moon is a six-foot blacksnake! As Ms. Byers shares the slices of her life that have to do with Moon and others of its ilk, she explains exactly how she writes. When youngsters fret over your requests for rewrites, point out—as the author does—that her manuscript was written approximately eighteen times before her publisher accepted it.

THE LOST GARDEN
Laurence Yep
B/w photographs
Messner (hb/pb), 1991
[j] 116 pages

Mr. Yep's parents owned a corner grocery store in San Francisco when he was a boy. His early life revolved around the store where he helped his parents who worked 12 hours a day, 7 days a week. As he traces his life from childhood to successful author, he explains how growing up Chinese in America prepared him to write science fiction about alienated people.

As you teach your students to identify good writing, also open their eyes to the splendid contributions made by the talented artists and photographers whose work they encounter. These professionals have often written and collaborated on many books for children—among them, their own stories (see below). Suggest youngsters locate other volumes that contain illustrations and photos by one or more of them. What is distinctive about their styles? Do they always approach the subject the same way? How do their techniques vary from book to book?

I WAS A TEENAGE PROFESSIONAL WRESTLER
Ted Lewin
Color and b/w illustrations and photographs by the author
Orchard (hb/pb), 1993
[j] 128 pages

In addition to the pleasure of learning about the seemingly incongruous milieu that provided the gifted Mr. Lewin the wherewithal for his artistic training, it is fascinating to see how he transformed snapshots of his fellow wrestlers into magnificent watercolors.

Add AuthorCards to your cache of giveaways. Whether received for noteworthy behavior, jobs well done, books read, or just-because, kids will enjoy the colorful, 2 1/4" x 3 1/2" collectibles. Printed on the back of each portrait card is a list of the author's books, a few biographical bits, selected vital statistics, and a word or two of advice. Ted Lewin, Pat Cummings, Gail Gibbons, Ruth Heller, Jim Arnosky, and Seymour Simon are among the 100+ authors and artists featured. Write to School Arts Materials, P.O. 94082, Seattle WA 98124 or call 1-800-752-4359 for more details.

TALKING WITH ARTISTS
Pat Cummings
Illustrations and b/w photographs
Bradbury, 1992
[i, j] 96 pages

Thirteen of her fellow children's books illustrators, among them Lois Ehlert, Tom Feelings, and Jerry Pinkney, spoke to Ms. Cummings about their early lives and answered questions about how they work. Photos and art from their childhood and adulthood accompany each dialogue.

I REMEMBER "121"
Francine Haskins
Illustrations by the author

Children's Book, 1991
[p, i] 32 pages

Storyteller/artist Francine Haskins describes growing up in a traditional African-American community at 121 S Street, the three-story, brick family home in Washington, D.C. She begins when she was three, awaiting the arrival of her baby brother; she stops six years later with the family's move to a new house.

BILL PEET: AN AUTOBIOGRAPHY
Bill Peet
B/w illustrations by the author
Houghton (hb/pb), 1989
[i, j] 190 pages

In between Bill Peet's childhood and his success as a children's book author/artist was a 27-year stint at Walt Disney Studios. His anecdotes of those days and his contributions to the Disney output are among the most enjoyable of all.

L. FRANK BAUM: ROYAL HISTORIAN OF OZ
Angelica Shirley Carpenter and Jean Shirley
Illustrations and photographs
Lerner (hb/pb), 1992
[i, j] 144 pages

This incisive biography reveals how a shy, dreamy child turned into an imaginative, productive adult and details the life and literary output of the Oz's creator from his boyhood years in the late 1800s to his death in 1919. The "Note to Readers" and extensive list of acknowledgments wonderfully demonstrate how a careful biography is compiled. David R. Collins' *Tolkien, Master Of Fantasy* (Lerner, 1992) and another Carpenter/Shirley collaboration, *Frances Hodgson Burnett: Beyond The Secret Garden* (Lerner, 1990) are two other equally engrossing and pertinent titles.

EZRA JACK KEATS: A BIOGRAPHY WITH ILLUSTRATIONS
Dean Engel and Florence B. Freedman
Illustrations by Ezra Jack Keats

Silver Moon, 1995
[i, j] 81 pages

When biographers know their subject personally, the resulting book becomes special. That's true here: The authors, long-time friends of Mr. Keats, have warmly portrayed the author/artist who began drawing at age four and worked until his death 63 years later producing nearly two dozen richly illustrated books for children.

THE MONSTER FACTORY
Richard Rainey
B/w illustrations by Ted Bernstein and b/w photographs
New Discovery, 1993
[j] 128 pages

The stories behind the stories of Frankenstein, Dracula, Dr. Jekyll and Mr. Hyde, and others of their kind are almost as spellbinding as the monsters themselves.

CHARLES DICKENS: THE MAN WHO HAD GREAT EXPECTATIONS
Diane Stanley and Peter Vennema
Illustrations by Diane Stanley
Morrow, 1993
[i, j] 48 pages

This literate, beautifully illustrated and designed volume exemplifies biography for young readers at its very best.

A final word about letters to authors and illustrators: Do not make letter writing a routine event with a perfunctory "Thank you, I liked your book. May I have your autograph?" or "Please draw me a picture." At an American Library Association Authors' Breakfast, I overheard a group of writers bemoan the sacks of dittoed or mimeographed, scarcely legible, impersonal form letters they sometimes receive.

Teach young people that a letter should be a sincere effort to communicate. Teach them to be specific, to introduce themselves, and to write what pleased them most, or least, or caused questions. Enclose a stamped, self-addressed envelope (essential in this age of ever-increasing postal costs) and chances are they'll receive a personal reply, particularly from nonfiction authors, who don't hear from as many children as do writers of popular children's fiction. Next to a smiling face, a sincere, involved letter from a young admirer is one of the nicest thank-yous an author or illustrator can get.

BATS

"...because bats are misunderstood and intensely feared, they serve as ideal animals for teaching basic principles about prejudice and fear of the unknown. As children come to understand how wrong they can be about bats, they may be encouraged to question basic assumptions often made about other unpopular animals and even people." Patricia A. Morton, *About Bats* (Bat Conservation International, 1991).

In addition to the thought-provoking comment above, you'll find other easily adoptable and adaptable suggestions in Ms. Morton's elementary-grade activity guide, including what first-grade teacher Carol Eklund calls "Thank you, Bat" salad. Each year her students enjoy the delicious blend of bananas, dates, and other bat-dependent fruits. Carol, who teaches at Susquenita Elementary, in South Central, Pennsylvania, has had bats on her agenda for many years and suggests you add them to yours.

FIRST LOOK AT BATS
Millicent E. Selsam
B/w illustrations by Joyce Hunt
Walker, 1991
[p] 32 pages

Very young readers are asked to discern similarities and differences as they compare the physical characteristics of the pictured flying mammals. The author also comments on bat diet, habitat, and echolocation and concludes with an illustrated glossary-like recapitulation.

BATS: CREATURES OF THE NIGHT
Joyce Milton
Illustrations by Judith Moffatt
Grosset (hb/pb), 1993
[p] 48 pages

The colorful cut-paper illustrations will attract beginning readers, and the flowing, fact-fill text will intrigue them with basic bat data.

Read aloud or recommend Ruth Horowitz's *Bat Time* (Four Winds, 1991) and Lorinda Bryan Cauley's *Stellaluna* (Harcourt, 1993) for fictional perspectives on bats. In the first, a little girl eagerly anticipates the twinkling starlight when she and her dad can watch for bats. In the second, which concludes with two pages of facts about the flying mammals, a baby fruit bat is adopted by birds.

SHADOWS OF NIGHT
Barbara Bash
Illustrations by the author
Sierra Club, 1993
[p, i] 32 pages

A lucid narrative and dark-of-night watercolors portray North America's most common chiropteran, the mouse-eared (*Myotis*), light-fleeing (*lucifugus*), Little Brown Bat during a typical spring-to-spring cycle.

BATS: NIGHT FLIERS
Betsy Maestro
Illustrations by Giulio Maestro
Scholastic, 1994

[p,i] 32 pages

Lifelike watercolors of more than 25 micro- and megabats illustrate this outstanding overview of bats, their habitats and diet, as well as social and physical characteristics. Ms. Maestro thoughtfully describes some features as attractive and appealing if sometimes strange or unusual. Beautiful!

Have handy Donald M. Silver's *Cave* (Freeman, 1993) so bat buffs can learn more about the dark habitat and the plants and animals it supports. Patricia J. Wynne's superb illustrations provide additional detail in this "One Small Square" volume.

BATMAN
Laurence Pringle
Photographs by Merlin Tuttle
Scribner's, 1991
[i] 42 pages

Open just about any bat book and Dr. Merlin Tuttle's name appears as photographer, consultant, founder of BCI (Bat Conservation International), or author. A dedicated scientist whose initiative, research, and perseverance have changed many people's opinion of bats from expendable to essential, the good doctor is someone youngsters should meet, even when bats aren't on the agenda.

Bats are nocturnal and sleep in caves during the day because once, long ago, the birds didn't keep their *Promise To The Sun* (Little, 1992), Tololwa M. Mollel explains in his charming version of an African tale.

THOSE AMAZING BATS
Cheryl Mays Halton
Photographs
Dillon, 1991
[i] 96 pages

Ms. Halton explains the origins of bat myths; describes their habitats and characteristics; and reveals the discovery of some bats' use of echolocation and, briefly, their role in medical research. From beginning (Merlin Tuttle in the middle of a Thai jungle in search of bats) to end (an introduction to the first American to build bat houses), this is a grabber.

Put Diane Ackerman's enthralling *The Moon By Whale Light* (Random, 1991; Vintage, 1992) on your must-read-to-myself-and-aloud-to-kids lists. The first of four chapters, "In Praise of Bats," recounts interviews with Merlin Tuttle at Bracken Cave and Big Bend National Park, Texas. The remaining chapters describe her equally enlightening adventures among penguins, crocodilians, and whales.

BEARS

They come in black, blue, brown, and white, can weigh less than 100 or more than 2,200 pounds; and stand from 4 to 11 feet tall. The black ones can be white or blue; the brown ones silver-tipped or almost black; the white ones are really yellowish; and the black-eyed, -eared, -armed, and -legged white ones are called pandas.

BEARS
Ian Stirling
Photographs by Aubrey Lang, b/w illustrations by Dorothy Siemens
Sierra Club (hb/pb), 1992
[i, j] 64 pages

BEARS
Helen Gilks
Illustrations by Andrew Bale
Ticknor, 1993

[i] 32 pages

These complementary books describe the physical characteristics, social behavior, and precarious status of the eight extant species, including the panda, now confirmed as a bear-family member. Though markedly different in design and layout, both will entice and satisfy inquiring youngsters with or without reports due.

Link youngsters to *The Moon Of The Bears* (Harper-Collins, 1993), one of Jean Craighead George's lyrical year-in-the-life-of series. Once again available for young readers, it is newly illustrated with colorful gouaches by Ron Parker.

BEARS IN THE FOREST
Karen Wallace
Illustrations by Barbara Firth
Candlewick, 1994
[pre, p] 28 pages

One of the excellent "Read and Wonder" series, this picture-book look at a North American black bear and her two cubs is twice told: Simple declarative statements describing the bears' activities are hand-lettered along the bottom margin and recast as a typeset narrative up above as the story within the pictures.

EVERY AUTUMN COMES THE BEAR
Jim Arnosky
Illustrations by the author
Putnam, 1993
[pre, p] 32 pages

Mr. Arnosky's sparely worded yet information-rich view of one of his winter neighbors portrays a magnificent black beast as it wends its way around a wooded hill to a cozy den, under the watchful eyes of the hill's year-round inhabitants.

HOW DO BEARS SLEEP?
E.J. Bird
Illustrations by the author
Carolrhoda (hb/pb), 1990
[pre, p] 32 pages

Do they "make up a bed/Of dry leaves and stones,/Or lie on the ground/Just resting [their] bones...?" Mr. Bird's poetic musings and amusing pastels are not to be missed when hibernating bears are on the agenda—or it's sleeptime for a toddler.

ALASKA'S THREE BEARS
Shelley Gill
Illustrations by Shannon Cartwright
Paws IV (hb/pb), 1990
[p] 32 pages

A delightful blend of fiction (how the polar, grizzly and black bear spread across Alaska) and fact (what differentiates the species, one from the other).

Much of what we know about black bears comes from Lynn Rogers, the wildlife biologist who has devoted his adult life to studying them. Keep handy *Bearman* (Scribner's, 1989), Laurence Pringle's insightful profile of Mr. Rogers, and author Joan Anderson's and photographer George Ancona's *Earth Keepers* (Gulliver, 1993), a chapter of which is devoted to Rogers and his work.

BEAR
John Schoenherr
Illustrations by the author
Philomel (hb/pb), 1991
[p, i] 32 pages

A spare narrative and evocative paintings portray an Alaskan grizzly, newly abandoned by his mother, as he develops into a competent predator.

GRIZZLIES
Lynn M. Stone
Illustrations by the author and others
Carolrhoda, 1993
[i, j] 48 pages

The habitats, diet, life cycle, and human interaction of North America's brown bears, which are now classified as a single species. Their notable size differences are attributed to diet, with salmon-feeding bears, e.g., the Kodiak (Island) brown, having become the largest over the centuries.

Read aloud or recommend Judy Allen's 32-page story of a 12-year-old American boy's unexpected encounter with a *Panda* (Candlewick, 1992) in Western China. Tudor Humphries's watercolors beautifully recreate its bamboo forest habitat.

BIOGRAPHIES

Biographies are natural links to other subjects, and I've chosen to weave many of them throughout the Guide, rather than group them all into this section. I've linked readers to architect Paul R. Williams in the Buildings section, for example, to Betsy Ross in the States section, and to Patricia D. Moehlman, the "Jackal Woman," in Wolves, Jackals, and Foxes.

When selecting biographies, remember to look for those that present the warts as well as the dimples, and reflect thorough research and respect for the reader through acknowledgments, notes, recommended readings, credits, indexes, and the like.

BIOGRAPHY TODAY: ANNUAL CUMULATION 1994
Laurie Lanzen Harris, Ed.
B/w photographs
Omnigraphics, 1995
[i, j] 342 pages

This annual hardback, an indexed, alphabetical cumulation of first-rate profiles published in three paperback issues during the year, is a must for every upper elementrary and middle school library—in single-issue paperback, cumulative hardback, or both forms. Each biography covers the childhood, youth, education, family, and career of people in the public eye: in this 1994 edition, Connie Chung, Steve Young, Ruth Bader Ginsberg, and Wilma Mankiller.

With the same fine qualities as the series above, Ms. Harris's *Biography For Beginners #1* (Omnigraphics, 1995) begins a twice-a-year series of hardbacks for younger readers. In her first edition are profiles of Beverly Cleary, Eric Carle, Bill Clinton, Nelson Mandela, twins Mary-Kate and Ashley Olsen of TV's "Full-House," and nine others.

CHAMPIONS: STORIES OF TEN REMARKABLE ATHLETES
Bill Littlefield
Illustrations by Bernie Fuchs
Little, 1993
[i, j] 132 pages

Mr. Littlefield's exceptionally fine writing will mesmerize readers. He humanizes athletes such as Satchel Page, Muhammad Ali, and Billie Jean King, fulfilling a statement in the foreword that "Champions may be larger than life, but they are never above life." Mr. Fuchs's paintings catch the spirit of the athletes and their sports.

WOMEN OF THE WORLD
Rebecca Stefoff
B/w photographs and illustrations
Oxford, 1992
[j] 151 pages

Ms. Stefoff has written an absorbing account of nine adventurers whose travels span the late 18th to mid-20th centuries. They include Austrian Ida Pfeiffer (1797-1858), the first woman to make traveling her life's work—she earned the money for her trips by writing books about them; and American Marguerite Baker Harrison (1879-1967), who became a distinguished reporter, spy, traveler, and epic film producer by the age of 41.

This is one of Ms. Stefoff's exemplary "Extraordinary Explorers" series which includes *Scientific Explorers* and *Accidental Explorers* (both Oxford, 1992).

Supplement Ms. Stefoff's book (see above) with Doreen Rappaport's *Living Dangerously: American Women Who Risked Their Lives For Adventures* (HarperCollins , 1991). Among the six whose bold achievements Ms. Rappaport describes are Annie Smith Peck, who, in 1908, was the first person to reach Peru's highest peak; Bessie Coleman, the world's first black pilot; and Thecla Mitchell, a triple amputee who completed the New York Marathon in a wheelchair. These inspirational stories, in whole or part, lend themselves to dramatized adaptations. Suggest youngsters choose, rewrite, and perform one as a TV or radio interview or you-are-there playlet.

SPIES
Penny Coleman
B/w photographs
Betterway, 1992
[i, j] 96 pages

These adventurers are of a different sort than the women above. Committed, ingeniously creative, very brave, and with deep political convictions, these women spied during the Civil War. Teenager Belle Boyd, for one, became the most famous spy on either side with exploits such as running through the battlefield to deliver military information to the rebels.

ANNE FRANK: BEYOND THE DIARY, A PHOTOGRAPHIC REMEMBRANCE
Ruud van der Rol and Rian Verhoeven

B/w and color photographs
Viking, 1993
[i, j] 113 pages

Those touched by Anne Frank's poignant diary will want to read this work by staff members of Amsterdam's Anne Frank House. Getting to know the Franks before they went into hiding makes you care even more about them. They are no longer faceless victims.

Slave Harriet Jacobs hid in a garret seven-feet wide, nine-feet long, with a ceiling that sloped up from the floor to a height of three feet for most of seven years to escape the abuse of her master. Mary E. Lyons recounts the life of this indomitable woman through a series of fictionalized *Letters From a Slave Girl* (Scribner's, 1992). They describe Harriet's childhood days, the harsh indignities of slavery, her escape to the tiny room, and eventual freedom. Ms. Lyons based her letters on Harriet Jacobs's 1861 autobiography and in a note to readers explains what is fact and what is fiction.

SHADOW CATCHER:
THE LIFE AND WORK OF EDWARD S. CURTIS
Laurie Lawlor
Photographs, mostly by Edward S. Curtis
Walker, 1994
[i] 132 pages

Edward S. Curtis dedicated his life (1868-1952) to documenting North American Indians from El Paso to Seattle, in words and, most importantly, in photographs. His respect for and acceptance by his subjects enabled him to assemble the most compelling look at Native Americans ever produced. The photographs leave the reader spellbound.

ELEANOR ROOSEVELT: A LIFE OF DISCOVERY
Russell Freedman
B/w photographs

Clarions, 1993
[j] 198 pages

As America's First Lady, Eleanor Roosevelt was both official host-
ess and avid champion of human rights. After her husband's death
in 1945, she continued to work for peace and earned the title
"First Lady of the World." The 125 archival photographs, which
show Mrs. Roosevelt with family, friends, and at work, illustrate a
work that captures both the private and public side of this greatly admired woman. Pair this with Mr. Freedman's equally perceptive portrait of *Franklin Delano Roosevelt* (Clarion, 1991).

BODIES

Guest author Linda Allison once asked teachers in my workshop to think of the six-inch cube of Styrofoam she'd placed on
a table as the 1/20 inch thick, 3/4 inch square patch of skin out-
lined on the back of her hand. She pierced the cube with 30 hairs
(using shish-ka-bob skewers) and proceeded to drape and drop
other sundry items around and atop it to represent what else such
a skin-patch would hold: nine feet of blood vessels (red yarn); 13
yards of nerves (twine); six cold and 36 hot heat sensors (white
and red thumb tacks) and so on, until she'd completed the list
itemized on page 17 of her *Blood And Guts* (Little, 1976). Every
time I look at the back of my hand, I think of Ms. Allison, what's
beneath that teeny bit of skin, her luckily still-in-print book, and
the power of imaginative teaching.

When human anatomy, its features, and their function are
on the agenda, teach à la Allison. And suggest students
do the same. Encourage individuals or small groups to

construct models of whatever body parts or systems are the subject of their reports. They'll find directions for the models and photographs of youngsters making them in Andrew Haslam's *Make It Work: Body* (Thomson, 1994). Wind up the unit with a whole-class collaboration — a complete body made of the individual models and whatever other found items fit.

ME AND MY BODY
David Evans and Claudette Williams
Photographs
Dorling, 1992
[pre, p] 28 pages

The authors' opening and closing notes help parents and teachers direct little ones through activities to learn about themselves—their gross body structure (size, reach, movement, etc.), five senses, and the foods to eat and to avoid for a healthy diet. Readers (and younger lookers) will see their peers engaged in the activities.

YOUR INSIDES
Joanna Cole
Illustrations by Paul Meisel
Putnam, 1992
[pre, p] 36 pages

A simple but not simplistic introduction to the skeleton, musculature, and digestive, nervous, and circulatory systems.

Preschool/primary-graders have the first-rate "Let's-Read-and-Find-Out" (HarperCollins) titles to turn to for information about their physiological selves: Among them, author/artist Aliki's *My Hands* (1962/1990), *My Feet* (1990), *I'm Growing* (1992), and *My Five Senses* (1962/1989); and Paul Showers's *Look At Your Eyes* (1962/1992), *Your Skin and Mine* (1965/1991), *Ears Are For Hearing* (1990).

WHAT'S INSIDE MY BODY?
Angela Royston
Photographs and illustrations
Dorling, 1991
[p] 17 pages

In simply stated, sharing-time fashion, two elementary graders show what's beneath the surface of their eyes, ears, and other body parts via a clever blend of photos and drawings. Young students can give similar oral reports by holding in front of themselves or a buddy life-size drawings of whatever segment of the body they've researched.

THE HUMAN BODY
Joan Western and Ronald Wilson
Illustrations
Troll, 1991
[i] 96 pages

An ideal volume for intermediate graders in search of a straightforward, coherent, substantive yet not overpowering reference for school reports. A general introduction to human anatomy is followed by short chapters on individual systems and respective components, related topics (i.e., family resemblances), and very brief reviews of landmark research.

Send report writers investigating the *Brain, Muscles, Heart And Lungs, Ears,* and *Eyes* (each Troll, 1992) to the appropriate 32-page, single-topic, volume in the fine "You and Your Body" series. And to Steve Parker's 64-page, 6" x 8" *Human Body* (Dorling, 1994), which includes one- or two-person experiments that help youngsters investigate and understand how their bodies function.

THE VISUAL DICTIONARY OF THE HUMAN BODY
Photographs and illustrations
Dorling, 1991
[j, ya] 96 pages

Stunning displays of annotated photographs and diagrams make visible almost every segment of human anatomy, from a microscopic single-cell to the largest bones and organs. Many photographs are of startlingly lifelike models, some life-size, others thousands of times larger than life.

Older readers, to whom the "Visual Dictionary" and similar Dorling Kindersley series are addressed, will understand that adjacent illustrations, though not so marked, are often to vastly different scales. When you are with younger students, help them appreciate that fact.

THE BODY ATLAS
Steve Parker
Illustrations by Giuliano Fornari
Dorling, 1993
[j, ya] 64 pages

Body layers are "peeled" away in illustrations interpreted by the narrative of a natural teacher. With insight, a conversational style, and sense of humor, Mr. Parker artfully manipulates details that could easily overpower into a sparklingly lucid description/explanation of how the human body works.

THE MAGIC SCHOOL BUS INSIDE THE HUMAN BODY
Joanna Cole
Illustrations by Bruce Degen
Scholastic (hb/pb), 1989
[p, i] 48 pages

The unflappable Ms. Frizzle leads her class on a tour through the body with stops at some "innerspace" systems. When back in the classroom, the kids outline a human body and identify the key parts and organs they "visited" on a bulletin-board-size poster.

Divide children into small groups, each one responsible for a different body system. Have the groups make their reports during a Body Fair produced learning-

center style with charts, drawings, information packets, and simple demonstration-type experiments at
each station.

OUTSIDE AND INSIDE YOU
Sandra Markle
Photographs
Bradbury, 1991
[p, i] 40 pages

An outstanding collection of X-rays, electron micrographs, ther-
mograms, and other images dramatically reveal what's happening
inside the body. Ms. Markle's descriptions are carefully worded
for very young readers/listeners, but the illustrations will attract
and intrigue readers of all ages.

SKELETON
Steve Parker
Photographs and illustrations .
Knopf, 1988
[i, j] 64 pages

Art and artifacts that focus on bones surround the human skeleton which stretches across the opening six pages of one of the
first and best of the "Eyewitness Book" series. What follows are
equally riveting displays which vividly illustrate similarities and
differences between people and a few of the other 40,000 species
with backbones.

Have youngsters trace each other's outlines on a roll of
butcher paper during the first day of school. When
they've completed life-size self-portraits (and added hand
and foot tracings along with current clothing sizes on the
wrong side) pin up the paper pupils—on the walls, ceiling, or anywhere where they can remain for nine months.
End of the year comparisons will reveal just how much
your boys and girls have grown since day one in your
room.

DISCOVER BONES
Lesley Grant
B/w illustrations by Tina Holdcroft
Addison (pb), 1991
[i, j] 96 pages

An imaginative, upbeat, fact- and activity-filled exploration of the science of skeletons from the Royal Ontario Museum people who know how to turn kids on to learning.

BONES BOOK
Stephen Cumbaa
Color illustrations
Workman (pb), 1991
[i] 64 pages

Awesome data about the body (e.g., your eye muscles contract 100,000 times a day) appear in a guide that virtually sparkles with the paleontologist/author's enthusiasm, expertise, and sense of humor. The 4 1/2" x 8" paperback is packaged with a twenty-five-piece make-your-own skeleton, whose assembly certainly makes its parts familiar — make no bones about that.

Challenge youngsters with the puzzles, brain teasers, experiments and other enjoyable mini-projects in Karen C. Anderson's and Stephen Cumbaa's *The Bones And Skeleton Gamebook* (Workman, 1993).

DINOSAURS ALIVE AND WELL
Laura Krasny Brown
Illustrations by Marc Brown
Little (hb/pb), 1990
[p] 32 pages

The Browns' whole-body guide will help young children establish the good habits that encourage a lifetime attitude toward keeping fit by eating well, dressing sensibly, exercising both body and mind, and learning to feel good about themselves and others. It's nonfiction with a sense of humor — a most effective kind.

•HUMAN SEXUALITY

The following will ease the often-awkward task of explaining human sexuality to children.

WHAT'S HAPPENING TO MY BODY? BOOK FOR BOYS: A GROWING UP GUIDE FOR PARENTS AND SONS
Lynda Madaras and Dane Saavedra

WHAT'S HAPPENING TO MY BODY? BOOK FOR GIRLS: A GROWING UP GUIDE FOR PARENTS AND DAUGHTERS
Lynda Madaras and Area Madaras
Newmarket, 1988
[i, j] 288 pages; 304 pages

These compelling guides, updated to include information about AIDS, reflect the insights Ms. Madaras gained teaching classes in puberty and sex education to teens and preteens. Whether they read these alone or with an adult, young adults will learn about their bodies in language they'll understand; with humor they'll appreciate; and a thoroughness they will find enlightening, comforting and respectful of their need to know.

My Feelings, My Self and *My Body, My Self* (both Newmarket, 1993), by Lynda and Area Madaras are noteworthy companions to the book for girls recommended above. The first is a workbook/journal that focuses on such teen concerns as peer pressure, communicating with parents, and learning strategies for win/win solutions to problems. The second is filled with quizzes, checklists, exercises, and room for entries on everything that has to do with a woman's body changes during puberty, from body image to emotional fluctuations to menstruation.

THE BODY BOOK
Sara Stein
B/w photographs and illustrations

Workman (hb/pb), 1992
[j] 294 pages

Ms. Stein's straightforward "owner's manual" answers just about any questions inquisitive middle-schoolers might have on our outer and inner physiological selves, including how we grow from single cell to adulthood, how we reproduce, and how our bodies are in a state of constant self-maintenance.

IT'S OK TO BE YOU:
A FRANK AND FUNNY GUIDE TO GROWING UP
Claire Patterson
B/w illustrations by Lindsay Quilter
Tricycle (pb), 1994
[i, j] 70 pages

IT'S PERFECTLY NORMAL:
CHANGING BODIES, GROWING UP, SEX & SEXUAL HEALTH
Robie H. Harris
Illustrations by Michael Emberley
Candlewick, 1994
[i, j] 89 pages

The authors' and illustrators' understanding of and respect for children is evident throughout both books. After assuring young readers that everyone is unique and explaining (and showing) how boys differ from girls, Ms. Patterson adroitly covers the fundamentals of maturation, sexuality, behavior, and the expression of feelings. The inclusion of Munchkin, a wise-cracking cat, in the lighthearted illustrations makes this introduction to puberty reader-friendly.

Ms. Harris covers the same material as Ms. Patterson, but treats the issue of homosexuality more explicitly and nonjudgmentally adds information about aborted pregnancies. She's also included information about sexual abuse and sexually transmitted diseases, including AIDS, and an index. A bird and a bee add light-hearted commentary here.

BRIDGES

BRIDGES GO FROM HERE TO THERE
Forrest Wilson
B/w illustrations by the author
Preservation, 1993
[i, j] 86 pages

With few words and whimsical drawings architect/builder Wilson shows and tells how bridges push against gravity's pull to hold things up. He provides a near-effortless way to teach children of all ages the principles of bridge design.

THE BRIDGE BOOK
Polly Carter
Two–color illustrations by Roy Doty
Simon, 1992
[i] 36 pages

With line drawings, brief copy blocks, and cartoons with voice bubbles, the writer/illustrator team provides historical perspective for various bridge types, from a simple log to a complex cable-stayed structure.

BRIDGES
Etta Kaner
Illustrations by Pat Cupples
Kids Can (pb), 1994
[i] 48 pages

In the guise of an engineer, the author explains how beam bridges, arch bridges, suspension bridges, and movable bridges are built and includes intriguing related projects for children working alone or in small groups. An index and glossary wrap up this delightful volume where men, women, boys, and girls are depicted working on bridge–building projects.

BRIDGING THE GOLDEN GATE
Kathy Pelta
B/w photos and illustrations
Lerner (hb/pb), 1987
[i, j] 96 pages

With the aid of archival photos, Ms. Pelta presents a comprehensive, pictorial explanation of the need for, debate about, and design and construction of the always-inspiring Golden Gate Bridge. Key facts (4,200-foot main span, 80,000 *miles* of wire, etc.), a bibliography, and a comprehensive index augment her excellent text.

BUILDIINGS

ROUND BUILDINGS, SQUARE BUILDINGS, BUILDINGS THAT WIGGLE LIKE A FISH
Philip M. Isaacson
Photographs by the author
Knopf (hb/pb), 1988
[j, a] 128 pages

Mr. Isaacson calls attention to buildings whose parts are in harmony with each other, buildings that have a "magical" feeling about them: Stonehenge and the Taj Mahal, among them, as well as Boston's Louisberg Square (of the "wiggling" bricks) and Chicago's Federal Center. His beautifully worded and photographed volume makes an ideal point of embarkation for all architectural excursions.

HOW THINGS WERE BUILT
David J. Brown
Illustrations
Random, 1992
[i, j] 140 pages

The two-page, cut-away illustrations of 60 structures, arranged in chronological order, range from simple reed huts of the ancient world to the twentieth century's largest engineering projects. Introductory paragraphs for each spread trace the development of building methods and materials. Annotations detail specific techniques and noteworthy particulars.

THE X-RAY PICTURE BOOK
OF BIG BUILDINGS OF THE ANCIENT WORLD
Joanne Jessup
Illustrations
Watts, 1994
[j] 48 pages

An oversize (10" x 12") view of what's beneath the surface of ten pre-17th century structures and the purposes they served. The first of the two spreads devoted to each recounts its history alongside a cutaway view. The second spread contains a description of its construction and highlights various operations along the way.

AMAZING BUILDINGS
Philip Wilkinson
Illustrations by Paolo Donati
Dorling, 1993
[i,j] 48 pages

The 21 buildings portrayed in this impressive 11" x 14" volume run the historical gamut from the Palace of Minos to the Toronto SkyDome, via a Mayan temple and Spain's Alhambra, among others. Each of the dramatic spreads is dominated by a cutaway drawing of the featured building; its floorplan and photograph are among the accompanying insets.

THE VISUAL DICTIONARY OF BUILDINGS
Photographs
Dorling, 1992
[j] 64 pages

The more-than-a-thousand parts pictured here furnish the most detailed look at buildings' tops, bottoms, sides—inside and out— I've seen. All are set against a white background to make their individually labeled components easily discernible. A chart of major architectural styles from Ancient Turkey to the 20th century concludes a pictorial presentation of the style and substance of architecture that will intrigue young and old.

WONDERS OF THE WORLD
Giovanni Caselli
Illustrations by the author
Dorling, 1992
[i] 64 pages

Buildings that make people "marvel at their existence" are arranged according to their similarity to the seven wonders of the ancient world. Grouped with Egypt's pyramids, for example, are other immense stone structures such as China's Great Wall; and Chicago's Sears Tower is grouped with the 400-foot tall Pharos (lighthouse) of Alexandria. Illustrations cleverly include side-by-side views, with one from above, so that readers can appreciate relative sizes.

UMM EL MADAYAN: AN ISLAMIC CITY THROUGH THE AGES
Abderrahman Ayoub et al.
B/w illustrations by Francesco Corni
Houghton, 1994
[j] 62 pages

Few books so dramatically demonstrate how the structures built to suit peoples' needs alter the face of cities than the "City Through the Ages" series. In each 9" x 12" volume, meticulous line drawings trace a fictitious city's growth, from an assemblage of primitive huts to a skyscrapered metropolis. Alternating with two-page overviews drawn from the same perspective are illustrations and text that detail building construction and provide an historical basis for each era's houses and public buildings.

Other volumes in this series are *San Rafael, Zebek*, and *Barmi* (Houghton, 1992, 1991, 1990), respectively a Central American, Northern European, and Mediterranean city.

Invite a member of your city's historical society to class to show children how their town has changed over the past few generations.

WHAT IT FEELS LIKE TO BE A BUILDING
Forrest Wilson
B/w illustrations by the author
Preservation, 1988
[i, j] 80 pages

An ingenious disclosure of how walls, beams, columns, and other building parts function. With few words and bold illustrations, the author/artist illustrates the internal stress and strain as being a bit of push and pull here, squash and squeeze there, here a droop, there a tug, everywhere some bend and brace. Readers of all ages will find themselves looking at the constructions around them with greater appreciation of the internal forces at work.

Patterns and designs found on buildings often reflect shapes in nature—spiral staircases like nautilus shells or onion-shaped church domes. Jane D'Alelio asks youngsters to pair natural to manufactured shapes in *I Know That Building!* (Preservation, 1989). She's also designed cards for a match-architect-to-building game; a covered bridge and two skyscrapers to trace or cut out and build; and an embossed image of a manhole on the back cover for rubbing. Her ideas make excellent springboards for projects children can create to become more aware of the old and new buildings that surround them.

THE WONDERFUL TOWERS OF WATTS
Patricia Zelver
Illustrations by Frané Lessac
Tambourine, 1994
[p, i] 32 pages

With broken bits of colored tiles, empty bottles, seashells, old shoes, and other found objects, Sam Rodia cemented together a magical city of streets, squares, fountains, steeples, spires, and lacey flying buttresses. Author and artist capture the simple life and artistry of this amateur architect/builder.

JULIA MORGAN: ARCHITECT OF DREAMS
Ginger Wadsworth
B/w photos and drawings
Lerner, 1990
[j] 128 pages

Architect Morgan's grit and determination shine throughout this vivid biography, from the architect's childhood through her fast-paced career, with detailed attention to her most famous project, Hearst Castle. Ms. Wadsworth has carefully researched the life of a publicity-shy, small-in-stature woman who ranks among the giants of American architecture.

THE WILL AND THE WAY
Karen E. Hudson
B/w and color photographs
Rizzoli, 1994
[i,j] 64 pages

Paul R. Williams was the first African-American member and Fellow of the American Institute of Architects. These notes to his first grandchild—edited by his granddaughter—comprise an inspirational story of talent and will overcoming great odds. Youngsters will profit by the distinguished architect's sage advice, which includes: "No matter what you decide to become, you must remember three things: Read, read, read!"

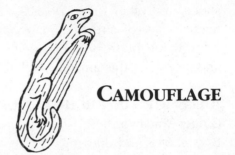

CAMOUFLAGE

ANIMAL CAMOUFLAGE
Joyce Powzyk
Illustrations by the author
Bradbury, 1990
[i, j] 40 pages

Ms. Powzyk describes the naturally misleading characteristics that help animals survive; protective coloration, mimicry, and masking, among them. She also lists the scientific names and whereabouts of the featured creatures.

HIDING OUT: CAMOUFLAGE IN THE WILD
James Martin
Photographs by Art Wolfe
Crown, 1993
[i] 32 pages

A stunning presentation of wildlife, from the Malaysian orchid mantis to the spotted leopard, all of which are virtually invisible when they want to be, within their native habitats.

Pair *Animal Camouflage* with *Hiding Out* so youngsters can compare close-ups of the Madagascan leaf-tailed gecko. The portraits nicely illustrate the complementary nature of hand-drawn and photographic images.

ANIMALS IN DISGUISE
Martine Duprez
Illustrations by Helene Appell-Mertiny
Charlesbridge, 1994
[i] 42 pages

Nine species are highlighted in this interestingly designed volume, where data on habitat, appearance, method of camouflage, and the like are arranged in columns for easy information gathering. Beautiful full-page portraits and smaller illustrations create continuity and an artistic whole.

SECRET FORESTS: A COLLECTION OF HIDDEN CREEPY CRAWLY BUGS AND INSECTS
Michael Gaffney
Illustrations by the author
Artists, 1994
[p,i] 32 pages

Six miniature habitats which include pine bark and leaf-littered grounds are the focus of dramatic 19" x 12" spreads which will grab and hold children's attention. The first two of the four pages devoted to each habitat contain individual portraits of the creatures. The second two show all of them in situ—scarcely discernible because of their natural blend–ability.

HOW TO HIDE AN OCTOPUS: AND OTHER SEA CREATURES
Ruth Heller
Illustrations by the author
Grosset (hb/pb), 1985/1992
[p] 32 pages

In light verse and lovely colors, Ms. Heller distinctively delineates eight sea creatures' ability to be there one moment and gone the next. Happily back in print are this and others of the author/artists's "How to Hide" series, among them *How To Hide A Butterfly* and *How To Hide A Crocodile And Other Reptiles* (all Grosset).

CANADA

THE STORY OF CANADA
Janet Lunn and Christopher Moore
Illustrations by Alan Daniel; photographs,
drawings, and reproductions
Key Porter, 1992
[j, ya] 320 pages

A "must" wherever the curriculum includes Canada, this handsome volume spans the period from 100 centuries ago to the late 1980s. It highlights women, Native Americans, Blacks, and Asians among other significant people in the country's history, as well as momentous places and events.

CANADA VOTES
Linda Granfield
B/w illustrations by Craig Terlson
Kids Can (pb), 1992
[i, j] 64 pages

An analogy- and anecdote-laden explanation of Canada's British-based system of "responsible government", including its major divisions, parties, election process, and limits on campaign spending. Ms. Granfield also explains voter registration and procedure, how women and minorities gained their once-denied right to vote, and how candidates wage winning campaigns.

CANADIAN FIRE FIGHTERS

CANADIAN POSTAL WORKERS

CANADIAN POLICE OFFICERS

CANADIAN GARBAGE COLLECTORS
Paulette Bourgeois
B/w illustrations by Kim LaFave
Kids Can (hb/pb), 1991/1992
[pre, p] 32 pages each

The responsibilities of Canadian community helpers are pretty much the same as their American counterparts. But there are differences, as youngsters will discover.

Before children meet a local "community helper," have them peruse and pair the appropriate volume from the above quartet with a book describing the American counterpart—Gail Gibbons's *Fire! Fire!* (HarperCollins, 1987), for example, and Gloria Skurzynski's *Here Comes The Mail* (Bradbury, 1992). Youngsters prepared with questions about similarities and dissimilarities between the two countries' professionals will make a visit from one much more effective.

LET'S CELEBRATE
Caroline Parry
B/w illustrations
Kids Can (pb), 1987
[i, j] 256 pages

This entertaining and enlightening look at northern North Americans' ethnic holidays and festivals is arranged by season and colored with historical and contemporary anecdotes, folklore, art activities, poetry, and recipes. Most of the events are those we also celebrate in the U.S.; those not on our calendars are worth discovering.

A PRAIRIE ALPHABET
Jo Bannatyne-Cugnet and Yvette Moore
Illustrations by Yvette Moore
Tundra, 1992
[i] 32 pages

The people, places, and things to be found in Canada's portion of the North American prairie—a habitat that provides them a self-sustaining, farming way of life—from annual agricultural fairs to the zucchini in their gardens.

O CANADA
Ted Harrison
Illustrations by the author
Ticknor, 1993
[p, i] 32 pages

Mr. Harrison shares impressions of each of his adopted homeland's provinces and territories on paired pages: heartfelt words on the left, vibrant paintings on the right.

CANADA: THE LAND

CANADA: THE PEOPLE

CANADA: THE CULTURE

CANADA CELEBRATES MULTICULTURALISM
Bobbie Kalman
Photographs and illustrations
Crabtree (hb/pb), 1993
[i] 32 pages each

Respectively, the four volumes provide a general introduction to, (1) Canadian geography, natural resources, and industry; (2) its multiculutural citizenry; (3) their holidays and other celebrations; and (4) artistic endeavors, from Cirque de Soleil to hockey.

CATS: WILD AND DOMESTIC

Feature felines. Encourage children to read, write, sing, speak, and paint pictures about cats—real and storybook, domestic and wild—for four weeks. If you start on April 12, you can end on May 12, and celebrate Cat Festival Day, as they do in Belgium. There, people parade costumed as cats from literature. Here, youngsters can march through neighboring classrooms after they've donned cat masks of their favorite factual or fictional felines. (Ron and Marsha Feller's *Paper Masks And Puppets* [Arts 1985] has step-by-step directions they can easily follow.) Let the students in each class play "20 Questions" and try to identify the cat breeds or characters represented by the masks.

•WILD CATS

BIG CATS

SMALL CATS
Susan Lumpkin
Photographs and illustrations
Facts on File, 1993
[i, j] 68 pages each

The big cats featured here are those that roam big areas to find enough big prey to survive. Well-designed with an eye-catching blend of fully annotated sidebars, insets, photographs, and drawings, these complementary presentations introduce the prey, habitats, unique characteristics, and endangered status of wild cat species.

 Primary graders will find Joyce Milton's *Big Cats* (Grosset, 1994) a manageable, information-packed, nicely illustrated read.

BIG CATS
Seymour Simon
Photographs
HarperCollins, 1991
[i] 40 pages

Mr. Simon describes the attributes that make seven of the largest feral felines superb predators and details the specifics that distinguish one from the other.

Hand youngsters artist/author Ted Lewin's *Tiger Trek* (Macmillan, 1990) for an imaginary yet realistic view of the striped predator, the wary creatures she passes, and the chital fawn she catches to share with her cubs in a hot, hazy jungle preserve where Maharajahs once reigned.

CHEETAH
Caroline Arnold
Photographs by Richard Hewett
Morrow, 1989
[i, j] 48 pages

Crisp closeups vividly illustrate a detailed description of this most endangered cat's attributes. The setting is an Oregon open-air wildlife park, where the study and breeding of cheetahs contribute toward their survival as a species.

MOUNTAIN LION
Sandra Chisholm Robinson
B/w illustrations
Roberts, 1991
[i] 62 pages

Puma, cougar, and panther are but three of the more than 40 different English names for the mountain lion, and there are about 60 more in Spanish and Indian dialects. This inexpensive paperback effectively combines information, stories, playlets, and games and activities based upon this cat of many names.

Introduce youngsters to Margaret Goff Clark's *The Endangered Florida Panther* (Cobblehill, 1993), to learn about this close cousin of the mountain lion and the efforts to keep the species from becoming extinct.

YOUR CAT'S WILD COUSINS
Hope Ryder
Full-color photographs by the author
Lodestar, 1991
[i] 48 pages

Ms. Ryden devotes two pages to each of the featured felines and illustrates each cat's history, habits, and habitat with two portraits and, for comparison's sake, a snapshot of her domestic longhair, Lily.

•DOMESTIC CATS

CATS
Juliet Clutton-Brock
Photographs, illustrations
Knopf, 1991
[i, j] 64 pages

This "Eyewitness Book" details the evolution and characteristics of domestic and wild cats. Two-page chapters focus on such topics as the agile predators' skeletal structure, extinct predecessors, senses, markings, and habitat — the stuff from which great school reports materialize.

CATS: IN FROM THE WILD
Caroline Arnold
Photographs by Richard Hewett
Carolrhoda, 1993
[i, j] 48 pages

Ms. Arnold's smoothly flowing, information-packed narrative highlights the domestic cat's history and highlights the parallels in its physiology and behavior and those of its wild forebears.

KNOW YOUR CAT: AN OWNER'S GUIDE TO CAT BEHAVIOR
Bruce Fogle
Photographs by Jane Burton

Dorling, 1991
[j] 128 pages

Dr. Fogle interprets feline body language; discusses various breeds' physical, social, and emotional characteristics; describes kittens' birth and growth; and suggests proper care and feeding through maturity to old age. A concluding questionnaire will help readers learn more about their cat's personality.

Perfect for preschoolers is author/artist Patricia Casey's *My Cat Jack* (Candlewick, 1994). Chances are their cats have much in common with Jack. Ask them.

KITTEN
Mark Evans
Photographs
Dorling, 1992
[p,i] 42 pages

In this "ASPCA Pet Care Guide for Kids," Dr. Evans stresses "pethood" responsibilities as well as its pleasures. His suggestions include the importance of spaying or neutering pets to avoid unwanted offspring.

Add Marilyn Baillie's and Brenda Clarks' scrapbooks of drawings, photos, and facts, *My Cat* and *My Dog* (Little, 1994), to your book-fair musts. Each inexpensive paperback is a compendium of fine drawings and pertinent facts with fill-in-the-blanks spaces for pet owners' comments about and photos of their favorite furry friends.

CHESS

For practice in logic and strategy, challenge youngsters with chess. Set out a set and let them teach themselves or learn more about the royal game.

THE KIDS' BOOK OF CHESS
Harvey Kidder
Two-color illustrations, w/chess set included
Workman (pb), 1970/1990
[p] 96 pages

The clear text interestingly links each piece and its movement to the medieval world that influenced its evolution: The pawn's diagonal striking power, for example, is traced to the medieval pikeman, who pointed his spike to either side of his protective shield. The new illustrations in this update are "the best diagrams I have ever seen in any beginners' book," according to a chess expert friend.

THE SIMON & SCHUSTER POCKET BOOK OF CHESS
Raymond Keene
Illustrations and archival photographs
Simon, 1989
[i] 192 pages

Mr. Keene's book, also highly recommended by my friend, is colorfully illustrated throughout with diagrams and contemporary and archival photographs. It explains basic moves, recommended attacks and defenses, and common errors. It also has a glossary of terms, an historical overview of the game, and an introduction to world champions — men and women.

 # CHILDREN AND THEIR FAMILIES

ALL THE COLORS OF THE EARTH
Sheila Hamanaka
Illustrations by the author
Morrow, 1994
[pre, p, i] 32 pages

BEIN' WITH YOU THIS WAY
W. Nikola-Lisa
Illustrations by Michael Bryant
Lee, 1994
[p,i] 32 pages

Two joyous books in rhyme that celebrate the diversity and one-ness of all peoples. In her picturebook for all ages, Ms. Hamanaka's lustrous oils illustrate the fact that "Children come in all the colors of the earth...." The refrain of Mr. Nikola-Lisa's playground-rappish rhyme points out that we're all "Different—/Mm-mmm,/but the same,/Ah-ha!"

Ann Morris's few words and Ken Heyman's photographs of children, families, and people of all ages are ideal story starters for creative writing or oral reminiscences of similar experiences when *On The Go* (Lothrop, 1990), using *Tools* (Lothrop, 1992, 1995), wearing *Hats, Hats, Hats* or *Shoes, Shoes, Shoes* (Lothrop, 1992,1995), eating *Bread, Bread, Bread* (Lothrop, 1989), or just sharing *Loving* (Lothrop, 1990).

MASAI AND I
Virginia Kroll
Illustrations by Nancy Carpenter
Four Winds, 1992
[p, i] 32 pages

Prompted by the "tingle of kinship," an African-American elementary grader compares her daily customs with those of the East Africans she studied in school. Were she Masai, she'd sleep on cowhide on the bare earth, she muses, and live among the African animals she sees in the zoo. Pair this with photoessayist Barbara A. Margolies's *Olbalbal: A Day In Maasailand* (Four Winds, 1994).

HOW MY FAMILY LIVES IN AMERICA
Susan Kuklin
Photographs by the author

Bradbury, 1992
[p, i] 32 pages

Kindergarten-age Sanu Dieng, Eric Cruz, and April Lee talk about the daily activities through which they learn and practice the traditions of their varied cultural heritages, respectively Senegalese, Puerto Rican, and Chinese. The children contribute favorite recipes that readers can try for a "taste" of their cultures.

Consider childhood games as you discuss cultural differences and similarities with Mary D. Lankford's *Hop-Scotch Around The World* (Morrow, 1992) as your jumping off point.

THE OTHER SIDE: HOW KIDS LIVE IN A CALIFORNIA LATINO NEIGHBORHOOD

CITY WITHIN A CITY: HOW KIDS LIVE IN NEW YORK'S CHINATOWN
Kathleen Krull
Photographs by David Hautzig
Lodestar, 1994
[i, j] 48 pages each

In each of these photoessays, two 12–year olds talk about their responsibilities (e.g., translators for their non-English speaking parents), school activities, aspirations, and other everyday events as they absorb the values of two worlds: their parents' and their American peers'.

KIDS EXPLORE THE GIFTS OF CHILDREN WITH SPECIAL NEEDS
Westridge Young Writers Workshop
B/w photographs and illustrations
Muir, 1994
[i, j] 118 pages

This superb antithesis to textbook/worksheet learning was written by 245 students in third to sixth grade classes with the help of sixteen teachers. For one year, the children spent time with one of ten disabled youngsters, then wrote about his/her life, drew appropriate illustrations, and ended each chapter/biography about that youngster with a q/a section about the disability.

FAMILIES: A CELEBRATION OF DIVERSITY, COMMITMENT, AND LOVE
Aylette Jenness
Photographs by the author
Houghton, 1990
[i, j] 48 pages

Families are, for all their differences, very much alike, as readers will discover in this eye-opening look at seventeen youngsters from many cultural backgrounds and their traditional, nontraditional, single- and two-parent, natural, and adoptive families.

Complement primary graders' family talk with Virginia Kroll's *Beginnings: How Families Come To Be* (Whitman, 1994). Like Ms. Jenness's (see above), this is a multicultural view of a family's many forms. Add a poetic touch with Mary Ann Hoberman's twenty-six poems about *Fathers, Mothers, Sisters, Brothers* (Joy Street, 1991; Puffin, 1993).

A FAMILY GOES HUNTING
Dorothy Hinshaw Patent
B/w photographs by William Muñoz
Clarion (hb/pb), 1991
[i] 64 pages

Avoiding its controversial aspects, Dr. Patent concentrates on hunting as a healthy family activity. Her focus is Roger and Carla Cox and their children who hunt to provide themselves low-fat, hormone- and antibiotic-free meat. The Coxes are portrayed as a closely knit family with a praiseworthy tradition of self-sufficiency.

Have youngsters share photos or memories of activities they've experienced with family members: A grandparent, perhaps, as in Francine Haskins's *Things I Like About Grandma* (Children's Book, 1992) and Margaret Wild's *Our Granny* (Ticknor, 1993); or a parent, as in Denizé Lauture's *Father And Son* (Putnam, 1993). A good book to bring to a family reunion is Wade Hudson's *I Love My Family* (Scholastic, 1993).

A MIGRANT FAMILY
Larry Dane Brimner
B/w photographs by the author
Lerner, 1992
[i, j] 40 pages

Juan Medina's family is one of the thousands whose income derives from the sowing and reaping of seasonal crops. Mr. Brimner's sensitive photoessay provides an insightful perspective on the difficulties that confront them as they strive to survive with dignity in communities that seek their help but too often remain insensitive to their needs.

VOICES FROM THE FIELDS
S. Beth Atkins
B/w photographs by the author
Joy Street, 1993
[j] 96 pages

The children of migrant farmworkers talk about themselves, their prose framed by poetry of their peers—all eloquent expressions of warmth, love of family, inner strength, and character undiminished by the peripatetic quality of their lives.

THE SACRED HARVEST: OJIBWAY WILD RICE GATHERING
Gordon Regguinti
Photographs by Dale Kakkak
Lerner (hb/pb), 1992
[i] 48 pages

One of the fine "We Are Still Here" series by Native American authors that sensitively reveals how cultural traditions are handed down from parent to child and blended into life in contemporary America. Among the other titles recommended in this series are *Shannon, An Ojbway Dancer* (1993), and *Children Of Clay: A Family Of Potters* (1992).

HOANG ANH
Diane Hoyt-Goldsmith
Photographs by Lawrence Migdale
Holiday, 1992
[i] 32 pages

The youngster and his family are shown as they blend Vietnamese and American traditions in their new roles as U.S. citizens. This is but one of the author/photographer team's many fine photo-essays about children in families that make ancient traditions the core of their contemporary lives. *Arctic Hunter* and *Cherokee Summer* (Holiday, 1992/1993) are two others.

LEAVING FOR AMERICA
Roslyn Bresnick-Perry
Illustrations by Mira Reisberg
Children's Book, 1992
[p, i] 32 pages

Ms. Bresnick-Perry recalls the days when she and her mother made ready to leave their little Jewish town of Wysokie Litewskie, in Russia, to join her father in America. With humor and affection, she recalls friends and relatives, the journey's preparations, the blend of excitement and sadness as the time of departure neared, and the tearful goodbyes.

THE YEAR YOU WERE BORN: 1981 THROUGH 1987
Jeanne Martinet
Illustrations by Judy Lanfredi
Tambourine (pb), 1994
[i] 56 pages each

A one-year-a-volume, day-by-day compilation of newsworthy events and historical tidbits for each of seven years (as of this writing). Youngsters can quickly discover—in class—notable events (other than their own arrival!) that happened during the year of their birth.

Send students to the library to read newspapers or magazines published when the adults in their homes were their age. You'll find that the assignment frequently prompts enthusiastic, memory-filled conversations at home. Have them pick one or more topics for additional research and updating. Those events, too, should stir dialogue at home—"Do you remember when...?"

KIDS FOR SAIL
Pamela and Sam Bendall
Photographs by the authors
Orca (pb), 1990
[i] 120 pages

A breathtaking, true-adventure story about nine-year-old Sam, his younger brother, and his parents, who travel by 40-foot sailboat from British Columbia to New Zealand. Ms. Bendall's third-person account, based on excerpts from son/co-author Sam's written-en-route diary and school reports will have you and your youngsters at one with the four on their exhausting, exhilarating, enriching, and occasionally life-threatening expedition.

ELIJAH'S ANGEL
Michael J. Rosen
Illustrations by Aminah Brenda Lynn Robinson
Harcourt, 1992
[p, i] 32 pages

Though subtitled "A Story for Chanukah and Christmas," this reminiscence of the author's boyhood friendship with 80-year-old Elijah Pierce is a marvelous read-aloud or -alone any time family, friendship, or tradition is on the agenda.

CHRISTMAS IN THE BIG HOUSE, CHRISTMAS IN THE QUARTERS
Patricia C. and Fredrick L. McKissack
Illustrations by John Thompson
Scholastic, 1994
[i, j] 68 pages

A plantation owner's family in their big house and the slave families in their quarters prepare and celebrate Christmas and New Year. The stark contrast is vividly reflected in words and pictures in this affecting account of life in Virginia, just before the Civil War.

FROZEN LAND

AMAZON BASIN
Jan Reynolds
Photographs by the author
Harcourt, 1994
[i, j] 32 pages each

When you and your children read each "About This Book" section of this "vanishing culture" series, you'll be as impressed and fascinated by the intrepid Ms. Reynolds as the people with whom she lived and whose day-to-day activities she described—respectively the Inuit and Yanomama. In *Sahara* (1991), *Himilaya* (1992), *Far North* (1992), *Down Under* (1992) (all Harcourt) she describes, respectively, Tuareg, Sherpa, Sami, and Aborigine families. Her intriguing photos and words reflect the skill and insight only an artist's first-hand experience can provide.

Ms. Reynolds's emphasis on children's roles in their respective families/cultures (see above) will provide readers the wherewithal for lively comparison (how are we alike/different?), thoughtful conjecture (in what ways might modern technology impinge?), and speculative discussions (will change be for better or worse?) of these endangered life-styles. All will inspire additional research.

THE CHILDREN OF MAURITANIA: DAYS IN THE DESERT AND BY THE RIVER SHORE
Lauren Goodsmith

THE CHILDREN OF INDIA
Jules Hermes
Photographs by the authors
Carolrhoda (hb/pb), 1993
[i, j] 56 pages, 48 pages

With striking photographs and terse descriptions, the authors of these and others in the fine "The World's Children" series vivify young people from all walks of life in their respective countries.

NEVE SHALOM/ WAHAT AL-SALAM: OASIS OF PEACE
Laurie Dolphin
Photographs by Ben Dolphin
Scholastic, 1993
[i] 48 pages

Neve Shalom/Wahat al-Salam (NS/WAS), which means Oasis of Peace, is a cooperative village of Israeli Jews and Arabs who want their children to learn to respect each other and coexist peacefully. Ms. Dolphin introduces readers to two 10½-year-old boys from outside the village (an Arab Moslem and a Jew), their families, and the friends they make as the first students to come to the NS/WAS school from other villages.

THE BOYS' WAR
Jim Murphy
Photographs
Clarion (hb/pb), 1990
[i, j] 110 pages

It has been estimated that between 10 and 20 percent of all soldiers in the Civil War were under 16 years of age — some 250,000 to 420,000 of them. In his remarkable account, Mr. Murphy traces the war's progress from the youngsters' perspectives, interweav-

ing his narrative with excerpts from their diaries, letters, and journals. The eager enlistees' evolution to disillusioned, battle-scarred,
and weary survivors is powerfully dramatized by the stark, sepia
photographs, particularly those of battlefields littered with the
dead. This is an invaluable resource for any discussion of war —
today's or yesterdays'.

TELL THEM WE REMEMBER:
THE STORY OF THE HOLOCAUST
Susan D. Bachrach
Color and b/w photographs from the
United States Holocaust Memorial Museum
Little, 1994
[i, j] 128 pages

More than one million children and teenagers were murdered by
the Nazis, including these, whose photographs and stories are
interwoven throughout this historical overview of the Holocaust.
Ms. Bachrach's stark reporting of the rise of Nazism, the persecu-
tion of non-Arayans and the handicapped, the operation of the
"killing centers," and the Nuremberg trials provides a look at
recent history all children should be taught, grim though it is.

COLUMBUS AND HIS TIME

As a fourth grader in 1942, I was fascinated that the year was
an anagram of the year when "heroic" Columbus and his cohorts
sailed into this hemisphere. I've changed quite a bit in five-plus
decades, and so has my view of the man and his cohorts. The
books of my childhood made no mention of the Spaniards' cal-
lous treatment of the natives.

As you prepare to teach about the explorers' impact on world
history, make certain your youngsters receive a balanced per-

spective. In addition to the books below, you'll profit by perusing Hans Koning's polemic, *Columbus: His Enterprise* (Monthly Review Press, 1976/1991). The real Columbus existed somewhere between the unblemished hero of my youth and Mr. Koning's archvillain.

DISCOVERY OF THE AMERICAS
Betsy Maestro
Illustrations by Giulio Maestro
Lothrop (hb/pb), 1991
[p, i] 49 pages

Ms. Maestro begins with the nomads who trekked the long-since buried land bridge beneath the Bering Strait. She introduces their now Native American descendants, mentions seafarers who preceded and followed Columbus, and highlights his and Magellan's voyages. Her addenda include an annotated table of noteworthy dates and a brief description of ancient and early American cultures.

Let Ms. Maestro's lucid distillation (see above) set the stage for the study of New World history. An excellent source for a student-drawn time line, each entry is a possible topic for individual or group research.

FORGOTTEN VOYAGER
Ann Fitzpatrick Alper
B/w illustrations
Carolrhoda, 1991
[i,j] 80 pages

An absorbing biography of Amerigo Vespucci, America's namesake and Columbus contemporary, an accomplished navigator and explorer who sailed and mapped much of the Atlantic coastline of Central and South America and some of North America's. Most notably, he was the first to realize that Columbus had not discovered the Indies, but a new continent.

Help children appreciate the scientific advances that

made possible Columbus's successful Atlantic crossing. As author/artist Leonard Everett Fisher explains in his book for intermediate graders, the New World's discovery might have been delayed for decades without the nautical research spearheaded and funded by Portugal's *Prince Henry: The Navigator* (Macmillan, 1990), the Fifteenth-century visionary who influenced the design of the caravel, improvement of nautical instruments, and keeping of ship's logs.

CHRISTOPHER COLUMBUS: GREAT EXPLORER
David Adler
B/w illustrations by Lyle Miller
Holiday, 1991
[i] 48 pages

Mr. Adler establishes a sense of time and place, paints a well-rounded portrait, and provides the particulars that appeal to and hold a reader's attention. Young readers and older, less fluent ones will find this a manageable, interesting resource for written or oral reports, as well as a good read.

I, COLUMBUS
Peter and Connie Roop
Illustrations by Peter E. Hanson
Walker, 1990
[i] 69 pages

These edited excerpts from the explorer's 1492-1493 log give youngsters access to Columbus's thoughts, penned during the ups and downs of his first transatlantic crossing. What better way to put children in touch with the past than to have them read the words of someone who lived it — and in a tastefully designed edition, at that.

FOLLOW THE DREAM
Peter Sis
Illustrations by the author

Knopf, 1991
[p, i] 40 pages

Words and pictures are beautifully synchronized in this read-aloud, look-together book for young and old, side by side. The few words, a smooth blend of fact and legend, capture the historic episode's essence: An ambitious, fifteenth century dreamer/explorer is determined to sail west across an uncharted ocean; he perseveres and does.

CHRISTOPHER COLUMBUS

Delno C. and Jean M. West
B/w illustrations
Atheneum, 1991
[j, y] 144 pages

How we know what we know about the man by a Columbus/medieval/ renaissance scholar and reading specialist, respectively. They have enhanced their fine work with highlighted commentary on the documents, journals, and other artifacts from which historians have reconstructed "the great adventure." Their joint effort will contribute to your own edification, as well as your youngsters'.

1492, THE YEAR OF THE NEW WORLD

Piero Ventura
Illustrations by the author
Putnam, 1992
[i, j] 94 pages

In this view of contemporaneous life in the old and "new" worlds, Mr. Ventura describes activities of typical young adults in each region and weaves historical facts throughout his narrative and in finely detailed illustrations. He sweeps an amazing amount of history into his few pages, aided by maps with which he compares 1492 boundaries with today's.

THE OTHER 1492

Norman H. Finkelstein

B/w illustrations
Beech Tree (pb), 1992
[i, j] 100 pages

The day before Columbus departed Palos, the last of 200,000 Jews who refused to renounce their religion fled Spain. Their expulsion and migration throughout Europe, Africa, and the western hemisphere is meticulously described with a focus on the accomplishments, contributions, and influence of Spanish Jews—some of whom were responsible for the funding of Columbus's venture.

THE TAINOS
Francine Jacobs
B/w illustrations by Patrick Collins
Putnam, 1992
[i,j] 112 pages

The "Indians" who welcomed Columbus had populated the region from the Antilles to the Bahamas since King Solomon's time. In a book as fascinating for its insights into *how* archaeologists unearthed Taino history, as well as *what* they discovered, Ms. Jacobs brings the people and their customs to life. About one million Tainos may have been present when Columbus arrived. There are none today.

COOKBOOKS

There are few easier ways to help children learn to read and follow directions carefully than to ask them to prepare something from a recipe. My favorite Non-Book-Report assignment for youngsters who select cookbooks is the preparation of any recipe they choose. I've received some marvelous notes from family members and acquaintances commenting on delicious successes—or spectacular failures!

PRETEND SOUP AND OTHER REAL RECIPES
Mollie Katzen and Ann Henderson
Illustrations by Mollie Katzen
Tricycle, 1994
[pre, p] 96 pages

These nutritious snacks, salads, and simple entrees are practicable for preschoolers with parents or older siblings as assistants. The "grown-up" directions, which supplement the recipes with cooking hints and safety tips, are followed by a series of numbered drawings that younger not-yet-readers can easily follow.

A CHEF
Douglas Florian
Illustrations by the author
Greenwillow, 1992
[p] 32 pages

With spare text and full-page illustrations, the author/artist depicts a chef and her assistants as they go about their business from early-morning marketing to the final preparation in behind-the-scenes tasks such as the washing, trimming, and/or chopping of meat and vegetables, mixing batter and frosting for desserts, and artistically arranging the food.

KIDS COOKING: A VERY SLIGHTLY MESSY MANUAL
Illustrations and measuring spoons
Klutz, 1987
[i] 80 pages

These recipes for young cooks and their grown-up assistants are easy-to-follow, clearly enumerated, and humorously illustrated on card stock, spiral bound to lay flat. The last four are "not-to-eat" recipes for Play Dough, face paint, finger paint, giant soap bubbles, and people crackers for dogs!

THE FANNIE FARMER JUNIOR COOKBOOK
Joan Scobey
Illustrations by Patience Brewster
Little, 1993
[i, j] 280 pages

A guide to basic foods and how to use them, introduction to the tools of a chef's trade, explanation of cooking terms, and safety pointers invaluable for cooks young and old precede the more than 100 recipes for basic foods—soup (French onion) to nut raisin cookies.

COOKING THE SWISS WAY
Helga Hughes
Photographs by Robert L. and Diane Wolfe
and b/w illustrations
Lerner, 1995
[i, j] 48 pages

When multicultural units are on the "table," suggest youngsters season studies and flavor facts with repasts related to the countries under consideration. Ms. Hughes's 8 ½" x 7" volume, one of the thirty plus "Easy Menu Ethnic Cookbooks" titles, begins with information about characteristic foods and customs, special ingredients, and cooking terms. Recipes in the series represent countries worldwide, from Africa to Vietnam.

A young girl discovers that *Everybody Cooks Rice* (Carolrhoda, 1991) differently in a multicultural neighborhood in Norah Dooley's story, which concludes with recipes for nine different rice dishes, including Vietnamese nuoc cham, Indian biryani, and Haitian rice and beans.

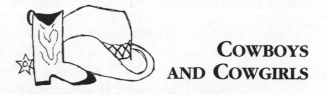

COWBOYS AND COWGIRLS

The cowboys of the Wild West were definitely not the romantic heroes seen in movies. They were often African, Mexican, or Native American, seldom wore a gun (never carried two), sang to their cattle (to calm them), and were killed more frequently in job-related tasks (trampled in a stampede or struck by lightning while herding) than by gunfire.

COWBOY COUNTRY
Ann Herbert Scott
Illustrations by Ted Lewin
Clarion, 1993
[p, i] 48 pages

An old cowhand explains the art of his craft to an aspiring youngster. Though some things have changed, he reflects, many will always be the same, "...knowing what an old cow is thinking before she knows herself..." for example. Inspired by interviews with old-time buckaroos, Ms. Scott's words ring true.

Send youngsters out for *Ranch Dressing, The True Story Of Western Wear* (Lodestar, 1993) by M. J. Greenlaw for the inside story on cowboy hats, belts, boots, and other distinctive paraphernalia.

COWBOYS OF THE WILD WEST
Russell Freedman
B/w photographs
Clarion (hb/pb), 1985
[i, j] 108 pages

Mr. Freedman's classic, illustrated with archival photographs, reveals the men for the hardworking, low-paid, highly skilled transients most were.

Some 5,000 to 8,000 African-Americans worked the cattle ranches and trails after the Civil War and one of them might have been *The Zebra Riding Cowboy* (Holt, 1992) pictured in Angela Shelf Medearis's version of a humorous old song. Maria Cristina Brusca's watercolors capture the joie de vivre of this bit of American folklore that youngsters will enjoy singing.

COWBOY: AN ALBUM
Linda Granfield
B/w, sepia, and full-color photographs and illustrations
Ticknor, 1993
[i, j, adult] 96 pages

Famous and infamous, real and movie, male and female cowboys star in this outstandingly written and designed history (I couldn't put it down). Ms. Granfield explains the origin of the word cowboy (Ireland 2,000 years ago), moves through the profession's heyday (from about 1866-1886, when the demand for beef was high and the range wide open), and ends with its contemporary practitioners.

Read aloud selections from Lois Brown's *Tales Of The Wild West* (Rizzoli, 1993), an outstanding blend of short stories (by Zane Grey, Louis L'Amour, O'Henry, and others) and factual pieces which include a cowboy's account of a longhorn drive and born-in-1841, 83-year-old Vittwia St. Clair Chapman Mickelson's reminiscences on the highlights of her life on the American frontier.

COWBOYS
Charles Sullivan
Color and b/w photographs and reproductions
Rizzoli, 1993
[p, i] 48 pages

Charles Sullivan's poetry accompanies twenty-two works of art that portray cowboys of the past and present. They include sculptures by Frederic Remington and Luis Jiminez, archival and contemporary photographs, and a "Wanted" poster for Frank and Jesse James. Suggest youngsters select one as a stimulus for poetry or prose of their own.

Youngsters intrigued by the "Outlaws and Lawmen of the Wild West" will enjoy Carl R. Green's and William R. Sanford's series of biographies which include *Jesse James, Billy The Kid, Bat Masterson* and *Belle Star* (all Enslow, 1992). Archival photographs create a sense of time and place.

ON THE PAMPAS

MY MAMA'S LITTLE RANCH ON THE PAMPAS
Maria Cristina Brusca
Illustrations by the author
Holt, 1991; 1994
[p, i] 40,32 pages

Ms. Brusca grew up in Argentina, where the cowboys, called gauchos, wear loose pants called bombachas, and dance the malambo. Her reminiscences will incidentally provide insight into the similarities and differences among North and South American ranch life and responsibilities—along with a glimpse of two fondly recalled summer vacations.

 **DINOSAURS**

DINOSAURS, DINOSAURS

BONES, BONES, DINOSAUR BONES
Byron Barton
Illustrations by the author

HarperCollins, 1989/1990
[pre, p] 40, 32 pages

The first of Mr. Barton's top-of-the-list books for the youngest set is an introduction to nine archosaurs. The second is a dynamic view of scientists as they trek to a dig, unearth their finds, and reassemble the fossils back at the museum. Bet you can't read it without singing..."Dem bones, dem bones, dem dry bones. . . . "

Follow *Bones, Bones...*(above) with a trip to a real *Dinosaur Mountain* (Clarion, 1988) via the Caroline Arnold/Richard Hewett photo-essay, so youngsters can see the paleontologists at Utah's Dinosaur Quarry extract, prepare, and reassemble their finds.

HOW BIG WERE THE DINOSAURS?
Bernard Most
Illustrations by the author
Harcourt (hb/pb), 1994
[pre, p] 32 pages

As in *The Littlest Dinosaurs* (1989), *Where To Look For A Dinosaur* (1993), *A Dinosaur Named After Me* (1991, all Harcourt) and other related titles, the astute author/artist tickles young readers' funny-bones with a blend of fact, fancy, and not-so-nonsensical specu-lation that simultaneously teaches and stirs imaginations.

Let your youngsters "Get to Know Bernard Most" (Harcourt) through the 20-minute video that shows him and schoolchildren talking about his work.

DINOSAUR ENCORE
Patricia Mullins
Illustrations by the author
HarperCollins, 1993
[pre, p] 32 pages

Were dinosaurs alive today, which could outrace an ostrich or outchomp a crocodile? These and other questions are posed and answered in this imaginative riddler illustrated with torn-tissue collages, some on horizontal and vertical gatefolds.

Save old editions when you update primary-grade dinosaur collections with Aliki's revised *Fossils Tell Of Long Ago* (1990), *My Visit To The Dinosaurs* (1985), and *Digging Up Dinosaurs* (1988, all HarperCollins). Have children compare old to new, discover the changes, and discuss why they think those changes took place.

DINOSAUR BONES!
C. E. Thompson
Illustrations by Paige Billin-Frye
Grosset, 1992
[p, i] 32 pages

Incipient dinosaur "detectives" will enjoy the chance to peruse the cut-paper skeletons and deduce—as paleontologists did with the real fossils—how some archosaurs may have moved, defended themselves, eaten, or performed other functions. This paperback is an ideal title for home/library bookfairs as well as the classroom library.

DINOSAUR QUESTION AND ANSWER BOOK
Sylvia Funston
Illustrations and photographs
Little, 1992
[i] 64 pages

Ms. Funston selected questions from readers of *Owl* and *Chickadee* magazines, made up a few of her own about recent discoveries, and added a touch of humor and scores of illustrations.

Have children peruse the illustration credits in the book above and they will discover that the pictured protoceratops and triceratops models were copyrighted by S & S Czerkas. Youngsters can meet Stephen and Sylvia Czerkas who live with *Dinosaurs All Around* (Clarion, 1993)— the scale and life-size models they create for museums and other exhibits. Caroline Arnold and Richard Hewett's photo-essay shows how the paleoartists make and display their incredibly lifelike sculptures.

DISCOVER DINOSAURS
Chris McGowan
Illustrations by Tina Holdcroft
Addison (pb), 1993
[i, j] 96 pages

Dr. McGowan smoothly weaves explanation and definition throughout an engaging narrative and he pauses appropriately, every other page or so, for projects that illustrate how paleontologists work. The just-right illustrations are straightforward depictions of the narrative and lighthearted renditions of kids engaged in the experiments. .

GREAT DINOSAUR ATLAS
William Lindsay
Illustrations by Giuliano Fornari
Messner, 1991
[i, j] 64 pages

At 11" x 14," the atlas is wide enough to display, among other spectacular spreads, a life-size illustration of the chicken-size *Compsognathus.* The large format also allows room for elaboration as well as identification; and Dr. Lindsay's words, though disjointed in appearance, form a coherent and unified narrative that makes this an unusually informative and well-balanced visual and verbal extravaganza.

DINOSAURS AND HOW THEY LIVED
Steve Parker
Illustrations by Giuliano Fornari
Dorling, 1991
[i, j] 64 pages

This useful supplement to the above atlas is on a somewhat smaller scale, but there is still ample room on the 9" x 11" spreads for elaboration as well as specifics. The occasional subtle and witty placement of people amid the dinosaurs keep readers mindful of their relative size.

TYRANNOSAURUS
William Lindsay
Dorling, 1992
Color, b/w and sepia illustrations and photographs
[i, j] 28 pages

Dr. Lindsay describes the fossils unearthed by Barnum Brown in 1908 and erroneously reconstructed in 1915 in a head-up, tail-down position. Paleontologists currently believe that head and tail were balanced over legs on a horizontal plane as demonstrated by models photographed here to simulate stop-motion shots of a live specimen as it hunts, devours its prey, and confronts an adversary. The author carefully points out that the behavior and coloring pictured is based upon educated guesses.

Barosaurus (1992), *Corythosaurus* (1993), and *Triceratops* (1993, all Dorling) are equally fascinating and similarly designed companion volumes that trace the discovery and reconstruction of the prehistoric beasts.

MACMILLAN CHILDREN'S GUIDE TO DINOSAURS
Philip Whitfield
Illustrations
Macmillan, 1992
[i] 96 pages

Each of five chapters focuses on a distinct dinosaur era and opens with an artist's rendering of life during that time. To help readers appreciate that the two-page scenes are an "idea, not fact...[but] not fantasy," each panorama is reduced and reproduced on the following page with an explanation of why the specific flora and fauna were included. The remainder of each chapter is, in effect, an illustrated catalog of selected dinosaurs and other reptiles common to the period.

If pop-ups are too fragile for the school library, recommend Tanner Ottley Gay's *Dinosaurs And Their Relatives In Action* (Aladdin, 1990) for inclusion in primary classroom, handle-with-special-care collections, book fairs, or lists of special-occasion gifts for parents. The colorful lifelike illustrations, relative simplicity of movable parts, and spare but informative text make it handy for very young readers.

DRAWING DINOSAURS
Jerome Goyallon
B/w illustrations by the author
Sterling, 1994
[i, j] 80 pages

Begin with a grid, Mr. Goyallon suggests, add midlines and diagonals to properly proportion sketches, draw key points, then fill in details: a useful technique, whatever the subject. Here, the artist/author accompanies his how-to drawing of more than 36 prehistoric creatures with a brief description of each, silhouettes that indicate its size relative to humans, and other pertinent facts.

AN ALPHABET OF DINOSAURS
Peter Dodson
Illustrations by Wayne D. Barlowe with b/w illustrations by
Michael Meaker
Scholastic, 1995
[p, i] 64 pages

Imaginative, full-page paintings, the most dramatic I've seen, make this an alphabet for all ages. Each realization is accompanied by a line drawing of the animal's skull or skeleton and a few descriptive sentences. A final guide provides the pronunciation and translation of each dinosaur's name, its size, diet, period of existence, and fossil site(s).

STEGOSAURS: THE SOLAR-POWERED DINOSAURS
Helen Roney Sattler
Illustrations by Turi MacCombie
Lothrop, 1992
[i] 32 pages

Ms. Sattler describes the general characteristics of these "plated lizards" and details the specifics that distinguish the eleven species so far unearthed. She makes clear how scientists make their deductions from fossils, what they have yet to learn, and how their theories change.

 Ms. Sattler provides tyranno-maniacs more about *Tyrannosaurus Rex And Its Kin: The Mesozoic Monsters* (Lothrop, 1989) in another volume as fine as the one above.

DINOSAURIUM
Barbara Brenner
Illustrations by Donna Braginetz
Bantam (hb/pb), 1993
[i] 48 pages

Readers tour through a dinosaur museum with chronologically arranged displays that replicate archosaurian life as it is currently conjectured. Special exhibits focus on such topics as dinosaur diet, possible coloration, family life, continental drift, the relative size of extinct and extant animal eggs, to scale, and a few important discoveries by young people. This is one of the best, easiest-to-access sources for report writers.

 Suggest youngsters think of as many reasons why *It's Probably Good Dinosaurs Are Extinct* (Green Tiger, 1993), have them compare theirs with Ken Raney's, then leave the author/artist's book around for repeated perusals of the incredibly fine art.

THE SEARCH FOR SEISMOSAURUS
J. Lynett Gillette
Illustrations by Mark Hallett and photographs

Dial, 1994
[i, j] 40 pages

Between 1985 and 1992, paleontologist David Gillette and his co-diggers moved over one million pounds of sandstone to unearth thirty-two vertebrae that spanned from tail to neck of the longest dinosaur ever discovered. Ms. Gillette describes the process from the time Dr. Gillette first learned of the fossils, through their unearthing with the help of magnetometry and ground-probing radar.

The indefatigable Joanna Cole and Bruce Degen have made it possible for you and your youngsters to ride *The Magic School Bus® In The Time Of The Dinosaurs* (Scholastic, 1994). Get on board!

INSIDE DINOSAURS AND OTHER PREHISTORIC CREATURES
Steve Parker
Illustrations by Ted Dewan
Doubleday, 1993
[i, j] 48 pages

In a lighthearted style, collaborators Dewan and Parker reveal what exists *Inside The Whale And Other Animals* (Dorling, 1992). Here, in a similar fashion, they fill in and flesh out dinosaur bones. Since no fossilized remains of prehistoric innards exist, however, the artist had to rely upon educated guesses for his re-creations. Mr. Parker's explanations of why Mr. Dewan drew what he drew neatly clarifies how paleontologists deduce the whole from its parts.

Connect kids to B. B. Calhoun's 11-year-old Fenton Rumplemayer, the amateur paleontological, private-eye protagonist of *On The Right Track, Fair Play* (Freeman, 1994) and others in B. B. Calhoun's "Dinosaur Detective" series.

DOGS

By sixth grade, I'd read every dog book in the children's room of my hometown library. I can recall only the fiction, however, and I don't know if that means nonfiction was absent or forgettable. Happily, today's children's books about real dogs and the people in their lives are both plentiful and memorable.

MY PUPPY IS BORN
Margaret Miller
Photographs by the author
Morrow, 1973/1991
[p,i] 48 pages

One pup's growth from a toothless, eyes-and ears-sealed, hand-sized ball of fur into a little girl's perky armful of the Norfolk-terrier kind.

WOODSONG
Gary Paulsen
B/w illustrations by Ruth W. Paulsen
Bradbury, 1990
[i,j] 144 pages

Mr. Paulsen's paean to his beloved sled dogs is one of the most moving books I've ever read. His eloquence borders on ardor as he vivifies individual dogs and the team that pulled him for 17 days in Alaska's 1,180 mile Iditarod.

Pair *Woodsong* to *Racing Sled Dogs* (Clarion, 1988), by Michael Cooper, for additional insight into what makes good sled dogs. Mr. Cooper begins with the breathtaking chronicle of Libby Riddle's winning 1985 race and continues with the dogs' history and details of their training. *Winterdance: The Fine Madness Of Running The Iditarod* (Harcourt, 1994) is Mr. Paulson's spellbinding account of his Iditarod race for young adult and older readers.

A GUIDE DOG PUPPY GROWS UP
Caroline Arnold
Photographs by Richard Hewett
Harcourt, 1991
[i, j] 48 pages

HUGGER TO THE RESCUE
Dorothy Hinshaw Patent
Photographs by William Muñoz
Cobblehill, 1994
[p, i] 32 pages

Behind the scenes with a golden retriever and a Newfoundland pup, as they are transformed into fully trained professionals, respectively a guide dog for the blind and a search-and-rescue dog for the lost.

UNDERSTANDING MAN'S BEST FRIEND
Ann Squire
B/w photographs
Macmillan, 1991
[i] 130 pages

Dr. Squire explains how dogs may have been selectively bred from their wolf ancestors into their various shapes and sizes. She describes the characteristics that make each breed good at what it was "designed" to do (guard livestock, hunt prey, or provide companionship), comments on the problems of excessive breeding and ends with a plug for the good, all-around mutt.

Ask kids what a Peruvian Inca Orchid, Fila Brasileiro and Xoloitzcuintli have in common, and chances are they'll never guess four legs! Until you share Susan and Daniel Cohen's *What Kind Of Dog Is That?* (Dutton, 1989). Their introduction to exotic canines provides enough detail on the temperament, color, history, and other distinctive characteristics of twenty-five of these breeds to make any one of them an interesting character in a short story. Suggest youngsters pick one as an hypothetical pet and proceed.

CAN DOGS TALK?

LOVING A HAPPY DOG

SECRET MESSAGES: TRAINING A HAPPY DOG
Mary Shields
Illustrations by Donna Gates
Pyrola, 1991; 1992; 1993
[pre, p] 32 pages

Ms. Shields (who treated me to my only dogsled ride) was the first woman to complete the Iditarod. In her perfectly paced and illustrated paperbacks, she explains how dogs communicate, the responsibilities of owning a dog from puppyhood to old age, and how to prepare a pup to pull a sled.

SUSAN BUTCHER: SLED DOG RACER
Ginger Wadsworth
B/w photographs
Lerner, 1994
[i] 64 pages

SUSAN BUTCHER AND THE IDITAROD TRAIL
Ellen M. Dolan
B/w photographs
Walker, 1993
[i, j] 112 pages

RACING THE IDITAROD TRAIL
Ruth Crisman
Photographs
Dillon, 1993
[i, j] 72 pages

Determined, single-minded youngsters will find a soul-mate in Susan Butcher. From early childhood, she knew what she wanted—a life filled with dogs far from the city. She worked hard, settled in Alaska, and became a four-time winner of the Iditarod. This hard-to-put-down trio of books about the outstanding athlete, her four-legged co-athletes, and their sport show that dreams can come true with hard work and perseverance.

Readers will discover that Susan Butcher's dyslexia didn't keep her from realizing her dreams. In *When Learning Is Tough* (Whitman, 1994), Cynthia Roby introduces eight children, between the ages of 9 and 13, who talk about how they are overcoming their learning disabilities.

ECOLOGY

Children have a natural curiosity about the world and an innate sense of fairness, two attributes that make them ideal candidates for the future guardians of our planet and the life forms that inhabit it. The books below encourage youngsters to appreciate, respect, and protect their world as they mature.

WHERE DOES THE GARBAGE GO?
Paul Showers
Illustrations by Randy Chewing
HarperCollins, 1994

RECYCLE
Gail Gibbons
Illustrations by the author
Little (hb/pb), 1992
[p] 32 pages each

Simple, succinct, and clear explanations of how recycling con-
serves energy and reduces pollution as it decreases waste. Both
show basic steps involved in making new-from-used paper, glass,
cans, and plastic; and conclude with a few specific recycling recommendations.

CARTONS, CANS, AND ORANGE PEELS:
WHERE DOES OUR GARBAGE GO?
Joanna Foster
Photographs
Clarion (hb/pb), 1991
[i, j] 64 pages

In this detailed description of current technology on environmentally sound refuse containment or transformation, Ms. Foster follows the progress of solid waste from household pickup to land-
fill, compost heap, waste-to-energy or resource-recovery facility,
and recycling center.

To introduce youngsters to the *Compost Critters* (Dutton,
1993) who transform garbage into the nutrient-rich soil,
have handy Bianca Lavies's fine photoessay on the sow
bugs, earthworms, mites, millipedes, nematodes, and the
others of their ilk in her backyard compost pile.

MY FIRST GREEN BOOK
Angela Wilkes
Illustrations
Knopf, 1991
[p, i] 48 pages

Dramatic, actual-size photographs illustrate the 10" x 13" volume
of eminently practical experiments with meticulous, easy-to-fol-

low instructions through which children learn about the consequences of environmental pollution and what they can do to reduce it.

DINOSAURS TO THE RESCUE
Laurie Krasny and Marc Brown
Illustrations by Marc Brown
Little (hb/pb), 1992
[p] 32 pages

Ecologically sensitive, elementary-school-age saurians describe and demonstrate effective strategies of the turn-off- the-tap-while-tooth-brushing, pick-up-litter, and plant-a-plant variety. All are well within the realm of little-hands practicability.

50 SIMPLE THINGS KIDS CAN DO TO RECYCLE
The Earth Works Group
B/w illustrations by Michele Montez
Earth Works (pb), 1994
[i] 144 pages

Upbeat and practical, this 5" x 8" paperback guide to the how, where, and what to recycle includes tips on how to pack a "no-garbage" lunch, recycle in class, and precycle a party and belongs in every classroom.

KIDS' GUIDE TO SOCIAL ACTION
Barbara Lewis
B/w photographs and illustrations
Free Spirit (pb), 1991
[i, j] 186 pages

Throughout her step-by-step handbook, Ms. Lewis shows how young people, from elementary through high school, can be a positive force for change. In addition to how-to's (e.g., initiate or change laws), she includes such whereby's as "power" interviews, proposals, and letter writing; and such where-to's and what-with's as petitions, letters, news releases and other forms for reproduction. Keep one copy of this extremely well-designed, practical, and useful resource in your classroom and at least two in the library.

REDUCING, REUSING AND RECYCLING
Bobbie Kalman
Photographs
Crabtree (hb/pb), 1991
[i, j] 32 pages

An upbeat, activity-packed, photo-illustrated handbook particularly useful for reluctant readers. Colorful two-page chapters with catchy subheads every paragraph or two that make it easy to skim for particulars.

3 Pandas Planting (Bradbury, 1994), 2 whales watching for polluters, and 1 elephant enjoying the earth are among the ecology-minded creatures doing their part to keep earth clean in Megan Halsey's delightful counting book. An addendum of recycling information concludes.

RECYCLING
Virginia and Robert Silverstein
Photographs
Putnam, 1992
[j] 32 pages

The Silversteins first view earth's natural recycling processes, then explain how wasteful habits came to replace waste-not, want-not ones. They discuss federal, state, local, and corporate waste-management efforts and the problems recycling presents, as well as noteworthy successes and creative ideas for its future.

LIVING TREASURE: SAVING EARTH'S BIODIVERSITY
Laurence Pringle
B/w illustrations by Irene Brady
Morrow, 1991
[i, j] 64 pages

Mr. Pringle amplifies the themes of observing and nurturing nature with startling facts on the range and variation of earth's lifeforms—more than 12,000 different kinds of beetles were found on one species of rain forest tree, for example. He warns that many species are being lost before their food or medicinal value can be established. He concludes his powerful argument for husbanding the earth's resources with a list of organizations dedicated to the cause.

GAYLORD NELSON
Jeffrey Shulman and Teresa Rogers
B/w drawings by Larry Raymond
21st Century, 1992
[i, j] 68 pages

An engaging biography of the man who, throughout public service as state senator, governor, and U.S. senator, made the preservation of natural resources his priority. Earthday 1970, possibly the largest demonstration in American history, was his most dramatic and perhaps most far-reaching accomplishment.

Did you know that *recycle*, as an ecological term, is a relatively new addition to the language? You'll not find in in any dictionary older than...well, rather than tell you, set your youngsters on a hunt for the oldest dictionary that lists it. You'll all be surprised.

RIVERKEEPER
George Ancona
B/w photos by the author
Macmillan, 1990
[i,j] 42 pages

"I love my work," John Cronin told photoessayist George Ancona. "This is all I want to do." Mr. Cronin, employed by the Hudson River Fishermen's Association, is responsible for the health and welfare of the 315-mile Hudson River, its flora and fauna. He defends the river against polluters and keeps track of the wildlife population. Students concerned with the environment will discover how one person can work within the system to change laws and attitudes about pollution.

**EARTHKEEPERS: OBSERVERS
AND PROTECTORS OF NATURE**
Ann T. Keene
Photographs and illustrations (b/w and color)
Oxford, 1994
[j] 222 Pages

In this splendid compendium, Ms. Keene vividly details, chronologically, the contributions of forty-six naturalists of the eighteenth through twentieth centuries. She briefly profiles scores more. Many are familiar: Muir, Mowatt, Carson, and Goodall; others less so: Bartram, Nuttall, Rothschild, and Maathai. I know of no single volume that is more useful as a resource on naturalists.

 **ELEPHANTS**

Thanks to radioimmunoassay, a technique through which the molecular structure of animals' bodies is analyzed and compared, scientists have verified that manatees are one of the elephant's closest relatives.

JUMBO
Rhoda Blumberg
Illustrations by Jonathan Hunt
Bradbury, 1992
[i] 40 pages

In as true an account as possible, considering the hype with which P.T. Barnum surrounded the eponymous beast, Ms. Blumberg entrancingly tells how the 11-foot tall, 18-feet round,

14,000-pound elephant and his caretaker-companion, Matthew
Scott, joined the "Greatest Show On Earth."

Read aloud or recommend Alice Fleming's *P. T. Barnum,*
and youngsters will discover how *The World's Greatest
Showman* (Walker, 1993) came to be.

ELEPHANT

Caroline Arnold
Photographs by Richard Hewett
Morrow, 1993
[i, j] 48 pages

ELEPHANTS

Eric S. Grace
Photographs and illustrations
Sierra Club, 1993
[i, j] 64 pages

Both authors describe the habitat, daily routines, and physical and
social characteristics of both African and Asian elephants: Ms.
Arnold with a focus on those in northern California's Marine
World Africa USA; and Dr. Grace, on wild Africans.

ELEPHANTS CALLING

Katherine Payne
Photographs
Crown, 1992
[i, j] 36 pages

Ms. Payne was the first to associate the throbbing that she sensed
when near elephants to low frequency sound waves. Using special equipment, she taped zoo and circus elephants and confirmed her suspicion that the elephants did indeed communicate
via infrasound. She describes her discovery, and African elephants
in general, in this volume which is centered around one newborn
in a Kenyan herd.

Link youngsters to Toshi Yoshido's *Elephant Crossing* (Philomel, 1989), whose vibrant illustrations depict a four-generation herd under the protection and leadership of its majestic, great-grandmother matriarch. Implicit in the simple, straightforward narrative is the message that a species' survival in the wild can be as dependent upon the presence of a leader old enough to remember where and how to get to nourishment as upon the nourishment itself.

IN THE VILLAGE OF THE ELEPHANTS
Jeremy Schmidt
Photographs by Ted Wood
Walker, 1994
[i] 32 pages

In a Southern Indian village near the Nilgiri Hills, working elephants are parked like cars next to the homes of their mahouts. Mr. Schmidt has captured the close relationship between a young boy who hopes to follow in his father's footsteps, and the elephant with which he'll work in a forest sanctuary.

From 1915 to 1927, Dr. John Symington practiced medicine in Duars, a wild region along India's northeastern border. During the rainy season he often became the *Doctor On An Elephant* (Holt, 1994), because no other means of transportation was feasible. Steven Kroll's account for young readers of one such trip, enlivened by Michael Chesworth's watercolors, fits nicely into any look at the people/pachyderm connection.

EXPERIMENTS

HOW SCIENCE WORKS
Color and b/w photographs and drawings
Reader's Digest Books, 1991
[j, a] 192 pages

This profusely illustrated volume, a virtual mini-course, sets out the basic equipment for a home laboratory (mostly standard kitchen/garage/workbench items); provides an historical overview for each chapter/subtopic; occasional biographical sketches; and step-by-step tests, experiments, and projects for investigators of all ages. It can be used by younger children with adult supervision.

PINT-SIZE SCIENCE
Linda Allison and Martha Weston
Illustrations by the authors
Little, 1994
[i, j] 48 pages

An excellent guide for adults or older siblings to introduce very young children to science ideas found in a walk, a sandbox, and a bath—all opportunities for instructive play.

MY FIRST SCIENCE BOOK
Angela Wilkes
Illustrations and photographs
Knopf, 1990
[p] 48 pages

Entice youngsters with life-size illustrations of equipment and smaller insets of their peers conducting experiments, step-by-step.

The first title is a general introduction to scientific experimentation; the second, to electricity and magnetism.

SOUND SCIENCE
Etta Kaner
B/w illustrations by Louise Phillips
Addison (pb), 1991
[i] 96 pages

SOAP SCIENCE
J. L. Bell
Illustrations by William Kimber
Addison (pb), 1993
[i] 64 pages

The first of these titles in this science activity series is an upbeat, humorously illustrated mix of activities, games, puzzles, historical anecdotes, riddles, and facts. In addition to explaining how people, other animals, and even plants hear, Ms. Kaner surrounds her experiments with such intriguing items as why owls have lopsided ears and when elephants communicate in infrasound.

The 36 experiments in the second title range from making soap and soap films of many shapes, to using it to make a soap battery.

THE SCIENCE BOOK OF SOUND
Neil Ardley
Photographs
Gulliver, 1991
[i] 40 pages

Each two-page experiment contains a brief introduction, step-by-step instructions (as easy to follow from the pictures as the text), and an example of the sound characteristic as found in nature (e.g., sound echoes used by bats). Others in this noteworthy "Science Book of..." series address, among other subjects, electricity, air, color, and water.

EXPLORABOOK
John Cassidy
Color illustrations
Klutz, 1991
[i] 100 pages

A powerful, plastic-encased magnet hangs from the spiral binding; a moiré spinner is riveted to the cover; and a four-power Fresnel lens, diffraction grating, mirror, and packaged agar growth medium are "pages" in this irresistible invitation to investigate magnetism, optical illusions, bacteria, and other natural phenomena.

Hand youngsters a prerecorded tape you don't mind losing, and suggest they play it once, then touch a magnet to it, and have them play it again. They'll discover for themselves why audio cassettes, VCR tapes, and computer disks should be kept far from magnets, including the one attached to the Explorabook above and those that accompany *Magnetic Magic* (Klutz, 1994), which encourages kids to explore magnetism.

WANNA BET? SCIENCE CHALLENGES TO FOOL YOU
Vicki Cobb and Kathy Darling
B/w illustrations by Merideth Johnson
Lothrop, 1993
[p, i, j] 128 pages

Add this to *Bet You Can! Science Possibilities To Fool You* (Avon, 1983; Lothrop, 1990) and *Bet You Can't Science Impossibilities To Fool You* (Lothrop, 1980; Avon Books, 1983) for an indispensable trio. I've yet to see elementary or college students (or their teachers) tire of "catching" friends and family with "tricks" gleaned from these one-per-page-or-two challenges.

THE SCIENCE BOOK FOR GIRLS
Valerie Wyatt
Illustrations by Pat Cupples
Kids Can (pb), 1993
[i] 80 pages

Perfect for girls who shy away from science, believing it to be a male domain. They'll start with girl-illustrated experiments as simple as making invisible ink, but be ready for a science fair project by book's end. Not chauvinistic, it is subtitled "and [for] other intelligent beings."

DR. ZED'S SCIENCE SURPRISES

SENSATIONAL SCIENCE ACTIVITIES

MORE SCIENCE SURPRISES BY DR. ZED
Gordon Penrose
Photographs by Ray Boudreau and illustrations
Simon (pb), 1989; 1990; 1992
[p, i] 48, 32, 32 pages respectively

The cleverly integrated photography and illustrations will attract young children. The more-than-a-dozen safe experiments employ materials easily found around home and school.

MEGA POWERS
Jack Weyland
Illustrations by Ken Steacy
Addison, 1992
[i] 80 pages

In comic-book format, Dr. Weyland explains why only comic characters have the power to see with X-ray vision, become invisible, or devise anti-gravity devices. Nevertheless, youngsters do have amazing powers—the ability to squeeze electricity from a lemon, for example—and the good doctor provides directions for experiments that illustrate them.

MIRRORS: FINDING OUT
ABOUT THE PROPERTIES OF LIGHT
Bernie Zubrowski

Illustrations by Roy Doty
Morrow (hb/pb), 1992
[i] 96 pages

In this "Boston Children's Museum Activity Book," Mr. Zubrowski cleverly combines optical theory with hands-on experiments to explain the principles of plane, transparent, and curved mirrors. Clear writing, upbeat illustrations, explicit directions, and diagrams of the student-tested experiments are the hallmark of this series on subjects that include *Tops*, and *Making Waves* (Morrow, 1989, 1994).

FOOD

WHERE FOOD COMES FROM
Dorothy Hinshaw Patent
Photographs by William Muñoz
Holiday, 1991
[p, i] 40 pages

Taking nothing for granted, Dr. Patent first explains that all food derives from the sun's energy. She then tells how fruit, vegetables, and grains grow and the role of animals in our food chain.

When "food" is on your lesson-plan menu, flavor activities with Lois Ehlert's *Eating The Alphabet* (Harcourt, 1989). You'll find a few "recipes" in the introduction to Alphabets on page 66.

AT THE SUPERMARKET
David Hautzig
Photographs by the author
Orchard, 1994
[p, i] 32 pages

With a clock on each page to record the hour, Mr. Hautzig chronicles 24 hours of behind-the-scenes supermarket activity from early morning baking, through the conversion of beef "primals" to recognizable steaks, roasts, and hamburger, to late night stocking of shelves.

👓 Supermarkets are supersites for enlightening assignments that extend classroom activities. On their next shopping trip, suggest youngsters scour supermarket shelves for food that traveled the farthest or least distance, then mark their finds on a classroom map; list prices of their three favorite foods/candies and, in class, compute cost per pound; note which items surround the cash register, or are stacked on the highest or lowest shelves and discuss marketing strategy.

COWS IN THE PARLOR: A VISIT TO A DAIRY FARM
Cynthia McFarland
Photographs by the author
Atheneum, 1990
[p, i] 30 pages

700 KIDS ON GRANDPA'S FARM
Ann Morris
Photographs by Ken Heyman
Dutton, 1994
[p, i] 32 pages

Ms. McFarland's book covers the meticulous care that dairy cows receive and the effort that goes into providing food for them. Ms. Morris's book does the same for goats, and then describes the production of goat cheese and its path to market.

👓 If your library has Aliki's twenty-plus-year-old *Green Grass And White Milk*, it's time to replace it with the author/artist's re-written and -illustrated *Milk From Cow To Carton* (Harper, 1992), one of the best for very young readers on how cows make milk and how it gets from farm to table.

THE AMAZING MILK BOOK
Catherine Ross and Susan Wallace
B/w illustrations by Linda Hendry
Addison (pb), 1991
[i] 80 pages

The coauthors describe milk's chemistry, nutritional value, production, and use as a component of cheese and other foods in
one of an outstanding series that I've found report-writing middle-
graders savor. It is upbeat; it approaches its subject from many
perspectives; and it is enriched with anecdotes, humor and practicable projects. Other similarly designed food-related titles are
The Amazing Egg Book (1990), *The Amazing Apple Book* (1990)
and *The Amazing Potato Book* (1991)–all Addison.

THE LIFE AND TIMES OF THE APPLE
Charles Micucci
Illustrations by the author
Orchard, 1992
[p, i] 32 pages

AN APPLE A DAY
Dorothy Hinshaw Patent
Photographs by William Muñoz
Cobblehill, 1990
[i] 64 pages

Effectively balancing illustrations and words, Mr. Micucci shows
and tells how apples are planted, cross-fertilized, grafted, and pol-
lenized. He identifies the parts of an apple blossom, portrays more
than a dozen apple varieties, and provides an apple time line.

Collaborators Patent and Muñoz cover much of the above plus
apple production in the field, the mechanical handling of apples
in a commercial packing plant, and the making of cider in a backyard press.

In *The Life And Times Of The Honey-Bee* (Ticknor,
1995) Charles Micucci provides youngsters as enter-

taining and eyeopening a perspective of the making of honey as he does the growing of apples in the book above.

PASTA FACTORY
Hanna Machotka
Photographs by the author
Houghton, 1992
[p, i] 32 pages

An elementary-grader takes classmates (and readers) through his dad's pasta factory. They see the machines that blend ingredients to make pasta in a variety of shapes, the cold storage room, the tool shop, and the quality control laboratory. And, of course, sample tastes of his dad's product. Made me hungry!

A TASTE OF INDIA
Roz Denny
Photographs and illustrations
Thomson, 1994
[i, j] 48 pages each

A prosaically designed but interestingly written series that succinctly introduces readers to a country's farming regions and regional foods, describes how meals are assembled, provides representative recipes, and concludes with a glossary and index. Among the other country's covered are France, Italy, Japan, China, Britain, West Africa, Mexico, the Carribean, and Spain.

To illustrate the cultures reflected in their favorite foods, suggest youngsters create a classroom version of *This Is The Way We Eat Our Lunch* (Scholastic, 1995). Edith Baer's peek at the midday repasts of children worldwide. Whether the focus is lunch or any other meal, your children will enjoy creating rhyming couplets like Ms. Baer's, to wit: "Amma savors beans and rice—cooked with fish, they're twice as nice!"

BACKYARD SUNFLOWER
Elizabeth King
Photographs by the author
Dutton, 1993
[p] 32 pages

What do children and birds have in common? Both love sunflower seeds. Ms. King shows and tells how primary-grader Samantha plants, cultivates, harvests, and eats the seeds from her backyard sunflower patch.

VANILLA, CHOCOLATE, & STRAWBERRY:
THE STORY OF YOUR FAVORITE FLAVORS
Bonnie Busenberg
Photographs and illustrations
Lerner, 1994
[i, j] 112 pages

Ms. Busenberg addresses the origins of these delicious flavors in a thorough discussion of the history of each source plant and its cultivation. She explains how the flavor is extracted, how derived products are manufactured, and includes favorite recipes for each. She even tells how taste buds and olfactory senses transmit flavors to our brains.

Mention food and Arnold Adoff waxes poetic. Don't discuss *Eats* (Lothrop, 1979) or *Chocolate Dreams* (Lothrop, 1989) without him.

THE CHEWING GUM BOOK
Robert Young
B/w photographs
Dillon, 1989
[i] 72 pages

The history, varieties, manufacture, and marketing of chewing gum are chronicled along with a gum time line and a useful index. Sticky business.

COOKIES
William Jaspersohn
B/W photographs by the author
Macmillan, 1993
[i] 48 pages

Every step in the making of Famous Amos chocolate chip cookies is detailed in this fascinating view of commercial chocolate chip cookie making, including a look at the die that helps the Ghiradelli Chocolate company turn out 3.5 million chocolate chips an hour—enough for almost 700,000 cookies.

HORSES

HORSES AND HORSEMANSHIP
Paula Rodenas
Photographs
Random House, 1991
[i, j] 180 pages

This artful interweaving of photographs, illustrations, narrative, and interviews reflect the unique interdependence of people and horses. The book's ten chapters cover anatomy, behavior, breeding and life cycle, as well as care, training, riding, and competing; it looks and feels as good in the hand as it is to read.

Remember *The Pony Express* (New Discovery, 1993) when the joint endeavors of people and horses are on the agenda. The historic 18-month-long venture into mail delivery literally rested upon the backs of hardy, intelligent, and speedy horses—mainly mustangs and thoroughbreds. Laurel Van der Linde's anecdote-laden account of the relatively short-lived service is first rate.

MAN AND MUSTANG

George Ancona
B/w photographs by the author
Macmillan, 1992
[i, j] 48 pages

Each year the U.S. Bureau of Land Management (BLM) rounds up and sells the mustangs that overpopulate western range lands. Youngsters will see and read how BLM specialists, wranglers, and vets trap, inoculate, brand (with liquid nitrogen), and transport wild horses to a corral just outside New Mexico State Penitentiary. There, minimum-security volunteers spend anywhere from a week to a month of eight-hour days transforming the animals from feral to ready-for-adoption.

In the book above, call youngsters' attention to the last-page "Thanks," below the addresses of BLM Wild Horse and Burro Adoption centers, for insight into the number of people involved in the planning and production of a book like this.

ASSATEAGUE: ISLAND OF THE WILD PONIES

Andrea Jauck and Larry Points
Photographs
Macmillan, 1993
[p, i] 32 pages

Seventeen years after the 1948 publication of Marguerite Henry's *Misty of Chincoteague*, Assateague Island (the fictional Misty's birthplace) became a national seashore. This view of the long barrier island, just off the coasts of Maryland and Virginia, portrays a year in the life of its resident wild ponies and a few of their fellow indigenes.

With photographs of the racers, their grooms, trainers, riders, and other attendants, Cynthia McFarland's *Hoofbeats* (Atheneum, 1993) shows a horse's life markedly different from the one on Assateague Island (see above). From birth to first race, the typical thoroughbred is gently trained to accept and feel comfortable on and around the track.

HORSES
Peggy Roalf
Illustrations
Hyperion, 1992
[p, i] 48 pages

In this volume of Ms. Roalf's fine introduction-to-art series, youngsters will discover works that reflect many cultures and range in age from a 17,000-year-old cave drawing to an optical illusion painted by Magritte 30 years ago. The pages facing each reproduction contain comments on the artist's background, his time (sadly, no women's works were included), and the work itself.

Add *The Ultimate Horse Book* (Dorling, 1991) to your class or library "wish list" when asked for class- or library-gift suggestions. This is browsing fodder for all ages. Where the text proves formidable, the pictures will entrance: notably the double-page photographic portraits, with supplementary annotated illustrations, of 80 breeds from Arabian horse to riding pony, including the Barb, Akhal-Teke, and other lesser known beauties. Words and pictures will absorb older readers with all of the above plus the basics of upkeep, equipment, care, feeding, riding, and dozens of other highlights of the horse world.

WILD HORSE WINTER
Tetsuya Honda
Illustrations by the author
Chronicle, 1992
[p, i] 36 pages

About 300 years ago, Japanese fishermen brought Nambu horses from their mainland to the island of Hokkaido. The horses were abandoned each winter to fend for themselves; and over the centuries, they developed into a tougher-hooved, longer-haired, and shorter-bodied species called Dosanko. With spare text and evocative paintings, Mr. Honda portrays a Dosanko colt's first migration from frozen, snow-covered forest to a milder, kelp-strewn coast.

BELLE'S JOURNEY
Marilyn Reynolds
Illustrations by Stephen McCallum
Orca, 1993
[p, i] 32 pages

In the early 1920s, when the author's mother was a child on the Canadian prairie, she rode her pony, Belle, eight miles to piano lessons. This account of their trip through a sudden, blinding snowstorm movingly portrays Belle's lifesaving perseverance during that journey and the events that surrounded it. You won't be able to read this just once!

Recommend Nancy Springer's *Music of Their Hooves* (Boyds Mills, 1994) for a view of horses from a poet's perspective.

A FIELD FULL OF HORSES
Peter Hansard
Illustrations by Kenneth Lilly
Candlewick, 1994
[p] 28 pages

Mr. Lilly's exquisite colored pencil/watercolors enrich a simply written book with parallel texts. One, set in serif type, is the narrator's description of what s/he sees while perched atop a fence; the other, in sans serif type, identifies the parts of the horse's body and other unique characteristics.

THEY DREAMED OF HORSES:
CAREERS FOR HORSE LOVERS
Kay Frydenborg
B/w photographs by Tanya Wood

Walker, 1994
[i, j, ya] 104 pages

Readers who want to spend the rest of their lives around horses will savor Ms. Frydenborg's introduction to 13 young women who do just that. Among them are a mounted police officer, equine perinatologist (specialist in the care of newborns shortly before and after birth), tack shop owner and saddler, farrier, and equine photographer.

 Mary Fields handled a team of horses well enough to become the first African-American woman to deliver mail. As written by Robert H. Miller, *The Story of Stagecoach Mary Fields* (Silver, 1995) makes fine reading.

INSECTS

Bug your kids! Have them establish, maintain, and study insects in a zoo that they can share with schoolmates throughout the year and feature during an Open House. Hand them the following guides which emphasize observation based on respect for habitats and the wildlife therein, and you'll find yourself smiling when you say, "My kids are driving me buggy!"

INSECTS
Jenny Tesar
Illustrations and photographs
Blackbirch, 1993
[i, j] 64 pages

Perfect for basic research, with clearly and simply written details on physical characteristics and how they function, how various species survive and reproduce, and the insects' niches in the food chain. Sidebars sprinkled throughout the well-annotated text call attention to specific insect features. Charts of the major insect orders, a taxonomy of the animal kingdom, and glossary conclude.

ENTOMOLOGY: WITH LOTS OF ADVENTURES, PROJECTS, AND IDEAS FOR EXPLORING THE WORLD OF BUTTERFLIES, ANTS, DRAGONFLIES, CRICKETS AND ALL THE OTHER INSECTS
Ellen Doris
Photographs and illustrations
Thames & Hudson, 1993
[i, j] 64 pages

Ms. Doris supplements her easy-to-follow procedures with fundamental information on insect classification and characteristics in general and specific to the species under consideration in a stimulating and inviting book.

Children planning a classroom live-insect collection will enjoy learning how the inhabitants of San Francisco's *Insect Zoo* (Lodestar, 1991) are collected, cared for, and displayed in Susan Meyer's photoessay. Once a year, the zoo hosts a "What's Bugging You? Day," with games, contests, and lectures about its inhabitants. An easily adaptable idea.

PET BUGS: A KID'S GUIDE TO CATCHING AND KEEPING CATCHABLE INSECTS
Sally Kneidel
B/w illustrations by Mauro Magellan
Wiley, (pb), 1994
[i, j] 117 pages

The title says it all. After an appropriate warning about insects that should not be handled, Ms. Kneidel tells how to find, catch, and keep—for a day or two—many that can be safely collected. Her appendix classifies, her glossary amplifies, and her bibliography and index complete this useful book.

👓 Have youngsters inspired by Ms. Kneidel's projects consider setting up one of the 49 science fair projects in H. Steven Dashefsky's guide, *Insect Biology* (Tab, 1992), for youngsters in the upper intermediate grades and older.

BUGWISE
Pamela M. Hickman
B/w illustrations by Judi Shore
Addison, (pb),1991
[i] 96 pages

These 30 "incredible insect investigations and arachnid activities" are in one of the perfect-for-kids handbooks written under the auspices of the Federation of Ontario [Canada] Naturalists. It includes directions for putting together a bugwatching outfit, keeping bugs away the natural way, and catching insects in a homemade pitcher plant.

👓 In *Backyard* (Freeman, 1993), Donald M. Silver describes and Patricia J. Wynne beautifully illustrates how to mark off a square of dirt and study the animal/vegetable life and the minerals on and under it. This excellent treatment of an old idea is all your kids will need to safely conduct a year-long project.

WHAT'S INSIDE INSECTS?
Angela Royston
Illustrations and photographs
Dorling, 1992
[p, i] 18 pages

In a clever juxtaposition of photographs and illustrations a side- or top-view photograph of an insect is paired with its duplicate, partially "peeled" to expose internal systems digestive, circulatory, etc. The one- or two-sentence introduction to each set describes the pictured insect's diet, and additional annotations highlight unique characteristics.

*👓 Suggest students present their insect research, aloud or in writing, in a similarly revealing show-and-tell style of layered images.

WHERE'S THAT INSECT?
Barbara Brenner
Illustrations by Carol Schwartz
Scholastic, 1993
[p, i] 32 pages

In this more than find-the-whatever book, readers learn about the look, habits, or food of the insect(s) pictured somewhere in the realistic illustrations. Seekers learn to discern male from female monarch butterflies, for example, and yellowjacket wasps from honeybees. Somewhat-to-scale silhouettes of the featured insects adorn the last page.

👓 With Stephen Gammell's exuberant paintings to look at and the melody of "Buffalo Girls won't you come out tonight..." to sing to, Jim Aylesworth's *Old Black Fly* (Holt, 1992) is a jolly experience—even when insects aren't on the agenda!

BIG BUGS
Jerry Booth
B/w and color illustrations by Edith Allgood;
b/w photographs
Harcourt (pb), 1994
[i] 48 pages

A brilliantly designed, 10" x 14" volume which takes full advantage of its size to present large illustrations and traceable masks of ants, flies, butterflies, and other insect fliers, farmers, builders, and predators alongside practical activities for insect inspectors. Mr. Booth also introduces and asks readers to join the "Greenpatch Kids," an alliance of environmentally concerned youngsters.

THE LIFE AND TIMES OF THE HONEYBEE
Charles Micucci
Illustrations by the author
Ticknor, 1995
[i] 32 pages

Mr. Micucci artfully interweaves illustration and text to explain, among other facts, the bee's life cycle, physiology, communication, and honey-making as well as a beekeeper's equipment.

Awe youngsters with the close closeups of insects—in whole or part—that only scanning electronic microscopes or their ilk make possible. You'll find the magnificent magnifications in black and white in Howard Tomb's and Dennis Kunkel's *Microaliens* (Farrar, 1993) and color-enhanced in Heather Amery's and Jane Songi's *Discover Hidden Worlds: Bugs* (Western/Golden, 1994).

INVENTIONS AND INVENTORS

INCREDIBLE CROSS-SECTIONS
Richard Platt
Illustrations by Steven Biesty
Knopf, 1992
[i, j] 48 pages

One of the first questions kids (and many adults) have about life on a space shuttle—or in castles, or ships before modern plumbing—is "How do they go to the bathroom?" Kid-wise Steven Biesty answers them with scrupulous details of those and fifteen other complex structures and machines across page spreads, some of which are double gatefolds that stretch more than three feet. With precise color drawings and interesting textual callouts, the artist and writer disclose how people live, things work, and vehicles go on land, sea, and in the sky. The perfect book for SSR, this will inspire long looks to absorb its intricacies. As will...

THE VISUAL DICTIONARY OF EVERYDAY THINGS
Photographs
Dorling, 1991
[i, j] 64 pages

This photographic exposé reveals what lies beneath the surface of items ranging from pens and pencils to a Burberry trenchcoat and an espresso machine. Whether low- or upscale, however, the neatly arrayed and identified components reflect the creative genius of designers who make the whole aesthetically more than the sum of its parts. Each spread includes a brief history and description of the item and how it works.

MACHINES AND HOW THEY WORK
David Burnie
Illustrations
Dorling, 1991
[i, j] 64 pages

THE RANDOM HOUSE BOOK OF HOW THINGS WORK
Steve Parker
Illustrations
Random, 1990
[i, j] 64 pages

These equally absorbing volumes reveal inside views of common devices and mechanisms on a less grand scale than the titles above. Mr. Burnie's subjects range from household appliances to commercial apparatuses. He begins with a definition and brief history of machines and ends, interestingly, with a sampling of inventors' attempts to achieve perpetual motion.

Mr. Parker's book, the most comprehensive of all the above, is divided into ten main sections; and includes cut-away or cross-section diagrams of in- and around-the-house appliances, farm equipment, and wildlife habitats, as well as home-entertainment, rock-concert, and film-set related instruments and equipment.

SCIENCE TO THE RESCUE
Sandra Markle
Photographs
Atheneum, 1994
[i, j] 48 pages

Ms. Markle focuses on eight creative solutions to real-life problems, among them the need for an artificial limb to help a young amputee run and jump. She states the need, describes the invention(s) that satisfied it, and challenges readers with related projects.

MISTAKES THAT WORKED
Charlotte Foltz Jones
Illustrations by John O'Brien
Doubleday, 1991
[i, j] 82 pages

You'll find how chocolate chip cookies, Popsicles™, Ivory® soap, Post-it™ notes, dog-guides for the blind, and other now commonplace essentials came to be in this perfect read-aloud.

AFRICAN-AMERICAN INVENTORS
Patricia and Fredrick McKissack
Photographs and illustrations
Millbrook, 1994
[i, j] 96 pages

The McKissacks' explanation of what patents are and how our patent system works precedes their tracing of inventions, from the time of slavery, through innovations in the shoe, railroad, electrical, and automobile industries, up to contemporary contributions in atomic energy and computers.

**THE REAL MCCOY: THE LIFE OF AN
AFRICAN-AMERICAN INVENTOR**
Wendy Towle
Illustrations by Wil Clay
Scholastic, 1993
[i] 32 pages

Because its imitations were inferior, locomotive workers insisted
on the "real" McCoy—the ingenious automatic oil cup that Elijah
McCoy patented in 1872. Ms. Towle recounts the life and many
accomplishments of the man whose name is synonymous with
perfection.

I'VE GOT AN IDEA!
Gloria M. Swanson and Margaret W. Ott
B/w photographs
Runestone Press, 1994
[i, j] 96 pages

Frederick McKinley Jones (1893-1961), son of an African-
American woman and Irish father, was on his own from age
seven. Ms. Swanson and Ms.Ott have written an absorbing
account of how the self-taught mechanical genius became an
automobile mechanic, race car designer, engineer, and inventor—
most notably, perhaps, of the Thermo-King cooling units on
refrigerated trucks.

WOMEN INVENTORS AND THEIR DISCOVERIES
Ethlie Ann Vare and Greg Ptacek
B/w photographs
Oliver, 1993
[j] 160 pages

Among the ten women are Stephanie Kwolek, Grace Hopper, and
S. Josephine Baker, whose innovations include, respectively, bul-
let-resistant Kevlar, automatic computer programming, and cap-
sules for the safe dispensation of medicine. The coauthors make
clear how each woman, through determination and perseverance,

overcame the strong male, institutional-led obstacles that confronted them throughout most of their lives.

MOTHERS AND DAUGHTERS OF INVENTION:
NOTES FOR A REVISED HISTORY OF TECHNOLOGY
Autumn Stanley
Scarecrow, 1993; Rutgers University Press, 1995
[j, a] 1,116 pages

Ms. Stanley's substantial volume belongs in every middle- and high-school library, and should be read by every teacher anticipating discussion about inventions. With assignments that require reference to her thoroughly researched history of inventions and innovators in fields from agriculture to artificial intelligence, all students will appreciate women's enormous contribution to technological progress.

SMITHSONIAN VISUAL TIMELINE
OF INVENTIONS: FROM THE FIRST
STONE TOOLS TO SATELLITES AND SUPERCONDUCTORS
Richard Platt
Photographs
Dorling, 1994
[i, j] 64 pages

A thorough perusal reveals that the *only* invention by a woman in this volume is Margaret Knight's Paper Bag Machine of 1879! Because I know few who see it will resist adding the lavishly illustrated and strikingly designed, 10" x 12" book to their collection, I recommend it only after you've purchased *Women Inventors and their Discoveries* (above), read the introduction to *Mothers and Daughters of Invention* (above), and browsed through Ms. Stanley's many chapters.

MAGNIFICATION

Bring the little things in life into focus. Set up a "Small Is Beautiful" corner replete with microscope(s) and magnifying glass(es).

LENSES! TAKE A CLOSER LOOK
Siegfried Aust
Full-color illustrations by Helge Nyncke
Lerner, 1991
[i] 32 pages

Information-packed chapters with lively illustrations reveal how people and animals see, and the history and development of eyeglasses, magnifying glasses, the microscope, and the telescope. Instructions for the construction of a periscope and kaleidoscope are included.

EXPERIMENTING WITH A MICROSCOPE
Maurice Bliefield
B/w illustrations
Watts, 1988
[j] 128 pages

THE WORLD OF THE MICROSCOPE
Chris Oxblade
Full-color illustrations
Usborne, (hb/pb), 1989
[i, j] 48 pages

Mr. Bliefield begins with a brief history of the instrument and devotes the main body of his book to the specific procedures for preparing and examining crystal, plant, and animal specimens. Have youngsters take special note of warnings about obtaining blood or saliva samples.

Mr. Oxblade's attractive book has single-topic, fully illustrated spreads with text and pictures thoroughly integrated. It includes details on the many kinds of microscopes, the optical principals that make them work, and their use in a wide range of disciplines.

THE HOME
Heather Amery and Jane Songi
Photographs
Western, 1994
[i,j] 40 pages

INCREDIBLY SMALL
Nina Canault
Photographs
New Discovery, 1993
[i, j] 48 pages

These representative titles are from two fine series: "Discover Hidden Worlds and "Frontiers of the Invisible," respectively. Both allow readers to explore views possible only through sophisticated photographic equipment and technology. Magnified images from *Nature* in general and *Bugs* specifically (both Western, 1994) are others in the first series; *Incredibly Far*, *Incredibly Fast*, and *Incredibly Hidden* round out the second.

MICROALIENS
Howard Tomb and Dennis Kunkel
B/w photographs and illustrations
Farrar, 1993
[j] 80 pages

Dr. Kunkel's micrographs of the animate and inanimate objects are awesome. They range from prickly surfaced grains of pollen to somewhat mysterious ribbon-like structures in human cells unknown before the invention of the electron microscope and magnified here 52,326 times. Mr. Tomb's accompanying narrative and annotations are equally mesmerizing.

MATH AND COUNTING

When it's time for them to count off, connect kids to books by the creative artists whose numerical excursions are as satisfyingly aesthetic as they are arithmetic.

FISH EYES: A BOOK YOU CAN COUNT ON
Lois Ehlert
Illustrations
Harcourt, (hb/pb), 1990
[p] 32 pages

With each flip of the page, a plain pilot fish leads the way from one to ten through bigger-by-one schools of brilliantly colored, Day-Glo-accented fish, whose diecut eyes cleverly add another dimension to the journey.

Provide scissors and an assortment of brightly colored wrapping or construction paper and suggest youngsters try their hand at collages similar to Ms. Ehlert's.

SEA SQUARES
Joy Hulme
Illustrations by Carol Schwartz
Hyperion, 1991
[p] 32 pages

In this imaginative, rhyming introduction to square numbers, readers simultaneously go from one to ten and one to a hundred: One whale has one strong tail, for example, and eight octopuses on the ocean floor result in "scrambled legs, 64." Two pages of facts about the ten featured creatures conclude the colorful volume.

THE TWELVE DAYS OF SUMMER
Illustrations by Karen Lee Schmidt
Elizabeth Lee O'Donnell
Morrow, 1991
[p, i] 32 pages

A resourceful preschooler acquires a beachful of new playmates, from twelve gulls a-gliding to a little purple sea anemone. All charmingly depicted in this read-aloud, sing-aloud book for any season.

👓 Use the book above to illustrate a familiar Christmas carol's adaptability. Suggest that youngsters similarly create lyrics to reflect a current topic of study: For example, "On a trip through the rain forest, guess what I did see...."

TEN LITTLE RABBITS
Virginia Grossman
Illustrations by Sylvia Long
Chronicle, (hb/pb), 1991
[p, i] 28 pages

Simple couplets that roll lightly from the lips and serene paintings that enchant the eye create a mellow ambiance in this just-before-nap or bedtime book. On the final pages, Ms. Grossman describes the costumes and customs of the ten tribes represented in the illustrations.

I SPY TWO EYES: NUMBERS IN ART
Lucy Micklethwait
Illustrations
Greenwillow, 1993
[all ages] 48 pages

NUMBERS AT PLAY
Charles Sullivan
Color and b/w photographs

Rizzoli, 1992
[all ages] 48 pages

Both books open youngsters eyes to an impeccable and exhilarating selection of fine art—paintings only, in the first, and contemporary and archival photographs, paintings, and sculpture, in the second.

THE LIFESIZE ANIMAL COUNTING BOOK
Photographs
Dorling, 1994
[pre, p] 28 pages

One greedy gorilla who's gobbled grapes greets readers at the start of this striking assortment of images. In a companion *Lifesize Animal Opposites Book* (Dorling, 1994), a four-page spread opens on a baby crocodile! Impressive!

ARCHITECTURE COUNTS
Michael J. Crosbie and Steve Rosenthal
Photographs
Preservation, 1993
[pre, p] 24 pages

One of an attractive trio of boardbooks that highlight architectural features. This book begins with no buildings in an unpeopled countryside and closes with ten columns of a college-campus building. Its companions are *Architecture Shapes* and *Architecture Colors* (both Preservation, 1993).

MOO, MOO, BROWN COW
Jacki Wood
Illustrations by Rog Bonner
Harcourt, 1992
[pre, p] 28 pages

Youngsters learn the names of animal babies ("Moo, Moo, Brown Cow have you any calves?...") when they read Ms. Wood's inviting picture book. Or, just as easily, sing it to the tune of "Baa, baa, black sheep."

THE LIBRARIAN WHO MEASURED THE EARTH
Kathryn Lasky
Illustrations by Kevin Hawkes
Little, 1994
[i] 48 pages

Over 2,000 years ago in ancient Greece, Eratosthenes, the brilliant head librarian of the Alexandria Museum, calculated the circumference of the earth within 200 miles. Ms. Lasky describes the man, his time, and his ingenious computation.

THE AMAZING BOOK OF SHAPES
Lydia Sharman
Illustrations by Janos Marffy and Grahame Corbett
Dorling, 1994
[p, i] 38 pages

A note to parents and teachers on how to use this book precedes the scores of facts about shapes, including those in tangrams, fractals, and kirigami flowers in this oversize (10"x13") book. Dozens of hands-on projects, a foil-coated bookmark/mirror, and a sturdy fold-out work surface grid complete with stencils make it a valuable and practical introduction to geometry.

WHAT AM I? LOOKING THROUGH SHAPES AT APPLES AND GRAPES
N. N. Charles
Illustrations by Leo and Diane Dillon
Scholastic, 1994
[pre, p] 40 pages

With geometrical die cuts, vivid illustrations of fruit, and verse, preschoolers learn colors and shapes.

SEA SHAPES
Suse MacDonald
Illustrations by the author
Gulliver, 1994

[pre, p] 32 pages

Ms. MacDonald's circle, square, triangle, and other shapes become a whale's eye, skate, shark's teeth, and other marine life, all of which she describes in her concluding "Sea Facts."

THE WHEELING AND WHIRLING AROUND BOOK
Judy Hindley
Illustrations by Margaret Chamberlain
Candlewick, 1994
[p] 28 pages

Ms. Hindley encourages children to look around and find things which are circular or derive from circles, including merry-go-rounds, rolled up newspapers, and seashells. With this start, author and illustrator then describe gears, axles, conveyor belts, whirlwinds, and, finally, our spiral galaxy.

EENIE MEENIE MINEY MATH! MATH PLAY FOR YOU AND YOUR PRESCHOOLER
Linda Allison
Illustrations by Martha Weston
Little (hb/pb), 1993
[pre] 48 pages

Though addressed to adults, this title in the delightfully upbeat "Brown Paper Preschool" series is perfect for young readers as a resource rich in mathematical activities they can share with very young siblings or cross-grade tutees. For equally idea-packed guides to wordplay, creative art and science, refer kids to *Wordsaroni* (Little, 1993), *Razzle Dazzle Doodle Art* (Little, 1994) and *Pint-Size Science* (Little, 1994), respectively.

CIRCLES

TRIANGLES
Catherine Sheldrick Ross
Illustrations by Bill Slavin

Addison, 1992: Kids Can, 1994
[i] 64 pages each

Ms. Ross extends boys' and girls' investigations of the respective shapes into architecture and construction with paper, toothpick, and chicken wire projects that relate math to everyday life. Prepare for a roomful of sundials, domes, bridges, and kaleidoscopes!

IS A BLUE WHALE THE BIGGEST THING THERE IS?
Robert E. Wells
Illustrations by the author
Whitman, 1993
[p, i] 32 pages

With cascading facts and whimsical art, Mr. Wells helps children visualize what can't be seen: The enormity of our universe, which is bigger than "...a jar of blue whales, a stack of Mount Everests, or even a crateful of sun-sized oranges!"

To help children visualize stupendous amounts, turn also to David M. Schwartz's *How Much is a Million* (Lothrop, 1985; Mulberry, 1993) and *If You Made a Million* (Lothrop, 1989; Mulberry, 1994): in the first, millions, billions, and trillions of things; in the second, a million dollars. All illustrated with Steven Kellogg's irresistible exuberance.

ONE HUNDRED HUNGRY ANTS
Elinor J. Pinczes
Illustrations by Bonnie MacKain
Houghton, 1993
[pre, p] 32 pages

In this delightful introduction to permutations, the littlest ant suggests that he and his 99 companions rearrange themselves from one long column into two, four, five, and finally ten columns to hasten their arrival at a picnic.

MATHNET CASEBOOKS
David D. Connell and Jim Thurman
B/w illustrations by Danny O'Leary
Freeman, 1994
[i] 64 pages

This first-rate blend of fact and fiction is based on Childrens' Television Workshop's "SQUARE ONE TV" programs in which Mathnetters George Frankly and Kate Monday crack jokes and solve mysteries by the numbers: in #3, *The Case of the Willing Parrot*, for example, Fibonacci numbers are introduced.

MUSIC MAKERS

MEET THE ORCHESTRA

MEET THE MARCHING SMITHEREENS
Ann Hayes
Illustrations by Karmen Thompson
Harcourt (hb/pb), 1991; 1995
[p, i] 32 pages each

These are humorously perceptive introductions of the finest picture-book kind to orchestral and marching-band musicians and their instruments. The players, animals all, hold their instruments as true professionals, with perfect embouchure and hand-position. Ms. Hayes aptly portrays each instrument's distinctive attributes in terms youngsters will readily appreciate.

**THE ORCHESTRA: AN INTRODUCTION
TO THE WORLD OF CLASSICAL MUSIC**
Alan Blackwood
Photographs and illustrations
Millbrook, 1993

[i, j] 94 pages

This is the place to send music-minded youngsters seeking an overview of the orchestra. It is divided into three sections: (1) a 300-year history of the orchestra's development; (2) an explanation of the operating principles and ranges of the instruments; and (3) a day in the life of an orchestral musician.

RATTLES, BELLS, AND CHIMING BARS
Karen Foster

MUSIC FROM STRINGS
BEATING THE DRUM
Josephine Paker

FLUTES, REEDS AND TRUMPETS
Danny Staples and Carole Mahoney
Photographs and illustrations
Millbrook, 1992
[i, j] 48 pages each

Shake, pluck, bang, toot: This series of instrument-specific books complements the general descriptions found in Mr. Blackwood's book (above) for the edification of youngsters interested in more detail about instruments from around the world as well as those found in a traditional symphony orchestra.

Hand youngsters Paul Fleisher's *The Master Violinmaker* (Houghton, 1993), with photographs by David Saunders, for a look at the way one master craftsman produces a stringed instrument.

MOZART TONIGHT
Julie Downing
Illustrations by the author
Bradbury (hb/pb), 1991
[p, i] 40 pages

LETTERS TO HORSEFACE
R. J. Monjo
B/w illustrations by Elaine Raphael and Don Bolognese
Puffin, 1975/1991
[p, i] 94 pages

These are faithful recreations of Mozart's life and time in slightly fictionalized books. In the first, the composer reminisces about surrounding events and the premiere of Don Giovanni. Richly hued watercolors reflect Ms. Downing's meticulous research into 18th century Europe and its customs.

Though none of the letters in Mr. Monjo's reissue were actually written by Mozart to his sister, their contents were based upon a thorough knowledge of the composer's biographies and collected letters. The author "recast and rephrased" previously recorded observations in the mischievous character of the 14-year-old prodigy.

WOLFGANG AMADEUS MOZART

LUDWIG VAN BEETHOVEN
Wendy Thompson
B/w and color illustrations
Viking, 1991
[i, j] 48 pages each

Clearly and concisely, Ms. Thompson summarizes the period and life of each composer. She describes the evolution of major works, and some minor ones; and she accompanies some with simplified excerpts scored for the piano. These superbly produced volumes (which, as of this writing include biographies of Schubert, Haydn, Tchaikovsky, and Debussy) will satisfy intelligent, inquisitive readers, young and old.

LIVES OF THE MUSICIANS: GOOD TIMES, BAD TIMES (AND WHAT THE NEIGHBORS THOUGHT)
Kathleen Krull

Illustrations by Kathryn Hewitt
Harcourt, 1993
[i, j] 96 pages

Ms. Krull has collected interesting anecdotes about 16 famous composers and their music—facts one is unlikely to find elsewhere. For example, it's estimated that if Mozart were alive today, he'd be earning $20 million a year from sales of his recordings. Ms. Hewitt's compelling watercolors of Vivaldi, Clara Schuman, Joplin, Guthrie, et al., are as intriguing as the text.

Barbara Mitchell's *Raggin'* and *America I Hear You* (both Carolrhoda, 1987) and Tom Streissguth's *Say it With Music* (Carolrhoda, 1994) are story-form biographies (there's a little dialogue) which make fine introductions to composers Scott Joplin, George Gershwin, and Irving Berlin, respectively, for intermediate grade readers.

JAZZ: MY MUSIC, MY PEOPLE
Morgan Monceaux
Illustrations by the author
Knopf, 1994
[i, j] 64 pages

Mr. Monceaux, the son of a jazz singer, has lovingly researched the careers and painted portraits of the "great [musical] rule breakers of our time," Louie Armstrong, Pearl Bailey, Art Tatum, Sarah Vaughn, The Modern Jazz Quartet...more than 50 singers and instrumentalists. His own recollections of many of them make this a warm, personal tribute to African-American music and musicianship.

PILGRIMS

Almost four centuries ago, Pilgrim and Wampanoag broke bread together in friendship. The English immigrants gave thanks for their bountiful harvest and the Native Americans who made it possible. When the holiday commemorating that day of thanksgiving appears on your agenda, open youngsters' eyes to the two communities represented at that long-ago picnic—perhaps the first multicultural potluck in North American history.

PEOPLE OF THE BREAKING DAY
Marcia Sewall
Illustrations by the author
Atheneum, 1990
[i] 48 pages

Ms. Sewall's evocative prose and earth-toned paintings artfully recreate the Wampanoag's time and place. In the first person plural, she articulates the woodland tribe's religious beliefs, social mores, and tribal customs.

> Have handy Russell M. Peters photoessay *Clambake* (Lerner, 1992), so youngsters can see how contemporary Wampanoags prepare for and celebrate a traditional feast. And read aloud Wampanoag tales as told by Manitonquat (Medicine Story) in *The Children of the Morning Light* (Macmillan, 1994).

N. C. WYETH'S PILGRIMS
Robert San Souci
Illustrations by N. C. Wyeth
Chronicle, 1991
[i] 36 pages

THE FIRST THANKSGIVING
Jean Craighead George
Illustrations by Thomas Locker
Philomel, 1993
[i] 32 pages

The times that preceded the settlers' first thanksgiving day in North America are brought to life in these complementary versions of the Pilgrims' progress. The first is set against the backdrop of murals painted in 1940. In the second, pages of text alternate with full-page illustrations.

THREE YOUNG PILGRIMS
Cheryl Harness
Illustrations by the author
Bradbury, 1992
[i] 48 pages

Young Bartholomew, Remember, and Mary Allerton spring to life in this superlative blend of fact and fiction which begins and ends with what is known: The cross section of a ship resembling the fully laden Mayflower, for example, and maps of the Pilgrims' travels. Between these "facts" is the story of the children's first year in America, portrayed in brightly colored, richly detailed, exuberantly animated art.

SARAH MORTON'S DAY

SAMUEL EATON'S DAY
Kate Waters
Photographs by Russ Kendall
Scholastic, 1989; 1993
[p, i] 36 pages each

Plimoth Plantation, the outdoor, living-museum of 17th century Plymouth, Massachusetts, is the locale where Mr. Kendall photographed first Amanda Poole as Sarah, then Roger Burns as

Samuel, as they and their colleagues dressed, worked, and spoke like the Pilgrims of 1627. Photos and a first-person-singular narrative provide historical verisimilitude.

Use a comparison of nine-year-old Sarah's, seven-year-old Samuel's, and your elementary-school students' clothes, homes, and sunup-to-sundown activities to stimulate a lively class discussion.

EATING THE PLATES
Lucille Recht Penner
B/w illustrations
Macmillan, 1991
[i] 36 pages

In this what, how, and why of Pilgrim food and manners, readers will discover that Pilgrims used fingers instead of forks, slept on the dinner table, drank beer instead of water, and washed clothes but twice a year. Ms. Penner also provides ten recipes for replicating a Pilgrim dinner—literally everything from soup to nuts. Bon appetit!

For a personal view of the Pilgrims' daily lives, share author/artist Gary Bowen's *Stranded at Plimoth Plantation* in 1626 (HarperCollins, 1994), the wood-cut illustrated journal of 13-year-old Christopher Sears, an "accidental" member of the colony from November 22, 1626, to August 23, 1627. The young Sears is fictional, but the setting, its inhabitants, and their behavior are the result of diligent research.

CRANBERRIES
William Jaspersohn
Photographs by the author
Houghton, 1991
[i] 32 pages

Many Thanksgiving menus include cranberries, one of the few fruits native to North America and doubtless a staple in the

Wampanoag fall/winter diet. Mr. Jaspersohn catches contemporary cranberry cultivators as they harvest (with helicopters!) the juicy red berry Pilgrims named crane-berry, after the bird their white blossoms resemble.

SQUANTO AND THE FIRST THANKSGIVING
Joyce K. Kessel
Illustrations by Lisa Donze
Carolrhoda, (hb/pb), 1983
[p] 48 pages

Between the time the earliest English settlers and the ones we call Pilgrims arrived in what is now Plymouth, a Patuxet Indian named Squanto had twice been enslaved, taken to Europe, freed, and returned to his homeland. On his second return, however, he found that all of his people had died from smallpox. Ms. Kessel tells how, ironically, the misfortune of the last of the Patuxets became the Pilgrims' blessing.

KING PHILIP
Robert Cwiklik
B/w illustrations
Silver, 1989
[j] 132 pages

Sixty-five years after they gave thanks for the friendship and help of Chief Massasoit and his people, English colonists beheaded the chief's son Metacom, whom they'd facetiously named King Philip. Mr. Cwiklik's riveting account, albeit with some "reconstructed" dialogue, thoughts, and descriptions, is a good way to help young people understand how and why the two cultures clashed and one was virtually obliterated.

ROCKS AND MINERALS

HOW THE EARTH WORKS: 100 WAYS PARENTS AND KIDS CAN SHARE THE SECRETS OF THE EARTH
John Farndon
Photographs by Michael Dunning
Readers Digest, 1992
[i, j, a] 192 pages

THE VISUAL DICTIONARY OF THE EARTH
Photographs and illustrations
Dorling, 1993
[i, j] 64 pages

Use these as your own refresher course and your students' introduction to things geologic. Mr. Farndon's profusely illustrated guide includes historical narrative; sketches of noteworthy scientists; and step-by-step tests, experiments and projects—with appropriate warnings.

Among the highlights of the *Visual Dictionary* is a two-page spread of the sedimentary layers of the Grand Canyon region.

ROCK COLLECTING
Roma Gans
Illustrations by Holly Keller and b/w photographs
HarperCollins, (hb/pb), 1984
[p] 28 pages

Ms. Gans explains how rocks are formed, their similarities, their differences, varieties and uses.

THE BIG ROCK
Bruce Hiscock
Illustrations by the author
Atheneum, 1988
[p, i] 32 pages

This profile of an enormous piece of granite begins with its formation 1,000 million years ago. The author explains how mountains form, are eroded by weather, and have lost chunks to ice-age glaciers which moved and deposited them far from their place of origin.

 Expand Mr. Hiscock's geological perspective with the poetic one of author/artist Peter Parnall whose paints and prose portray *The Rock* (Macmillan, 1991) as home, shelter, or roothold for forest life.

THE AMAZING DIRT BOOK
Paulette Bourgeois
Addison, (hb/pb), 1990
[i] 80 pages

Ms. Bourgeois gives kids the dirt on rocks in their smallest form—from dust under the bed to flower beds—in another of her activity enhanced "amazing" books.

ROCKS & MINERALS
R. F. Symes
Photographs and illustrations
Knopf, 1988
[i, j] 64 pages

CRYSTAL & GEM
R. F. Symes and R. R. Harding
Photographs and illustrations
Knopf, 1991
[i, j] 64 pages

In the first of this natural pair, readers learn how rocks and minerals are formed, mined, or otherwise freed from the earth and used. In the second, the authors elaborate on crystals' various colors, shapes, values, and technological and fashionable uses.

Hand youngsters Milton Meltzer's *Gold!* (HarperCollins, 1993), for "the true story" of why people search for, mine, trade, steal, mint, hoard, shape, wear, fight, and kill for one of the most precious metals found in rocks.

ROCKS AND MINERALS
Steve Parker
Photographs and illustrations
Dorling, 1993
[i, j] 58 pages

This backpack-sized (6"x8") "Eyewitness Explorer" is a distillation of the above R. F. Symes books with added activities for collecting and examining properties.

Chris Pellant's *Rocks and Minerals* (Dorling, 1992) is an ideal reference book for the avid amateur rock hound. Mr. Pellant's explanation of how to collect, record, and store specimens precedes close-up photographs of hundreds of rocks and minerals which are annotated with concise data and an illustration of each mineral's crystal shape.

SING SONGS

When I was young, singing was a daily class activity, a natural part of family get-togethers, and standard fare at most movie theaters where we followed the bouncing ball. Today, when I ask audiences to join me in song, their enthusiasm and pleasure vividly demonstrate that singalongs are anything but dated.

Unfortunately, the National Arts Education Research Center of the National Education Association reports that general music instruction in the elementary classroom has steadily decreased since 1962. Fewer and fewer children sing in school. Buck the trend. Make words and music an essential ingredient in your youngsters' lives.

Sing daily; join in song with the class next door; assemble for monthly all-school songfests (if weekly or bi-weekly ones aren't feasible); and wind up the year with an open-house sing-along for parents, teachers, and kids.

Transfer words to transparencies and, if you have a laser pointer, let a child guide it over the projected lyrics, so everyone can follow a bouncing ball that has nothing to do with win/lose sports and everything to do with win/win singing!

FROM SEA TO SHINING SEA: A TREASURY OF AMERICAN FOLKLORE AND FOLK SONGS
Amy L. Cohn
Illustrations by Caldecott artists
Scholastic, 1993
[all ages] 416 pages

This eyeopener will enrich the lives of everyone who hears, reads, sings, or otherwise partakes in the pleasures to be found within its four pounds of pages. Impeccably researched, solidly organized, and exquisitely illustrated, Ms. Cohn's compilation is a sine qua non for every school, public, or private children's library.

IN THE DAWN'S EARLY LIGHT: THE STORY OF THE STAR SPANGLED BANNER
Steven Kroll
Illustrations by Dan Andreasen
Scholastic, 1993
[i, j] 40 pages

Read aloud or hand youngsters this dramatized story of the events that led Francis Scott Key to pen what has become the lyric of our national anthem. The every-other-page illustrations are supplemented with an etching of Francis Scott Key, a photograph of the original manuscript of the poem, and J. Stafford Smith's melody (with piano accompaniment) to which it was set.

Enhance Mr. Kroll's history of *The Star Spangled Banner* (Dell, 1992) with author/artist Peter Spier's reissued perspective of the anthem and its meaning. Connect both books to James Weldon Johnson's *Lift Ev'ry Voice and Sing* (Scholastic, 1995), beautifully illustrated by Jan Spivey Gilchrist in a picture book for young children. Set to music by J. Rosamond Johnson, the poet's brother, it is considered by many people to be the African-American National Anthem.

SONGS OF THE WILD WEST
Metropolitan Museum of Art
Illustrations
Simon, 1991
[i, j, adult] 128 pages

Forty-five folksongs celebrate America's westward expansion in this music/art book illustrated with reproductions and photographs of art and artifacts that depict or were used by adventurers and settlers who explored the frontier. With (1) biographies of the artists or artisans who created the works of art; (2) histories of the works themselves; and (3) stories of the songs' heroes or villains, it is a glorious volume to sing by or peruse—and a must whenever you teach any aspect of the settling of America. Piano accompaniments are simple yet musically interesting, and guitar chords are noted.

THE SESAME STREET SONGBOOK
Illustrations
Macmillan, 1993
[pre, p] 220 pages

Sixty-four perfect songs to grow by—eminently singable, rhythmically varied, harmonically rich, and within the range of children's singing voices. And the lyrics are on target to help little ones learn to accept themselves and others; discover the world around them; dance, sing, count, and learn the alphabet. All arranged with piano accompaniments and guitar chords.

CARIBBEAN CARNIVAL
Irving Burgie, composer/arranger
Illustrations by Frané Lessac
Tambourine, 1992
[p, i] 32 pages

"Day-O," "Yellow Bird," and "Jamaica Farewell" are among these calypso classics. With raspers they've made out of notched dowels and simple shakers of pea-, rice-, or bean-filled bottles, cans, and cardboard tubes, have children form a rhythm section to accompany themselves as they sing these lively tunes. The very simple piano accompaniments have guitar chords noted.

THE LAURA INGALLS WILDER SONGBOOK
Eugenia Garson, Editor/compiler
B/w illustrations by Garth Williams
HarperCollins, 1968.
[i] 160 pages

It's good to have this back in print so that children can become familiar with the music they read about in Ms. Wilder's stories. The songs are grouped by topic and their source in the "Little House" series is identified. The simply written piano accompaniments also indicate guitar chords. Ms. Garson's description of her research is fascinating.

CLIMBING JACOB'S LADDER: HEROES OF THE BIBLE IN AFRICAN-AMERICAN SPIRITUALS
John Langstaff
Illustrations by Ashley Bryan
McElderry, 1991
[all ages] 24 pages

A brief distillation of the Old Testament story precedes "Ezekial Saw the Wheel," "Joshua Fit the Battle of Jericho," "Go Down, Moses," and the other spirituals in this handsome anthology. Harmonically rich and rhythmic piano arrangements accompany all.

AMAZING GRACE
Jim Haskins
Two-color illustrations
Millbrook, 1992
[i,j] 48 pages

The hauntingly beautiful and spiritually uplifting hymn of the title was written, ironically, by a man whose logs, journals, and other writings make up "one of the most detailed records of the slave trade that has ever existed." This biography of the Englishman, John Newton (1725-1807), reveals his troubled youth, experiences on slave ships as crewmember and captain, and eventual change of heart. Put this on your "Good Book, Bad Cover" shelf when you get it, for its unimaginative cover will otherwise attract few readers.

"Amazing Grace" and thirty-six other songs of *Praise For the Singing* (Little, 1993), especially for children, have been collected by Madelaine Gill and Greg Pliska, with illustrations by Ms. Gill and piano arrangements by Mr. Pliska. The songs reflect the traditions of many cultures and include "Praise God from Whom All Blessings Flow," "Havenu Shalom Alechem," "This Little Light," and "Tis the Gift to Be Simple."

ARROZ CON LECHE
Lulu Delacre
Illustrations by the author
Scholastic, 1989/1992

LOS POLLITOS DICEN/ THE BABY CHICKS SING
Nancy Abrahan Hall and Jill Syverson-Stork
Illustrations by Kay Chorao
Little, 1994
[pre, p] 32 pages each

Enrich your youngster's repertoires with the songs in Spanish and English from the popular and traditional songs, musical games, and nursery rhymes in these two nicely illustrated bilingual collections, 12 in the first and 17 in the second.

TWO BY TWO
Barbara Reid
Illustrations by the author
Scholastic, 1993
[all ages] 32 pages

In her inimitable style, Ms. Reid rolled, flattened, and otherwise manipulated plasticene until it came to life as Noah, his family, and their myriad animal charges. The lively characters seem to build, board, abide in, and disembark the ark as they bounce to the rhythm of the lyrics the artist has adapted to the traditional folksong "Who Built the Ark?"

SWIM THE SILVER SEA, JOSHI OTTER
Nancy White Carlstrom
Illustrations by Ken Kuroi
Philomel, 1993
[pre, p] 40 pages

A wonderfully soothing nap or nighttime read- or sing-aloud that introduces little ones to Alaskan coastal wildlife as Joshie passes them, guided home by his mother's voice. Once you've sung the original melody, it will seem you've always known it.

TODAY IS MONDAY
Eric Carle
Illustrations by the author
Philomel, 1993
[pre, p, i] 24 pages

In this oversize (9" x 12") book you can hold up for the class to see and sing from, tissue-paper collages illustrate the cumulative song in which a different food is featured each day of the week—

by one of a septet of animals. In conclusion, a multiethnic gathering of kids enjoy a meal of everything previously mentioned.

THREE BLIND MICE
John W. Ivimey
Illustrations by Lorinda Bryan Cauley
Putnam, 1991
[pre, p] 32 pages

Almost everyone knows they were blind and tailless, but not how they got nor whether they stayed that way. All questions are answered in this warm and witty rendition of the classic rhyme.

YANKEE DOODLE: A REVOLUTIONARY TAIL
Illustrations by Gary Chalk
Dorling, 1993
[p, i] 32 pages

The traditional verses of this merry tune plus 15 original ones are amplified with historical anecdotes and jaunty illustrations in which George Washington, the colonists, Red Coats, et al., are portrayed as animals.

JANE YOLEN'S OLD MACDONALD SONGBOOK
Jane Yolen, Ed.
Illustrations by Rosekrans Hoffman
Boyds Mills, 1994
[pre, p] 96 pages

These 43 songs about barnyard animals include "The Old Grey Mare," "Be Kind to Your Web-Footed Friends," and "Go Tell Aunt Rhody." Adam Stemple's simple arrangements are well within the grasp of youngsters with a year's piano lessons behind them. Guitar chords are also marked.

SLEEPY TIME

Reading aloud isn't just a school activity. Encourage the habit at home by suggesting children read aloud to younger members. Retirers and retirees both will enjoy these just-before-lights-out books:

ASLEEP, ASLEEP
Mirra Ginsburg
Illustrations by Nancy Tafuri
Greenwillow, 1992
[pre, p] 26 pages

The gently rocking rhythm of questions and answers assure little ones that in the woods, fields, streams, and home, all rest peacefully.

> Suggest young read alouders use Karen Wallace's clever *Why Count Sheep?* (Hyperion, 1993), wherein "A teacher counts children...a librarian counts books...," as inspiration for bedtime musings about what different people count to get to sleep.

GOING TO SLEEP ON THE FARM
Wendy Cheyette Lewison
Illustrations by Juan Wihngaard
Dial, 1992
[pre, p] 28 pages

A father satisfies his son's curiosity about the slumbering stances of barnyard inhabitants: "A cow lies down in the soft sweet hay,..." and "...A horse, of course, stands up all night...."

ANIMALS DON'T WEAR PAJAMAS
Eve B. Feldman
Illustrations by Mary Beth Owens

Holt, 1992
[p] 32 pages

Though animals don't wear pajamas, snuggle under cozy quilts, or otherwise behave like their human counterparts, they do know how to keep warm, find comfortable places, and fall asleep contented—as evidenced in a depiction of kids and creatures at their drowsing best.

IN THIS NIGHT...
Irmgard Lucht
Illustrations by author
Hyperion, 1993
[p] 24 pages

In the quiet of moonlight, wild geese travel, cats prowl, rabbits spar, and other animals go about their natural lives in a vivid evocation of the arrival of spring.

GOODNIGHT TO ANNIE: AN ALPHABET LULLABY
Eve Merriam
Illustrations by Carol Schwartz
Hyperion, 1992
[pre, p] 32 pages

From alligators dozing in the soft mud to zebras sleeping in the "zzzzzzzzzzzzzzzzzzzzzoo, with neither a xylophone nor X-ray, in between.

What bedtime rhymes do the adults in your student's lives remember from their childhood days? Have youngsters collect and illustrate them for a class- or schoolroom version of *Sleep Rhymes Around the World* (Boyds, 1994), edited by Jane Yolen.

SNAKES

SNAKES
Patricia Demuth
Illustrations by Judith Moffatt
Grosset, (hb/pb), 1993
[p] 48 pages

Ms. Demuth introduces beginning readers to snake locomotion, diet, coloration, methods of predation, and other such characteristic traits.

Katy Hall's and Lisa Eisenberg's *Snakey Riddles* (Puffin, 1990), of the "Why doesn't the cobra call his mother collect? He likes to call poison to poison!" ilk, are perfect for primary gigglers. Especially as illustrated by Simms Taback.

TAKE A LOOK AT SNAKES
Betsy Maestro
Illustrations by Giulio Maestro
Scholastic, 1992
[p, i] 40 pages

That Ms. Maestro is a fine teacher is clearly evident in her well-integrated blend of words and pictures that tell and show what makes a snake a snake, how it survives as both predator and prey, and that it has a positive role in the balance of nature. Readers will finish with an understanding and appreciation of an animal more to be respected than feared.

SNAKE
Caroline Arnold
Photographs by Richard Hewett
Morrow, 1991
[i] 48 pages

Readers who dread all snakes may find nonvenomous ones somewhat less frightening when they see how matter-of-factly, gently, and with pleasure men, women, and children hold Rosy,

218 • EYEOPENERS II •

a two-foot-long rosy boa. Though the subject is snakes in general, focus is primarily boas and pythons.

SNAKES
Seymour Simon
Photographs
HarperCollins, (hb/pb), 1992
[i] 32 pages

With a superb selection of photographs to illustrate, Mr. Simon describes the physical characteristics and habits of snakes in general, both venomous and harmless.

THE SECRETIVE TIMBER RATTLESNAKE

A GATHERING OF GARTER SNAKES
Bianca Lavies
Photographs by the author
Dutton, 1990; 1993
[p, i, j] 32 pages each

Smooth, rich narratives effortlessly lead readers through the snakes' life cycles and reveal their physical and behavioral characteristics en route. The first volume focuses on the less aggressive cousin of the western diamondback; and the second, the red-sided garter snakes that winter in limestone caverns in Manitoba, Canada.

Point out the last-page portraits of Ms. Lavies "shooting" her subjects. Children will find them as awesome as her closeups.

SNAKES
Lucy Baker
Photographs and illustrations
Puffin, (pb), 1990
[p, i] 32 pages

The simple, spare, but informative text includes directions for mask-making and other activities and concludes with the day-in-the-life-of story about a young constrictor. Ms. Baker's inexpensive paperback is attractive for the fairly fluent as well as the reluctant reader.

SEA SNAKES
Sneed B. Collard III
Illustrations by John Rice and photographs
Boyds Mills, 1993
[i] 32 pages

Mention snakes and chances are youngsters will think only of the land variety—until they read this fascinating introduction to the reptiles that spend their entire lives at sea.

SPACE AND ASTRONOMY

THE VISUAL DICTIONARY OF THE UNIVERSE
Illustrations and photographs
Dorling, 1992
[j, a] 64 pages

THE SPACE ATLAS
Heather Couper and Nigel Henbest
Illustrations by Luciano Corbella and photographs
Gulliver, 1992
[j, a] 64 pages

The dictionary allows independently inquisitive reader/browsers or report-bent students to name what they only recognize by sight and to see what they only know by name, for every pictured detail is labeled and the index contains more than 2,000 entries. The atlas's absorbing narrative conveys the exhilaration of the search and discovery inherent in astronomy, while amplifying maps, charts, and other illustrations with explanations, descriptions, and pertinent history.

Seymour Simon's painstakingly selected, first-rate photographs of *Stars* (Morrow, 1986), *Galaxies* (Morrow, 1988), *Comets, Meteors and Asteroids* (Morrow, 1994) provide a stellar background for descriptions and analogies that transform usually difficult concepts into terms children—and adults—can easily picture. When explaining that the galaxy is mostly empty space, for example, Mr. Simon writes that a dozen tennis balls spread out across the U.S. would be more crowded than most of the stars in the galaxy. He brings the heavens down to earth for readers of all ages.

SPACE, STARS, PLANETS, AND SPACECRAFT
Sue Becklake
Photographs and illustrations
Dorling, 1991
[i, j] 64 pages

ILLUSTRATED WORLD OF SPACE
Iain Nicholson
Illustrations
Simon, 1991
[j] 64 pages

Ms. Becklake's emphasis is on technology and how observers gather data; Dr. Nicolson's is on the history of astronomy and what data they've gathered. In both overviews, dramatic, detail-filled drawings, photographs, and computer-enhanced images are integrated with and provide background for two- to four-page chapters.

Connect kids to Leonard Everett Fisher's *Galileo* (Macmillan, 1992). Mr. Fisher's dark illustrations convey the oppression Galileo must have felt when secular and religious authorities condemned him for maintaining that the sun was the center of our universe.

LOOKING AT THE INVISIBLE UNIVERSE
James Jespersen
B/w illustrations
Atheneum, 1990
[j] 160 pages

An eye-opening view of what can't be seen when you look up at the night sky—quasars, pulsars, and other aspects of radio astronomy. Through analogy, illustration, and anecdote, the authors present a balanced history of radio astronomy discoveries that notes women's as well as men's discoveries and contributions to the field.

PLANETS
Gail Gibbons
Illustrations by the author
Holiday, (hb/pb), 1993
[p] 32 pages

An excellent first look at such planet basics as distance from the sun, length of day and year in earth terms, and natural satellites.

PLANETARIUM
Barbara Brenner
Illustrations by Ron Miller
Bantam, (hb/pb), 1993
[i] 48 pages

THE GRAND TOUR
Ron Miller and William K. H. Hartman
Photographs and paintings
Workman, (pb), 1993
[j, a] 208 pages

The first of these follows a group of children as they visit solar system displays, one per planet, from the sun to Pluto. The second starts readers on Jupiter and proceeds, in order of decreasing size, with stops at the 25 worlds larger than a thousand kilometers across, their satellites, and selected comets and asteroids.

Norma Cole's one-to-twenty-and-back "space counting book" *Blast Off* (Charlesbridge, 1994), has bottom-of-the-page captions for older readers or read-alouders. Suggest cross-grade tutors bone up on the text, then paraphrase it as they hold up the book for little ones to see and count by.

MY PLACE IN SPACE
Robin and Sally Hirst
Illustrations by Joe Levine and Roland Harvey
Orchard, (pb), 1990
[i] 36 pages

"Are you sure you know where you live," the bus driver teases. So Henry tells him. Precisely. From his house on Gumbridge Street to the farthest known galaxies! Whimsically detailed drawings of Henry's small town and realistic paintings of the heavens above illustrate this simplest, clearest, and wittiest introduction I've seen to where we are in the universal scheme of things.

Henry's recitation, as noted above, is bound to pique incipient astronauts' galactic curiosity. You can simultaneously satisfy and stimulate more if you put them aboard Joanna Cole's *The Magic Schoolbus® Lost in the Solar System* (Scholastic, 1992) with Ms. Frizzle and her class.

START EXPLORING SPACE:
A FACT-FILLED COLORING BOOK
Dennis Mammana
B/w line drawings by Helen I. Driggs
Running, (pb), 1991
[i] 126 pages

Line drawings accompany enlightening words on topics which include night-sky sights, past and present stargazers, and basic facts about planets, stars, and related phenomena. As they color between the lines, young crayon- or felt-tip-pen-pushers will discover details they might otherwise miss.

I WANT TO BE AN ASTRONAUT
Byron Barton
Illustrations by the author
HarperCollins, (hb/pb), 1989
[pre, p] 32 pages

Mr. Barton's five sentences, brilliant colors, and bold strokes tell it like it is for today's toddlers, tomorrow's space walkers.

Have children pretend they are 31st-century travel agents responsible for filling regularly scheduled rocket flights to other planets. Have them select a planet and create a magazine advertisement, a poster, or a travel brochure that will describe the sights and experiences to be had during a vacation there.

ONE GIANT LEAP
Mary Ann Fraser
Illustrations by the author
Holt, 1993
[i] 36 pages

Exactly 109 hours, 24 minutes, and 15 seconds after he left Earth, Neil Armstrong stood on the moon. Ms. Fraser's art provides a dramatic backdrop to her highlights of the Apollo 11 mission from 2:28:11 hours before its July 16, 1969, launch, to splashdown, 195:17:52 hours later.

SPACE CAMP
Anne Baird
Photographs by Robert Koropp

Morrow, (hb/pb), 1992
[i] 48 pages

THE U.S. SPACE CAMP BOOK OF ROCKETS
Anne Baird
Photographs by David Graham
Morrow, 1994
[i] 48 pages

A week at the Huntsville, Alabama, Space Camp will top kids' wish lists after they peruse this orientation-to-graduation chronicle of 12-year-olds exposed to a seven-day-smidgen of NASA's astronaut-training program. Campers also visit the nearby Rocket Park and Space Museum to learn how space flight became a reality. Even at arm's length, the respective experiences are exciting, enriching, and insightful highs.

LIVING IN SPACE
Don Berliner
Color and b/w photographs
Lerner, 1993
[i, j] 64 pages

Learn how astronauts go to the bathroom, brush teeth, wash hair, and attend to other personal routines with limited water in zero gravity in this look at the hygienic, group dynamic, and other aspects of space-station design.

Turn to *Space & Astronomy* (Tab, 1992) for science fair projects for (1) middle school students working alone or with a buddy, (2) upper elementary graders receiving occasional help from a cooperative parent, or (3) classroom exercises you oversee.

VOYAGER: AN ADVENTURE TO
THE EDGE OF THE SOLAR SYSTEM
Sally Ride and Tam O'Shaughnessy
Photographs

Crown, 1992
[i] 36 pages

VOYAGERS
Gregory Vogt
Photographs
Millbrook, 1991
[i,j] 112 pages

Much of what we know about Jupiter, Saturn, Uranus, and Neptune was revealed by the Voyagers 1 and 2. Introduce their discoveries with the straightforward, strikingly illustrated, Ride/O'Shaughnessy collaboration. Proceed to Mr. Vogt's account which also covers the problems Voyager encountered and how scientists and engineers overcame them. A superb teacher, he defines and elaborates in exactly the right places—I kept thinking, "So *that's* how they do that...Now I see!"

The above title and Mr. Vogt's others in the "Missions in Space" series, as well as his planet-titled, eight-volume, "Gateway Solar System" series (Millbrook) is invaluable for your own and your students' edification.

SPACE MACHINES
Norman Barrett
Illustrations and photographs
Watts, 1994
[p, i, j] 48 pages

This "visual guide" of first-rate illustrations, annotations, and descriptive prose is a fascinating compendium of the sophisticated contraptions with which scientists explore and use space: communication and other satellites, space craft and probes, telescopes, space stations and bases. The diagrams are perfect for tracing via overhead projectors for bulletin-board size posters or murals.

Highlight robotics and simulation, two of the technologies upon which space research relies, with *Robots* (Bradbury,

1990) and *Almost the Real Thing* (Bradbury, 1991). In the first, Gloria Skurzynski traces robot development from rudimentary mechanical playthings to prototype astrobots. In the second, she traces the evolution of replicating devices from wind tunnel to virtual reality.

Suggest youngsters synthesize what they've learned about space travel, planets, and robots with the design and construction of an astrobot model specifically configured to land on, roam about, gather, and transmit information about a planet of their choice.

 **SPIDERS**

SPIDERS
Gail Gibbons
Illustrations by the author
Holiday, 1993
[p] 32 pages

AMAZING WORLD OF SPIDERS
Janet Craig
Illustrations by Jean Helmer
Troll, (pb), 1990
[p, i] 32 pages

Start young readers with Ms. Gibbons's introduction and they'll segue smoothly into Ms. Craig's. Both authors explain how the eight-legged arthropods differ from insects, describe their general characteristics, and focus on the unique ways in which different species spin their webs—Ms. Craig in more depth.

SPIDERS
Jenny Tesar
Photographs and illustrations

Blackbirch, 1993
[i, j] 64 pages

A lucid, refreshingly designed overview of spider anatomy, reproduction, growth, web-building, and habitat—just the place to
send student spider researchers. A taxonomy of the animal kingdom, glossary, and up-to-date list of relevant titles is appended.

OUTSIDE AND INSIDE SPIDERS
Sandra Markle
Photographs
Bradbury, 1994
[p, i] 40 pages

This awesome collection of photographs and micrographs is clar-
ified by lucid descriptions and explanations aimed at young readers but is mesmerizing for all ages. Among the views is a tarantu-
la's lung which, like all spiders' aptly named "book lungs," resem-
bles stacked pages.

Mention spider and what happens? Of course! Kids start
"climbing" up the water spout with thumbs and forefin-
gers as they sing "Eensie Weensie Spider..." So have
handy elementary-school-teacher (of course!) Jill
Sardegna's delicious parody *The Roly-Poly Spider*
(Scholastic, 1994). This plump predator finds the water-
spout a close squeeze after satisfying snacks on, rather
than with, "friends" invited to dine.

SPIDERS NEAR AND FAR
Jennifer Owings Dewey
Illustrations by the author
Dutton, 1993
[i] 48 pages

With flowing narrative and meticulous depictions, the
author/artist compares web builders and wanderers, the two basic
spider types, in an oversized (10" x 10") format which provides
plenty of space for close-up detail of body parts, web designs,

and burrow construction. She concludes with life-size portraits of 22 types of spiders.

STATES

To help his sixth graders learn basic skills in a creative and imaginative way, James Plummer suggested they write a book. From a list he, his kids, their parents, and others helped assemble, the youngsters wrote to noteworthy authors and artists in their state, as well as people in its various government agencies. The students explained their project and requested a contribution of one activity, something creative that kids could do by themselves. One artist sent an original picture map of Maine and suggested children draw their own with scenic sites or otherwise interesting places they'd visited. An auctioneer-appraiser suggested children ask about the stories behind family items that have been passed down from one generation to another. The Fish and Wildlife Department suggested children use the Maine animal track chart they sent as inspiration for the creation of imaginary paw prints and the animals that would have made them. Mr. Plummer's kids illustrated and supplemented some of the suggestions and wrote their own, one of which included ideas and topics readers could include in a book about their own towns. .lm5

James Plummer's *A Gift From Maine* is unfortunately out of print, but you don't need to see the book to adapt his ideas. Try it, for whether your youngsters contact creative artists statewide or locally, they will learn about their state's people, places, and things — and themselves — in a way they'll probably never forget.

HOW PROUDLY THEY WAVE
Rita D. Haban
Illustrations

Lerner, 1989
[i, j] 111 pages

A picture of its state flag precedes each two-page state history which includes the how and when of statehood, the flag's designer(s), and the significance of its colors and design elements.

I PLEDGE ALLEGIANCE
June Swanson
Illustrations by Rick Hanson
Carolrhoda, (hb/pb), 1990
[p, i] 40 pages

Ms. Swanson defines the sentence Francis Bellamy penned in 1892, and recounts its inspiration, intent, and evolution from the original twenty-three, to today's thirty-one words.

> In Bette Bao Lord's wonderful *In the Year of the Boar and Jackie Robinson* (HarperCollins, 1984), Shirley Temple Wong recites, "I pledge a lesson to the frog of the United States of America, and to the wee puppet for witches hands...."

STATE BIRDS
Virginia Buckley
Illustrations by Arthur and Alan Singer
Dutton, 1990
[i] 64 pages

There are 50 states, but only 33 state birds! The author comments on their selection as state symbols and most easily recognized attributes. Each is portrayed in its native habitat.

HELLO U.S.A. Series
Color and b/w photographs and illustrations
Lerner, (hb/pb), 1991-1994
[i,j] 72 pages each

This one-volume-per-state series is as enjoyable to learn by as to learn from. Each comfortably sized book (7 $\frac{1}{2}$" x 5 $\frac{3}{4}$") is attractively designed and interestingly conversational. Special features include an historical time line, list of famous native sons/daughters, assorted facts-at-a-glance (population, average temperatures, natural resources, etc.), glossary, and index.

THE DOUBLEDAY ATLAS OF
THE UNITED STATES OF AMERICA
Illustrations and photographs
Doubleday, 1990
[i] 126 pages

Two-pages are devoted to each state, arranged alphabetically within three geographical groupings. For each state there is a brief profile, a relief map, annotated illustrations which identify the state bird, tree, and flower, usually two to three photographs of people and places, and a list of noteworthy facts. In sum, a useful one-volume resource for typical school-report, fact-finding missions.

IT HAPPENED IN AMERICA:
TRUE STORIES FROM THE FIFTY STATES
Lila Perl
Two-color illustrations by Ib Ohlsson
Holt, 1993
[i,j] 288 pages
   The engaging stories about men and women from many backgrounds and times in their state's history are prefaced by a brief introduction to the state that includes the origin of its name, the date of its admittance into the Union, and a trivia question and answer. Here are 50 superb read alouds, short enough to fit into the few minutes before lunch-, recess-, bus-, or any other time.

BETSY ROSS
Alexandra Wallner
Illustrations by the author

Holiday, 1994
[p, i] 32 pages

It is possible, but not provable, that Betsy Ross sewed the first American flag. Her story, as recounted here, was passed down by relatives and friends. Whether true or not, Ms. Ross was a hardworking colonial businesswoman and Ms. Wallner's introduction is worth reading.

FACTS PLUS
Susan C. Anthony
B/w illustrations
Instructional, (pb), 1995
[i, j] 250 pages

The capital, governor, song, tree, nickname, highest and lowest points, and tourist information 1-800 numbers are among the state facts in this first-rate reference must for report-writing youngsters.

 **TIDE POOLS**

MARINE BIOLOGY
Ellen Doris
Photographs
Thames & Hudson, 1993
[i, j] 64 pages

Chock full of excellent suggestions for investigating coastal water flora and fauna, this volume is equally packed with fundamental information about the classification of marine life in general—from whale to seaweed—and about a few species in particular. Many photos show students from Woods Hole (MA) Children's School of Science engaged in the recommended activities. Ms. Doris clearly notes appropriate safety precautions and provides information on how to order specimens and supplies for further study.

SEASHORE
Donald M. Silver
Illustrations by Patricia J. Wynne
Freeman, 1993
[i] 48 pages

In this focus on "One Small Square" of rocky tidepool, Dr. Silver explains tides, describes the plant and animal life that have adapted to their ebb and flow, and, in margins and sidebars, suggests strategies for close-up studies and related art projects.

TIDE POOLS
Ronald Rood
Illustrations by Martin Classen
HarperCollins, 1993
[p, i] 48 pages

Among the beguiling "secrets and surprises" that await tide pool explorers are sea cucumbers who devour the entrapped sea creatures off their tentacles "just as you'd lick jelly off your fingers." The colorful imagery of both author and artist inform, stir imaginations, and stimulate curiosity in a "Nature Study Book" just right for very young readers and listeners.

EXPLORING AN OCEAN TIDE POOL
Jeanne Bendick
B/w illustrations by Todd Telander and photographs
Holt, (hb/pb), 1992
[p, i] 56 pages

After a general description of the "neighborhood" she dubs one of the most crowded on earth, Ms. Bendick describes its plants and the process of photosynthesis. She explains the animal life from a who-eats-whom-and-how perspective. Her prose flows in this handy (6" x 7$\frac{1}{2}$") little Redfeather nonfiction series title.

For a closer look at *Who Eats What?* (HarperCollins, 1995), as well as who eats whom (see above), hand primary graders Patricia Lauber's introduction to food chains and food webs, one of the "Let's Read and Find Out" series perfect for very young readers with a high curiosity quotient.

SEASHORE
David Burnie
Photographs and illustrations
Dorling, 1994
[i] 62 pages

One of the "Eyewitness Explorers" series designed as take-alongs to introduce young readers to nature's niches, it supplements descriptive data with suggestions for observing, experimenting, and creating art. The many chapters offer readers starting points for independent first-hand research, from making sand or tidepool profiles to examining the life on and around wooden pilings.

TIDE POOL
Christiane Gunzi
Photographs and illustrations
Dorling, 1992
[i, j] 28 pages

A few specimens from around the world, from strawberry anemones to sea lemon slugs, are in tight focus in one of the "Look Closer" series that features photo enlargements which allow readers to see details not discernible otherwise. Illustrations of elementary-grade youngsters holding or looking at the featured plants or animals show relative size.

TREES

Adopt a tree as your class mascot. As with any other pet, youngsters can name, write stories and poetry about, photograph, paint or sketch it. They can measure and compare its school-year growth to theirs and study others like it. They can also sit next to, dance around, relax under, make rubbings of, and hang bird feeders from it. Best of all, there's neither a cage to clean nor concern to be had about care on holidays and long weekends.

Start out each day with a poem by X. J. Kennedy, David McCord, Edna St. Vincent Millay, or other poets extolling trees and other growing things in Barbara Brenner's garden of poems about our planet, *The Earth is Painted Green* (Scholastic, 1994).

A GIFT OF A TREE
Greg Henry Quinn
Illustrations by Ronda Krum
Scholastic, 1994
[p, i] 32 pages

Aptly titled, Mr. Quinn's book comes with seeds and directions for starting and nurturing the enclosed sprouter. Whether or not youngsters sow the seeds successfully, his presentation on trees' gifts—oxygen to breathe, wood to build with, fruit to eat, and more—is noteworthy.

TREE TRUNK TRAFFIC

MANGROVE WILDERNESS
Bianca Lavies
Photographs by the author

Dutton, 1989, 1994
[i] 32 pages each

The author/photographer's camera "froze" two-, four-, six-, and eight-legged creatures as they fluttered, scampered, crept, crawled, or swam about their business on the thoroughfares provided by a 70-year-old oak and the red mangroves off the southwest coast of Florida, respectively.

👓 Suggest students schedule five-minute turns monitoring nearby tree trunk traffic. How does it compare to the hustle and bustle on Bianca Lavies's trees?

A B CEDAR
George Ella Lyon
Three-color illustrations by Tom Parker
Orchard, 1989
[all ages] 32 pages

The illustrations are simply hands holding leaves. Ah, but the hands! Men's and women's of all shades and ages. And next to them, the tree's blossom or seed. And beneath, a miniature silhouette of the whole tree, with people nearby for scale. Stunning!

TREE
David Burnie
Photographs, illustrations
Knopf, 1988
[i, j] 64 pages

A multitude of facts await perusers of these photographs and drawings that expose trees from every angle, inside and out. Two-page chapters focus on what trees are, their life cycle, various parts and species, life around and within them, and how to learn more about them.

👓 Ask children to name the heaviest things that ever lived and they'll probably call out "whale" or "dinosaur" before even thinking "tree," if plants come to mind at all. But

California's giant Sequoias can weigh as much as 6,000 tons! Have youngsters read all about the three species of redwoods, the complex community of plants and animals they support, the myths and legends that surround them, and the movement to preserve what few remain, in Bill Schneider's colorful *The Tree Giants* (Falcon, 1988).

BE A FRIEND TO TREES
Patricia Lauber
Illustrations by Holly Keller
HarperCollins, 1994
[p] 32 pages

Beginning readers will discover what trees are, why we need them, and how, by recycling, we can reduce their destruction.

RED LEAF, YELLOW LEAF
Lois Ehlert
Illustrations by the author
Harcourt, 1991
[p, i] 36 pages

Brilliant collages of paper, fabric, leaves, twigs, and the like vivify a simple story (in large type for young readers) and the underlying facts (in small type for older readers) which describe a sugar maple's growth from seed to mature tree in all its fall regalia.

In *How Leaves Change* (Lerner, 1986), Sylvia Johnson clearly explains (and colorful photos illustrate) a leaf's function on the living plant and after it falls, chlorophyll and the process of photosynthesis, and exactly what causes the brilliant displays Ms. Ehlert so brilliantly portrays.

OUTSIDE AND INSIDE TREES
Sandra Markle
Photographs
Bradbury, 1993
[p, i] 40 pages

This clear, concise, smoothly flowing guide identifies and explains the function of trees' various parts, from bark to heartwood and roots to leaves. It can serve as refresher course and lesson-plan outline for the study of earth's largest plants, as well as your youngsters' resource.

GIANTS IN THE LAND
Diana Appelbaum
B/w illustrations by Michael McCurdy
Houghton, 1993
[i, j] 32 pages

The only trees tall enough to become masts on ships in King George the Third's Royal Navy grew in New England. How 18th-century colonists felled and ferried the pines from forest to Britain's shipbuilders is an impressive historical anecdote, exceptionally well-told, here, in words and pictures.

North America's English settlers discovered a far different forest from the one we see today. They gazed at a *Temperate Deciduous Forest* (Twenty-First, 1994) alive with wildlife and crowned by often mile-wide flocks of passenger pigeons. Connect kids to April Pulley Sayre's small (6" x 9") but information-packed introduction to the climate, geology, plant and animal life, ecology, and environmental problems of this habitat—one of six titles in the excellent "Exploring Earth's Biomes" series.

HOW THE FOREST GREW
William Jaspersohn
B/w illustrations by Chuck Eckart
Greenwillow, (hb/pb), 1980; Mulberry, 1992
[p] 56 pages

A TREE IN A FOREST
Jan Thornhill
Illustrations by the author

Simon, 1992
[i] 32 pages

Use Mr. Jaspersohn's step-by-step narrative of the two-century transformation of cleared acreage from abandoned farmland to dense woodland as prelude to Ms. Thornhill's 212-year life cycle of a sugar maple tree. Both books make clear that no tree stands alone but rather relies on and is relied upon by the flora and fauna that congregate in, on, or around it.

CHRISTMAS TREE FARM
Sandra Jordan
Hand-colored, sepia-toned photographs by the author
Orchard, 1993
[i] 32 pages

This evocative photoessay traces an ongoing Rhode Island happening that has parallels throughout the states: In early spring, baby trees are planted in clear spaces between other trees on land Mrs. Clark's great-grandfather farmed; in November, families come to dig up or cut their special tree for the holidays.

THE BIG TREE
Bruce Hiscock
Illustrations by the author
Atheneum, (hb/pb), 1991
[p,i] 32 pages

Along with information on how a tree lives and breathes, Mr. Hiscock's perspective emphasizes the social history encompassed within a sugar maple's life span from Revolutionary War days, through peaceful years in the nineteenth century, and as backyard witness to family reunions as the century turns.

THE BLOSSOM ON THE BOW: A BOOK OF TREES
Anne Ophelia Dowden
Full-color & b/w illustrations by the author
Ticknor, 1975/94

[i, j] 71 pages

The title is poetic, but Ms. Dowden's well-written prose is a coherent explanation of the way trees grow. Much of her book is a description of the seven forest regions of the United States, including a list of the common trees found in each: The northeastern forest, with more than 300 species of wild trees, reigns supreme. Her watercolors of representative tree leaves, flowers, fruits, and seeds reveal details hard to capture with photography.

You'll find detailed instructions for seasonal tree projects in Monica Russo's *The Tree Alamanac: A Year-Round Activity Guide* (Sterling, 1993): how to start trees in bottles in spring; press leaves in summer; collect specimen leaves and explore for insects, mosses, and lichens in fall; identify dormant trees and make waxed-paper leaf decorations in winter.

CRINKLEROOT'S GUIDE TO KNOWING THE TREES
Jim Arnosky
Illustrations by the author
Bradbury, 1992
[p, i] 32 pages

My elementary school leaf-collecting-and-identifying assignments would certainly have been more successful with this easy-to-read-and-learn-from handbook with its clear illustrations of leaves, seeds, needles, and seed cones.

THE EVER-LIVING TREE:
THE LIFE AND TIMES OF A COAST REDWOOD
Linda Vieira
Illustrations by Christopher Canyon
Walker, 1994
[i] 32 pages

Born in the time of Alexander the Great, Ms. Vieira's *Sequoia sempervirens* reached 300-feet high when Washington was president and was felled during the gold rush. Its roots sprouted new trees by the time of the first Moon-walk and will continue to give life to the forest for years to come. The borders of Mr. Canyon's vivid illustrations include a time line and contemporary historical scenes.

 **TRUCKS**

SAM GOES TRUCKING
Henry Horenstein
Photographs by the author
Houghton (hb/pb), 1989
[pre, p] 32 pages

Little ones who dream about riding the white lines in a semi will enjoy traveling alongside Sam as he accompanies his trucker-dad on an average workday, from morning meal, through cargo pick-up and delivery, to nighttime homecoming.

TRUCKER
Hope Herman Wurmfeld
B/w photographs by the author
Macmillan, 1990
[j] 64 pages

Sober, but not somber, this is a warm and insightful down-to-earth portrayal of the day-to-day activities of big rig owner/operator Phil Marcum. Though he hauls merchandise some 3,000 miles a week between Canada and Florida, he still makes the time to drive his rig to daughter Hillary's school to show and tell her primary-grade classmates how trucks help us get the things we need.

BIG RIGS
Hope Irvin Marston
Photographs by the author
Cobblehill, 1993
[p, i] 48 pages

Big rigs, or the mostly diesel-burning eighteen-wheelers, are the largest trucks on the highway. There are "reefer" refrigerated vans, "possum belly" livestock haulers, "gooseneck" low-to-the-ground heavy-haulers, and more. Crisp portraits of the various tractors, trailers, and their logos; a simple descriptive narrative; and a two-page glossary of truckers' CB radio terms comprise this super photoessay.

HERE COME THE MONSTER TRUCKS
George Sullivan
Photographs
Cobblehill, (hb/pb), 1989
[i, j] 64 pages

Powered by supercharged motors, these monsters are the 10 to 15-feet tall, extraordinarily modified pickup trucks that sit atop 66" to 120" tires and are maneuvered by drivers who crush and jump over old automobiles for the sport of it. Whether its a pastime you promote or disdain, the trucks, the people who built them, and the activity itself will fascinate anyone who likes to read about giants and record breakers—and what young reader doesn't!

FIRE TRUCK NUTS AND BOLTS
Jerry Boucher
Photographs by the author
Carolrhoda, 1993
[i, j] 40 pages

Firemen are among the first "city helpers" preschoolers meet in a trip highlighted by a closeup inspection of the fire truck. Mr. Boucher shows how they are constructed, from planning to delivery. Each one a work of art—as well as craft.

Trucks and math? Of course! Bruce McMillan found diamonds on the accelerator pedal, circles on the light lenses, a hexagonal throttle, and more when he aimed his camera at a *Fire Engine* looking for geometric *Shapes* (Lothrop, 1988). With this clever and natural introduction to the shape of things, automotive or otherwise, hand youngsters the class camera to focus on similar figures on the school bus or anywhere else.

TRACTORS
Caroline Young
Illustrations
Usborne, (hb/pb), 1992
[p, i] 32 pages

Attractively arranged, annotated pictures of spreaders, sprayers, lifters, combines, and other around-the-farm equipment, enhanced by sidebars detailing their specialized parts and movements.

POWER MACHINES
Ken Robbins
Hand-tinted b/w photographs by the author.
Holt, 1993
[p, i] 32 pages

Mr. Robbins's 12" x 8" full-page, somewhat-fuzzy photos admirably capture the awesome power of thirteen machines, from payloader to car flattener. Youngsters will be fascinated by the photos and descriptions of motorized devices that lift, lower, relocate, smash, spin, or otherwise manipulate otherwise immovable objects.

VOLCANOES AND EARTHQUAKES

VOLCANOES

EARTHQUAKES
Seymour Simon
Photographs and illustrations
Morrow, (hb/pb), 1988; 1991

[p, i] 32 pages each

Mr. Simon's brief, tight narrative on four major types of volcanoes is accompanied by striking full-page photographs that include Mt. St. Helens's eruption, the island of Surtsey's formation, and Hawaiian volcanic activity. The second equally impressive (10" x 10") volume includes words about and views of collapsed buildings from the 1964, 1985, and 1989 earthquakes in Alaska, Mexico City, and San Francisco, respectively.

In appropriate pop-up fashion, Jean Cassels's *Volcanoes and Earthquakes in Action* (Macmillan, 1993) introduces young readers to the whys and types of volcanoes and earthquakes and includes a moving tsunami as it approaches a tropical island.

VOLCANO & EARTHQUAKE
Susanna Van Rose
Illustrations and photographs
Knopf, 1992
[i, j] 64 pages

This "Eyewitness Books" indexed assemblage of hundreds of annotated photographs and illustrations, in the manner of a museum exhibit, is a useful reference source for the causes and effects of natural phenomena and people's responses to them.

Franklyn M. Branley explains *Volcanoes* (HarperCollins, 1985) and *Earthquakes* (HarperCollins, 1990) to very young readers in two of his many titles in the "Let's Read and Find Out" series especially for inquisitive primary graders.

VOLCANO: THE ERUPTION
AND HEALING OF MOUNT ST. HELENS
Patricia Lauber
Photographs and illustrations
Bradbury, 1986; Aladdin, 1993
[i, j] 64 pages

One of the last decade's most impressive rock events created a "stone wind" of steam and rocks that traveled at speeds up to 200 miles an hour, leveling 150 square miles of countryside. Ms. Lauber documents and explains how nature heals its self-inflicted wounds in a moving testimony to the precarious balance between plants and animals and their life-sustaining interdependence.

SURTSEY: THE NEWEST PLACE ON EARTH
Kathryn Lasky
Photographs by Christopher G. Knight
Hyperion, 1992
[i, j] 64 pages

This wife and husband team were among the first 100 people allowed on the island that emerged from the sea near Iceland's coast in 1963. Ms. Lasky's lyrical prose and Mr. Knight's truly spectacular photographs recount Surtsey's development, from its birth through the establishment of grasses and the presence of birds in 1970; a photo-essay at its best.

Hand Helen Roney Sattler's posthumously published *Our Patchwork Planet* (Lothrop, 1995) to technically inclined, highly motivated middle-school students who are fascinated by the causes of the phenomena highlighted above: Mt. St. Helens's eruption, for example, Surtsey's birth, or awesome earthquakes. Ms. Sattler's explanation of the forces that shaped the earth's far-from-stable crust is a careful and enlightening exposition of plate tectonics.

WEATHER

WHAT WILL THE WEATHER BE?
Linda DeWitt
Illustrations by Carolyn Croll

HarperCollins, 1991
[p, i] 32 pages

Ms. DeWitt explains what meteorologists do, what their instruments measure, what causes changes in the weather, and why it is often unpredictable.

WEATHER FORECASTING
Gail Gibbons
Illustrations by author
Four Winds, 1987
[p] 32 pages

WEATHER WORDS AND WHAT THEY MEAN
Gail Gibbons
Illustrations by the author
Holiday, 1990
[p] 32 pages

Readers visit a small weather station in the first of these books and discover how meteorologists collect and report data from the instruments within and without their station. In the second, Ms. Gibbons simply and succinctly illustrates and defines temperature, air pressure, moisture, wind, and their related terms.

WEATHERWATCH
Valerie Wyatt
B/w illustrations by Pat Cupples
Addison, (pb) 1990
[i, j] 94 pages

This data- and idea-packed paperback lures readers with world records, atmospheric anomalies, and folklore. Ms. Wyatt also explains map symbols, cloud classification, and similar meteorological matter; and suggests experiments, record keeping, and other activities for home/school weather stations.

THE SIERRA CLUB BOOK OF WEATHERWISDOM
Vicki McVey
B/w illustrations by Martha Weston
Sierra Club, 1991
[i, j] 104 pages

Dr. McVey tells youngsters how and what to watch, as well as why, to become weatherwise—able to forecast the weather without technologically sophisticated instruments. She connects chapters on basic weather principles and experiments with stories about 11- and 12-year-olds from Tuareg, Navajo, and other cultures that have learned to survive by watching weather patterns, animal behavior, and other natural signs.

For additional meteorological experiments, hand elementary grade youngsters Neil Ardley's *The Science Book of Weather* (Gulliver, 1992) and Muriel Mandell's *Simple Weather Experiments with Everyday Materials* (Sterling, 1990). Mr. Ardley's 14 projects are in one of the "The Science Book of..." series, which is noteworthy for the clarity of its step-by-step photo/directions.

Ms. Mandell's easy-to-follow 50-plus experiments include an explanation of what youngsters will discover and why, as well as charts, tables, and a data-rich narrative.

THE WEATHER SKY
Bruce McMillan
Photographs by the author
Farrar, 1991
[i, j] 40 pages

To show the effects of the simplest weather fronts and the clouds associated with each, Mr. McMillan presents a year's worth of sky changes via juxtaposed color photographs of the sky, b/w drawings of a vertical cross-section of that slice of sky, and a local-area weather map that pinpoints it.

THE BIG STORM
Bruce Hiscock
Illustrations by the author
Atheneum, 1993
[i] 32 pages

Snow? In April? In New York? Enough to delay the Yankee's 1982 season-opener four days! Mr. Hiscock profiles the unprecedented blizzard as it proceeded from its Pacific start to its Atlantic end. He smoothly integrates explanations of the storm's manifestations en route, which included tornadoes in Texas, hail in Kentucky, and record-low temperatures in the Appalachians.

Have youngsters close their eyes when you share excerpts from Nathaniel Tripp's evocative *Thunderstorm* (Dial, 1994). After they've sketched what they saw in their minds' eyes as you read aloud, compare and discuss similarities and differences between their views and artist Juan Wijngaard's.

A RAINY DAY
Sandra Markle
Illustrated by Cathy Johnson
Orchard, 1993
[p] 32 pages

Ms. Markle's illustrated explanation of why it rains, what happens when it does, and where the rain goes is perfectly tuned to primary graders.

Artist/author Ashley Bryan illustrates and tells *The Story of Lightning and Thunder* (Atheneum, 1993) as Southern Nigerian youngsters have heard it told for generations.

WINTER

SPRING

SUMMER

FALL
Ron Hirschi
Photographs by Thomas D. Mangelsen
Cobblehill, 1990/1991
[p, i] 32 pages each

The artistry of Mr. Hirschi's spare prose and Mr. Mangelsen's photography makes these collaborations an aesthetic delight for browsers of all ages.

EXPLORING WINTER

EXPLORING SUMMER

EXPLORING SPRING

EXPLORING AUTUMN
Sandra Markle
B/w illustrations by the author
Atheneum, 1984-1991; Avon, (pb), 1991-1992
[i] 154; 170; 122; 152 pages

This eminently browsable quartet is filled with ideas and facts about natural events, suggestions for related experiments, directions for crafts, games, and other activities that will entertain and enlighten youngsters throughout the year.

The long, hot summer will seem that much shorter and cooler when kids are involved in the activities designed by Linda Allison in *The Sierra Club Summer Book* (Sierra, 1977/1989) and Jane Drake's and Ann Love's *The Kids' Summer Handbook* (Ticknor, 1994), subtitled a "cottage, cabin, camping, and canoeing official activity book." Recommend both, along with *Exploring Summer* (see above), in your just-before-summer-vacation letter to parents.

ARCTIC SUMMER
Downs Matthews
Photographs by Dan Guravich
Simon, 1993
[p, i] 36 pages

HERE IS THE ARCTIC WINTER
Madeleine Dunphy
Illustrations by Alan Janes Robinson
Hyperion, 1993
[p, i] 32 pages

Mr. Matthews's prose highlights native and summer-only animals, as well as a few flowering plants. Ms. Dunphy's this-is-the-house-that-Jack-built cumulative rhyme focuses on natives only—ten of them.

GLOBAL WARMING
Laurence Pringle
Photographs
Arcade, 1990
[i, j] 42 pages

A thoughtfully balanced presentation of scientists' observations, interpretations, theories, and disagreements concerning global warming. Mr. Pringle explains the "greenhouse" effect, changing weather patterns, and what people can do to adapt to a warmer world and slow down Earth's rising temperature.

THE GREENHOUSE EFFECT
Rebecca L. Johnson
Illustrations and photographs
Lerner, (hb/pb), 1990
[j] 112 pages

This calm discourse is as essential for your understanding as it is for students who seek a detailed exposition of atmospheric phenomena. Excellent charts, diagrams, and photographs further clarify Ms. Johnson's knowledgeable elucidation of the causes and effects of global warming, her description of life on a warmer planet, and the worldwide cooperation necessary to reduce the release of carbon dioxide and other greenhouse gases.

With author/artist Betsy Bowen's *Antler, Bear, Canoe: A Northwoods Alphabet Year* (Little, 1991) as inspiration, suggest boys and girls create a similar my-town-through-the-year block-printed alphabet. If wood or linoleum isn't available for printing, Styrofoam trays will do.

NATURE ALL YEAR LONG
Clare Walker Leslie
Illustrations by the author
Greenwillow, 1991
[i] 56 pages

This information- and activity-packed, month-by-month guide traces seasonal changes in animal and plant behavior. The naturalist/artist suggests easily doable ideas for observing those changes with occasional notes on timely festivals. Though specific to New England, with few exceptions (e.g., looking at snowflakes) they are appropriate throughout the States.

WHALES, DOPHINS, AND PORPOISES

Wrap a great white or humpback around your school wall. Instead of the temporary murals that adorn the classroom or hallway bulletin boards during an investigation of these fascinating sea creatures, let children permanently preserve whales by painting them on the outside walls, where the community-at-large can enjoy them for many years.

BABY WHALES DRINK MILK
Barbara Juster Esbenson
Illustrations by Lambert Davis
HarperCollins, (hb/pb), 1994
[pre, p] 32 pages

Begin primary graders' search for cetacean information with this introduction to the physical and social traits that characterize mammals of the cetaceous kind. Move on to...

GREAT WHALES
Patricia Lauber
B/w photographs; b/w illustrations by Pieter Folkens
Holt, 1991
[i] 64 pages

...a conversational exposition on whale family differences and recently discovered characteristics: E.g., right whales, which are so fat they float, will raise their flukes as sails to let the wind push them along. A brief history of whaling and its effects on specific whale populations concludes.

How does it feel to be a whale? However your youngsters imagine it feels, as Joanne Ryder guides them through a metamorphosis from human to cetacean and back in *Winter Whale* (Morrow, 1991). Read aloud this poetic evocation of a humpback's seasonal sojourn near the Hawaiian Islands, and have children listen with closed eyes. Be prepared with sense-ational words you can add to their vocabularies when you discuss their vicarious adventures.

HUMPBACK WHALES
Dorothy Hinshaw Patent
Photographs
Holiday, 1989
[p] 32 pages

BABY WHALE
Lynn Wilson
Illustrations by Jean Cassels
Grosset, 1991
[p] 32 pages

These two are natural companions to Ms. Ryder's *Winter Whale*, and will increase youngsters familiarity with the vital statistics, life and times of the barnacle-encrusted, long-flippered, singing cetaceans.

WHALES AND DOLPHINS
Steve Parker
Illustrations and photographs
Sierra, 1994
[i, j] 56 pages

This superlatively designed blend of lucid text and get-at-a-glance charts, diagrams, gatefolds, and other illustrative devices vivifies the unique physical and social characteristics of marine mammals. It has a glossary, index, and no bold face type to interrupt the reader's concentration.

The seventeen poems Myra Cohen Livingston chose for *If You Ever Meet a Whale* (Holiday, 1992) sing of the marine mammal's power and glory. Leonard Everett Fisher's paintings, among his best, portray the mammal's grandeur.

MIGHTY GIANTS OF THE SEA
Judith E. Rinard
Illustrations by Ned and Rosalie Seidler
National, 1990
[p] 14 pages

Brief descriptions accompany illustrations that lift, pop-up, or unfold (in one instance to reveal a 38-inch blue whale and her calf) for a wonderfully dramatic introduction to twelve species of whales and dolphins. A $2^{1}/_{2}$-minute, 33-rpm "sound sheet" of humpback songs is included.

For a closer look at individual whale species, hand older readers David O. Gordon's and Alan Baldridge's *Grey Whales* (Monterey, 1991), Francois Gohier's *A Pod of Gray Whales* and *Humpback Whales* (both Blake, 1987;1990); and Vicki León's *A Pod of Killer Whales* (Blake, 1988).

GOING ON A WHALE WATCH
Bruce McMillan
Photographs by the author
Scholastic, 1992
[p, i] 40 pages

Whenever I'd seen pictures of whales breaching, blowing, or otherwise breaking the ocean's surface, I'd wonder what the whole whale looks like, not just the part above the water. Now I know, for Mr. McMillan paired his photos with drawings outlining what the camera couldn't catch—the complete whale. A brilliant idea.

The dedication page of the book above is a nautical map highlighted with the course Mr. McMillan sailed to photograph the whales. Use it to inspire a display of nautical, aeronautical, road, weather, and whatever other maps you can acquire of a given area to show children a few of the many ways people can picture the same place.

THE SEARCH FOR THE RIGHT WHALE
Scott Kraus and Kenneth Mallory
Photographs
Crown, 1993
[i, j] 36 pages

In 1980, when the species seemed close to extinction, 26 North Atlantic right whales were found swimming in the Bay of Fundy, their northern feeding grounds. Readers will sense the excitement of the chase in this description of the subsequent research that revealed the winter calving grounds and migration route of the whale dubbed the "right" one to hunt for oil.

WHALING DAYS
Carol Carrick
Woodcuts by David Frampton
Clarion, 1993
[i] 40 pages

Powerful woodcuts vivify a gripping history of whaling from the first scavenging of beached beasts through the heyday of whaling fleets and the invention of the harpoon cannon to the contemporary, almost universal ban on its practice.

Jill Bailey's *Project Whale* (Steck-Vaughn, 1991), a deft blend of fact and fiction, is ready-made for fourth- to sixth-graders' readers' theater. The cast of characters is professionally involved with whales and their information-packed dialogue is ready to read as it is. Delegate chapters or smaller sections to groups of youngsters and let them select roles, practice their parts, then come up to the front of the room and read. Work with the class as a whole to explain how the descriptive prose can be divided among two or more narrators or rewritten as additional dialogue, and set youngsters to work on adaptations they can then read aloud.

IN THE COMPANY OF WHALES:
FROM THE DIARY OF A WHALE WATCHER
Alexandra Morton
Photographs
Orca, 1993
[i, j] 62 pages

A compelling and insightful view of killer-whales off the west coast of British Columbia from a professional whale watcher who has studied the black and white mammals in the wild for more than 14 years.

WHALES
Lesley Dow

DOLPHINS AND PORPOISES
Janelle Hatherly and Delia Nicholls
Photographs and illustrations
Facts, 1990
[i, j] 68 pages each

These oversize (9½" x 13") volumes are divided into two- to six-page chapters that cover each group's unique physical and social characteristics, habitat, and diet. Sidebars highlight noteworthy specifics; and a glossary and index complete presentations which abound with well-annotated, full-color photographs and detailed illustrations.

DOLPHIN ADVENTURE
Wayne Grover
B/w illustrations by Jim Fowler
Greenwillow, (hb/pb), 1990.
[p, i] 48 pages

An ideal read aloud. From the moment you begin, you and your listeners will "be there"; and once you've finished, they'll want to read it again themselves, to relive the author/scuba diver's incredibly satisfying, other-world experience. The other world, here, is the watery one off the coast of Florida, where it really happened that one father asked another to save his child—but not in so many words.

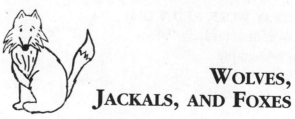

WOLVES, JACKALS, AND FOXES

Wolves are essential to the balance of nature and merit respect and admiration, not the fear or destruction encouraged by classic children's tales. Help children fix the "big, bad wolf" firmly in fiction's realm. Open their eyes to the fact that healthy, wild wolves pose no danger to humans.

WHEN THE WOLVES RETURN
Ron Hirschi
Photographs by Thomas D. Mangelsen
Cobblehill/Dutton, 1995
[i] 32 pages

In his paean to the natural order of things, the author explains how carnivores maintain nature's balance; and that to survive, they need everyone's help. He challenges youngsters to keep in mind that the survival of healthy predators means healthier prey in numbers the land can support. Mr. Mangelsen's photographs eloquently illuminate Mr. Hirschi's words.

Read aloud excerpts and recommend older readers enjoy at their own pace Bruce Thompson's *Looking at the Wolf* (Roberts, 1987), an information-laden explication of the biology and behavior of the "direct ancestor of every paper-fetching, car-chasing, bone-chewing, tail-wagging domestic dog alive today...." It is nature writing at its best.

WOLVES
R. D. Lawrence
Photographs
Sierra, 1990
[i, j] 64 pages

GRAY WOLF, RED WOLF
Dorothy Hinshaw Patent
Photographs
Clarion, 1990
[i, j] 64 pages

Both indexed volumes address the physical characteristics, social behavior, and precarious status of North American wolves. Mr. Lawrence concentrates on attributes and provides full-page drawings that detail such specifics as wolf body language and skull structure. Dr. Patent also highlights research and recovery projects, including the reintroduction of the red wolf to North and South Carolina, and the wolf-protection program in Minnesota.

WOLVES
Seymour Simon
Photographs
HarperCollins, (hb/pb), 1993
[i] 32 pages

THE EYES OF GRAY WOLF
Jonathan London
Illustrations by Jon Van Zyle
Chronicle, 1993
[p] 32 pages

The riveting cover portraits and equally compelling contents guarantee both volumes to be short-time-on-the-shelf, long-time-on-the-lap books. Mr. Simon alternates full-page pictures with narrative on the unjustifiably maligned wolf's physical and social characteristics, its hunting strategies, and its pup rearing practices. Mr. London's sparely worded tale traces the winter night's progress of a solitary male as it roams the frozen north's forests and ridges in search of food and a mate.

The wolf's role in maintaining a balanced environment becomes evident when a family is inadvertently removed from a small island in Celia Godkin's *Wolf Island* (W. H. Freeman, 1993).

TO THE TOP OF THE WORLD
Jim Brandenburg
Photographs by the author
Walker, 1993
[i, j] 44 pages

On assignment to photograph arctic wolves, Mr. Brandenburg flew to Ellesmere Island in Canada's Northwest Territories, about 500 miles from the North Pole. The striking photographs and observations in this volume comprise his account of the trip and provide a glimpse of the relatively rare Canis lupus arctos during the springtime when life in the pack revolves around nurturing newborn pups.

On his first trip to Ellesmere Island, Mr. Brandenburg accompanied wildlife-biologist L. David Mech, who described their stay in the May 1987 *National Geographic* article "At Home with the Arctic Wolf." Send youngsters to the library to read the article for additional information about this subspecies of grey wolf and to note the similarities and differences in the two perspectives and presentations.

JACKAL WOMAN
Laurence Pringle
Photographs by Patricia D. Moehlman
Scribner's, 1993
[i] 42 pages

Mr. Pringle introduces young readers to behavioral ecologist Patricia D. Moehlman whose study of two species of jackal in the Tanzania's Serengeti Plain has shown them to be caring parents and skilled hunters.

RED FOX
Karen Wallace
Illustrations by Peter Melnyczuk
Candlewick, 1994
[pre, p] 28 pages

In larger type and simple though not simplistic sentences, this charming and informative picture book allows beginning readers to follow a meadow fox on an average day. In smaller type along the bottom of the page, for older readers, is more detailed information—how, when trotting, for example, the fox leaves a straight line of prints. The whole is a fine blend of fact and factual fiction.

Eve Bunting's lyrical poem *Red Fox Running* (Clarion, 1993), beautifully rendered in gouache and watercolors by Wendell Minor, follows a red fox as it hunts one cold wintry night. Link it to Peter Spier's *Fox Went Out on a Chilly Night* (Doubleday, 1961/1989), and Tejima's *Fox's Dream* (Philomel, 1987/1990) for three very different interpretations of the nocturnal activities of foxes.

WORDS

Fine writers aren't flimflam artists jibber-jabbering gobbledygook. Nor are their deliberations humdrum, their imagery wishy-washy, or their similes so-so. First-rate authors shape phrases as savory as cinnamon, in styles as joyful as jubilees, in books as scintillating as...

SUPERDUPERS: REALLY FUNNY WORDS

IT FIGURES! FUN FIGURES OF SPEECH
Marvin Terban
Illustrations by Giulio Maestro
Clarion, (hb/pb), 1989; 1993
[i] 64 pages each

In the first of Mr. Terban's words on words, he's asssembled such colorful contrivances as "flimflam" and "jibber-jabber" and explained their origins. In the second, he expounds on similes, metaphors, onomatopoeia, and the like. Add both to your collection, lickety-split.

Strike while the iron is hot and drop Bobbie Kalman's demystified *Settler Sayings* (Crabtree, 1994) into the pot when Mr. Terban's collection of colorful words are on the menu. You'll whet youngsters' appetite for collecting and creating their own colorful phrases.

UP, UP AND AWAY: A BOOK ABOUT ADVERBS
Ruth Heller
Illustrations by the author
Grosset, (hb/pb), 1991
[p, i] 48 pages

MERRY-GO-ROUND: A BOOK ABOUT NOUNS
Ruth Heller
Illustrations by the author
Grosset, (hb/pb), 1990
[p, i] 48 pages

Bold, bright illustrations and playful rhymes introduce the particulars and peculiarities of the parts of speech in 10"-square books easy to hold up in front of a group as you sensitize youngsters to what makes good English. Ms. Heller's similar *Many Luscious Lollipops* (1989), *Kites Sail High* (1988), and *A Cache of Jewels* (1987) target adjectives, verbs, and collective nouns, respectively.

With Ms. Heller's books as guides, suggest each student select one part of speech; jot down a short, original list of such words; then, with a buddy or two, use their combined lists as the basis for a story, dramatization, or poem to be read aloud, enacted, or put between covers for the classroom collection of original works.

OTTER NONSENSE
Norton Juster
Illustrations by Michael Witte
Morrow, 1994
[i] 64 pages

This handy little (5" x 6") collection of such animated witticisms as "oxidentally on porpoise, larks and bagels," and "wrenagade" is sure to stimulate similar puns on an animal nature. My students came up with seal-ing tape, horse-cents, and cat-acombs, among others.

HIPPOPOTAMUS HUNT
Bernard Most
Illustrations by the author
Harcourt, 1994
[p, i] 40 pages

Mr. Most's infectious wit and delight in wordplay will encourage youngsters to try their own variations on his themes—here and in *Pets in Trumpets* (Harcourt, 1991) and *Can You Find It?* (Harcourt, 1993), the words in words.

HO HO HO! THE COMPLETE BOOK OF CHRISTMAS WORDS
Lynda Graham-Barber
B/w illustrations by Betsy Lewin
Bradbury, 1993
[i, j] 122 pages each

Ms. Graham-Barber digs into the history of mistletoe, reindeer, yuletide, and their ilk. She's also turned her investigative skills to words related to Independence Day in *Doodle Dandy!* (Bradbury, 1992), Valentine's Day in *Mushy!* (Bradbury, 1991), and Thanksgiving Day in *Gobble!* (Bradbury, 1991).

FRANK AND ERNEST ON THE ROAD
Alexandra Day
Illustrations by the author
Scholastic, 1994
[p, i] 42 pages

In this, their third adventure, Frank, the elephant, and Ernest, the bear, drive a semi and learn to talk like truckers. The temp workers extraordinaire mastered the lingo of short order cooks in *Frank and Ernest* (Scholastic, 1988) and baseball players in *Frank and Ernest Play Ball* (Scholastic, 1990) on their first two "jobs." Kids will find all three bodacious reads, good buddy.

THE SCHOLASTIC RHYMING DICTIONARY
Sue Young
Two-color illustrations by David Sheldon
Scholastic, 1994
[i, j] 213 pages

Composing verse will be much easier with this, the best I've seen. Ms. Young provides 15,000 words organized by rhyming sounds—aste, oodle, uzzle, etc. All are listed alphabetically by number of syllables and include phrases, idioms, and place names.

ANTICS
Cathi Hepworth
Illustrations by the author
Putnam, 1992
[i] 32 pages

Whimsical, one-to-a-page illustrations catch and hold the eye as readers move from ANTique to ANTzzzzzzZ, passing RembrANT and VigilANTes along the way.

MY FIRST WORD BOOK
Angela Wilkes

MI PRIMER LIBRO DE PALABRAS EN ESPAÑOL
Angela Wilkes and Rubí Borgia

MON PREMIER LIVRE DE MOTS EN FRANÇAIS
Angela Wilkes and Annie Heminway
Photographs
Dorling, 1993
[pre, p] 64 pages each

Only the language differs in these oversized (10" x 13") volumes lavishly illustrated with pictures of everyday items, all named and indexed.

LET'S GO/VAMOS

MY DAY/MI DIA
Rebecca Emberley and Alicia Marquis
Illustrations by Rebecca Emberley
Little, (hb/pb), 1993
[pre, p] 28 pages each

English and Spanish words identify Ms. Emberley's cut-paper images of things youngsters might encounter at the zoo, beach, or circus and at home, school, or play. *My House/Mi Casa* and *Taking a Walk/Caminando* (both Little, 1990) were the first of Ms. Emberley's charming introductions to Spanish—or English—for the very young.

THE DANCER
Fred Burstein
Illustrated by Joan Auclair
Bradbury, 1993
[pre, p] 32 pages

English, Spanish, and Japanese words and phrases accompany the full-page illustrations of a little girl and her dad and the people and places they pass en route to her ballet lesson. The translations and phonetics are vetted by Berlitz.

AT THE BEACH
Huy Voun Lee
Illustrations by the author
Holt, 1994
[p] 28 pages

Ms. Lee's blend of fact and fiction introduces readers to ten Chinese characters and their Mandarin pronunciation. Young Xiao

Ming's mother draws the ideograms in the sand and explains how closely they resemble what they name: The symbol for water, for instance, looks like a big splash.

**CODES AND CIPHERS: HUNDREDS OF
UNUSUAL SECRET WAYS TO SEND MESSAGES**
Christina Ashton
B/w illustrations
Betterway, (pb), 1993
[i, j] 110 pages

Ms. Ashton's handy, hands-on compendium on how to make and break codes and ciphers includes fascinating historical anecdotes of broken, unbroken, and misinterpreted secret messages.

LETTER JESTERS
Cathryn Falwell
Illustrations by the author
Ticknor, 1994
[i] 48 pages

Ms. Falwell's creative manipulation of typefaces wonderfully illustrates their impact on the reader. With humor and insight she demonstrates how a taken-for-granted aspect of the words people read dramatically influences their interpretation.

Bibliography

APPRAISAL: SCIENCE BOOKS FOR YOUNG PEOPLE. The Science Education Department, Boston University School of Education and The New England Roundtable of Children's Librarians. Boston, quarterly.

BOOKLINKS: CONNECTING BOOKS, LIBRARIES, AND CLASSROOM. Chicago: American Library Association, Bimonthly.

BULLETIN OF THE CENTER FOR CHILDREN'S BOOKS. University of Chicago Press, monthly except August.

CHILDREN'S CHOICES. International Reading Association and Children's Book Council, Chicago, annual annotated listing.

THE FIVE OWLS. Minneapolis: THE FIVE OWLS, Bimonthly.

Freeman, Evelyn B. and Person, Diane Goetz, ed. USING NONFICTION TRADE BOOKS IN THE ELEMENTARY CLASSROOM: FROM ANTS TO ZEPPELINS, NCTE, 1992.

Fox, Mem. RADICAL REFLECTIONS: PASSIONATE OPINIONS ON TEACHING, LEARNING, AND LIVING. New York: Harcourt, 1993.Friedberg, Joan Brest, June B. Mullins, and Adelaide Weir Sikiennik. PORTRAYING PERSONS WITH DISABILITIES: NONFICTION. New Jersey, Bowker, 1992.

Hearne, Betsy. CHOOSING BOOKS FOR CHILDREN: A COMMONSENSE GUIDE. New York: Delacorte, 1990.

THE HORN BOOK. Boston: The Horn Book, bimonthly.

THE KOBRIN LETTER: CONCERNING CHILDREN'S BOOKS ABOUT REAL PEOPLE, PLACES AND THINGS. Palo Alto, CA: Dr. Beverly Kobrin, six issues per year.

Lieberman, Jan. TNT: TIPS & TITLES OF BOOKS; grades K-8. Santa Clara, CA: three issues per year.

Lima, Carolyn W. and John A. A TO ZOO: SUBJECT ACCESS TO CHILDREN'S PIC-TURE BOOKS - 4TH Edition. New Jersey, Bowker, 1993.

Loewen, James W. LIES MY TEACHER TOLD ME: EVERYTHING YOUR AMERICAN HISTORY TEXTBOOK GOT WRONG. New York: The New Press, 1995.

THE MUSEUM OF SCIENCE AND INDUSTRY BASIC LIST OF CHILDREN'S SCIENCE BOOKS. Chicago: American Library Association, 1994.

Miller-Lachmann, Lyn. OUR FAMILY, OUR FRIENDS, OUR WORLD: AN ANNOTATED GUIDE TO SIGNIFICANT MULTICULTURAL BOOKS FOR CHILDREN AND TEENAGERS. New Jersey: Bowker, 1992.

NOTABLE CHILDREN'S BOOKS. Chicago: Association for Library Service to Children, American Library Association, listed annually.

"Notable Children's Trade Books in the Field of Social Studies," SOCIAL EDUCATION. New York, National Council for the Social Studies and Children's Book Council, list-ed annually.

OUTSTANDING SCIENCE TRADE BOOKS FOR CHILDREN. New York, National Science Teachers Association and Children's Book Council, listed annually.

PARENTS' CHOICE. Newton MA: Parents' Choice Foundation, quarterly.

PUBLISHERS WEEKLY. New York. Bowker.

THE READING TEACHER. Newark, DE: International Reading Association, eight issues per year.

Routman, Regie. THE BLUE PAGES: RESOURCES FOR TEACHERS FROM INVITA-TIONS. New Hampshire: Heinemann, 1994.

Saul, Wendy, Jeanne Reardon, Anne Schmidt, Charles Pearce, Dana Blackwood, Mary Dickinson Bird. SCIENCE WORKSHOP: A WHOLE LANGUAGE APPROACH. New Hampshire: Heinemann, 1993

SCHOOL LIBRARY JOURNAL, New York: Bowker, Monthly.

Sinclair, Patti K. E FOR ENVIRONMENT: AN ANNOTATED BIBLIOGRAPHY OF CHIL-DREN'S BOOKS WITH ENVIRONMENTAL THEMES. New Jersey: Bowker, 1992.

Stanley, Autumn. MOTHERS AND DAUGHTERS OF INVENTION: NOTES FOR A REVISED HISTORY OF TECHNOLOGY, New Jersey: Scarecrow, 1993; New Jersey: Rutgers University Press, 1995.

SCIENCE BOOKS & FILMS, American Association for the Advancement of Science. Washington, nine issues per year.

Trelease, Jim. THE NEW READ-ALOUD HANDBOOK. New York: Penguin, 1989.

Tsuruda, Gary. PUTTING IT TOGETHER: MIDDLE SCHOOL MATH IN TRANSITION. New Hampshire: Heinemann, 1994.

THE WEB: WONDERFULLY EXCITING BOOKS. Columbus, OH: College of Education, Ohio State University, quarterly.

Goodman, Kenneth S., Yetta M. Goodman, Lois Bridges Bird. THE WHOLE LAN-GUAGE CATALOG. Santa Clara, CA: American School Publishers, 1991.

Wurman, Richard Saul. INFORMATION ANXIETY, New York: Doubleday, 1989; Bantam, 1990.

Key to Publishers

Clarion .... Clarion Books
Cobblehill .... Cobblehill Books
Crabtree .... Crabtree Publishing Company
Crown .... Crown Books for Young Readers
Dawn .... Dawn Publications
Delacorte .... Delacorte Books for Young Readers
Dell .... Dell Publishing
Dial .... Dial Books for Young Readers
Dillon .... Dillon Press
Dorling .... Dorling Kindersley, Inc.
Doubleday .... Doubleday & Co., Inc.
Dutton .... Dutton Children's Books
Earth .... Earth Works Press
Enslow .... Enslow Publishers, Inc.
Facts .... Facts on File, Inc.
Falcon .... Falcon Press
Farrar .... Farrar Straus Giroux Books for Young Readers
Four Winds .... Four Winds Press
Free Spirit .... Free Spirit Publishing, Inc.
Freeman .... W.H. Freeman and Company
Green Tiger .... Green Tiger Press
Greenwillow .... Greenwillow Books
Grosset .... Grosset & Dunlap
Gulliver .... Gulliver Books
Harcourt .... Harcourt Brace Children's Books
HarperCollins .... HarperCollins Children's Books
Holiday .... Holiday House Books for Young People
Holt .... Henry Holt and Company Books for Young Readers
Houghton .... Houghton Mifflin Company
Hyperion .... Hyperion Books for Children
Instructional .... Instructional Resources Co.
Joy Street .... Harcourt Brace & Company Children's Books
Just Us .... Just Us Books, Inc.
Key Porter .... Key Porter Books
Kids Can .... Kids Can Press
Klutz .... Klutz Press
Knopf .... Alfred A. Knopf Books for Young Readers
Lee .... Lee & Low Books
Lerner .... Lerner Publications
Little .... Little, Brown and Company
Lodestar .... Lodestar Books
Lothrop .... Lothrop, Lee & Shepard Books
Macmillan .... Macmillan USA Children's Books
McElderry .... Margaret K. McElderry Books
Messner .... Julian Messner
Millbrook .... The Millbrook Press
Monterey .... Monterey Bay Aquarium
Morrow .... Morrow Junior Books

Mulberry .... Mulberry Books
Muir .... John Muir Publications
National .... National Geographic Society
Network .... Network Publications
New Discovery .... New Discovery Books
Newmarket .... Newmarket Press
North .... North Light Books
Oliver .... The Oliver Press, Inc.
Omnigraphics .... Omnigraphics, Inc.
Orca .... Orca Book Publishers
Orchard .... Orchard Books
Owen .... Richard C. Owen Publishers, Inc.
Oxford .... Oxford University Press
Paws IV .... Paws IV Publishing
Pelican .... Pelican Publishing Co., Inc.
Philomel .... Philomel Books
Preservation .... The Preservation Press
Puffin .... Puffin Books
Putnam .... G.P. Putnam's Sons
Pyrola .... Pyrola Press
Quilt Digest .... The Quilt Digest Press
Random .... Random House
Reader's Digest .... Reader's Digest Kids
Rizzoli .... Rizzoli Books for Children
Roberts .... Roberts Rinehart Publishers
Rosen .... The Rosen Publishing Group
Running .... Running Press Book Publishers
Scarecrow .... Scarecrow Press
Scholastic .... Scholastic Hardcover
Scribner's .... Charles Scribner's Sons Books for Young
                                              Readers
Sierra .... Sierra Club Books for Children
Silver .... Silver Burdett Press
Silver Moon .... Silver Moon Press
Silver Press .... Silver Press. Paramount Publishing
Simon .... Simon & Schuster Children's Book Division
Sterling .... Sterling Publishing Co., Inc.
Tab .... TAB Books
Tambourine .... Tambourine Books
Thomasson .... Thomasson-Grant, Inc.
Thomson .... Thomson Learning
Ticknor .... Ticknor & Fields Books for Young Readers
Tricycle .... Tricycle Press
Troll .... Troll Associates
Tundra .... Tundra Books
Twenty-first .... Twenty-First Century Books
Usborne .... Usborne Publishing
Viking .... Viking Children's Books

The Quick-Link Index

Index of Authors, Illustrators, and Book Titles

KEEP THE GOOD IDEAS COMING!
SUBSCRIBE TO THE KOBRIN LETTER

Until *Eyeopeners III* is published, you can keep abreast of the best non-fiction by subscribing to The Kobrin Letter. I publish six issues a year from September to May, group books by topic (just as you'll find them in *Eyeopeners II*), and you may begin your subscription at any time. Simply photocopy the coupon below, fill it out, and mail it to:

Dr. Beverly Kobrin, 32 Greer Road, Paolo Alto CA 94303.

__Absolutely! Sign me up for one year. I've enclosed a $12 check.
__Absolutely! Sign me up for one year and bill me $14.

Name _____

Address _____

City, State, Zip _____

Canadian sunscribers: Please remit U.S. funds and add $1.50/yr. for postage.

If you are ever dissatified with The Kobrin Letter, simply cancel and the price of unmailed issues will be promptly refunded.